ABOUT THE AUTHOR

As a second-generation migrant **A. K. Karla** has first-hand knowledge of the foreigner's life and an obsession with difference, the meaning of belonging and the incessant, often unconscious search for a homeland that can no longer be found. Through richly woven 'world' stories A. K. continues to journey, guiding the reader and writing with words that are never far from the heart.

A. K. also writes psychological fiction under the pen-name **Jack Duval**.

MR GUPTA'S HARDWARE STORE

A. K. Karla

Matador
9 Priory Business Park,
Wistow Road, Kibworth Beauchamp,
Leicestershire. LE8 0RX
Tel: 0116 279 2299
Email: books@troubador.co.uk
Web: www.troubador.co.uk/matador
Twitter: @matadorbooks

ISBN 978 1838594 732

British Library Cataloguing in Publication Data.
A catalogue record for this book is available from the British Library.

Printed and bound in Great Britain by 4edge Limited
Typeset in 11pt Minion Pro by Troubador Publishing Ltd, Leicester, UK

Matador is an imprint of Troubador Publishing Ltd

There is only one moment in time
when it is essential to awaken.
That moment is now.

(Attributed to the Buddha)
(C.563BC – 483BC)

CHAPTER
ONE

1972

Meera Gupta sat by the window and looked down at the busy street, her head covered in a loosely draped, sage green sari. She had made a gap in the fabric to see out, but her mouth was covered as was her beautiful long black hair, now in a tight oiled plait which fell down her back reaching almost to her waist.

She wasn't actually wearing the sari, not in the way it should be worn, anyway. More she had placed it over herself, almost like a tent. It had become something to hide under, and this she did, maintaining her innate modesty in any way she could whilst Mr Gupta was downstairs in the hardware store. She rubbed the thick, silver embroidered border rhythmically between her fingers, mumbling quietly to herself as she did so.

'Crimplene, Crimplene, this is all I hear. "Do you not want to be like a modern English lady, Mrs Gupta?"' She mimicked her husband's excellent English from that morning, the lilting Indian accent rising and falling perfectly. '"Why do you persist with this sari – pari rubbish? We live in England now, and you must behave and dress like an English lady. Wear the beautiful Crimplene suit I have bought for you. You are going to see Mrs Kumar this morning, I believe? You must set an example, Mrs Gupta. You must set an example to those beneath our standing in life."' She let out a loud humph.

'An example of what, Mr Gupta? That I am a foolish Indian woman, pretending to be an even more foolish English woman?'

She continued to rub the sari border, now rocking slightly – backwards and forwards. She was due at the Kumars' room in a nearby boarding house at ten-thirty. Chandu Kumar was her husband's employee, and it was his wife that she would be visiting. The previous evening she had made Jalebi, a traditional Indian sweet much loved by her friend, Babita Kumar. This morning she noticed that two were missing, eaten no doubt by her husband despite his protestations about fatty Indian foods, and his preference for the 'Rich Tea biscuits' which she detested. She spoke out loud again, her head moving from side to side as she did so, a sneer on her smooth dark face and her eyes flashing with anger.

'Mrs Gupta – Mr Gupta, what have we become? My name is Meera, Mr Gupta – Meera! And you are Vasu – Vasuman, if you must. You are a crazy man that you do not even know your wife's name! Perhaps you should have

2

married an English woman instead of me? Yes, an English woman in a mini-skirt! Let us divorce, Mr Gupta, the English do it all the time, so that should suit you very well,' she almost shouted, her good but heavily accented English becoming even more so as her rage grew. She swore in Hindi, which along with the head gesture was banned by Mr Gupta, then banged her fist down on the wooden arm of the chair before roughly swiping at the tears that now careered down her face. She swore again, more quietly this time, the anger cooling almost as quickly as it had come.

Glancing upwards through the glass, she noted the grey suburban London sky, laden with rain that would no doubt empty itself upon her just as she was walking to see Babita. Perhaps for the thousandth time she longed for the hot Indian sun; for proper monsoon storms, for the sights and smells of home, and mostly for her family – her father, her brother and his children, and for the close, almost indistinguishable lives that they had shared. Here, she had nothing. The husband that she came to England with had changed beyond recognition, as had her life, and she let out a sob of despair and longing for that which had been lost.

Once again, although this time more gently, she raised her hand to wipe the tears from her cheeks before standing up – the green sari falling softly to the floor. Pulling the thick nightdress over her head, she flung it down onto the linoleum, kicking it away as she walked quite naked to the bathroom. Mr Gupta would not approve of such wanton non-English behaviour, she thought, as she slammed the door behind her. But Mr Gupta was in the shop amongst his beloved paint and screwdrivers and, for now, at least, she would do as she pleased.

CHAPTER
TWO

Downstairs, Mr Gupta stood behind the wooden counter, smiling broadly as he opened the till. This was one of the main pleasures of his life as a shopkeeper – pressing the buttons and seeing the pile of notes grow under their clip as the day progressed. He handed over two brown paper packages of screws, a paintbrush and a large tin of mushroom-coloured paint.

'Thank you for your custom as always, Mr Jackson. Do please come again,' he said, in his finest English.

Mr Jackson, who was a regular at the store nodded his head, half an inch of ash falling onto the quarry-tiled floor from the cigarette that appeared to be permanently wedged between his lips. Waiting until the customer had gone, he then went through to the back storeroom to fetch the dustpan and neatly swept up the ash.

'Filthy habit you have, Mr Jackson,' he said aloud. Mr Jackson was long gone by now, but Mr Gupta often entertained himself by saying what was on his mind when each customer was no longer in earshot. Sometimes he would be complimentary, perhaps ingratiatingly so, but more often it was critical, these comments rarely failing to provide him with endless personal amusement. He never shared this with anyone else, and was particularly careful that Chandu didn't hear these sarcastic and often denigrating verbal asides aimed at the customers, preferring to keep this other side of himself hidden.

He had just pulled out a duster to polish the wooden counter when Chandu walked through the door, the bell announcing his return from delivering a parcel to a customer nearby. As slight as Mr Gupta was full-figured, he was little more than five-feet-five inches in height and compared to Gupta's nearly six feet, appeared at a quick glance to be little more than a child. A child however he was not, at just eight years younger than his employer who was soon to be forty-four years old. Another difference between them was that Chandu's complexion was dark, considerably darker than Mr Gupta's who wrongly liked to pride himself on the fact that he might easily be mistaken for having southern European origins. Chandu's narrow face was lined beyond his thirty-six years, and his expression was almost always one of anxiety – especially when he was in the hardware store.

'You delivered the parcel?' asked Mr Gupta.

Chandu nodded.

'Then give the money please, Mr Kumar,' he continued, his voice caustic and accusatory, implying that Chandu had not intended to give it to him at all.

5

Chandu put his hand in his khaki overall pocket, pulled out a five-pound note and some loose change, and placed it on the counter. 'He gave me fifty pence as a tip for climbing twelve flights of stairs,' he said, his eyes lowered. 'The lift was broken.' He looked up at his employer, quite aware of what the reply would be.

'You know very well that I do not hold with tips,' replied Mr Gupta. 'I pay you more than enough as it is. Any extra given belongs to the store.' Before he had even finished speaking, the money, including the tip, was dropped into the till which was then loudly slammed shut.

Chandu turned away, muttering under his breath in Hindi. 'Filthy mean devil.'

'What was that, Mr Kumar? Did you say something?'

'Yes, I said shall I make your tea now, Mr Gupta?'

'Please do, and make sure it's strong enough.'

Chandu walked behind the counter and into the storeroom. He was happier in here than at any other time during his working day. The dark room was lit by a single bare bulb, and the mixed smells of floor wax, cleaning products, oil and paint, reminded him of his uncle's furniture workshop back home in India. He had spent much of his childhood in the workshop, fetching and carrying, listening to the men laughing, teasing and joking – the smell of their strong black cigarettes mingling with the ever-present fragrance of fresh sappy wood. His Uncle Jay had injured his back when a huge piece of timber fell on him, and the man who was left in charge turned out to be a thief. He was eventually sent to jail, but not before the shop was ruined and eventually closed down for good. It was this that brought him and his wife, Babita, to England some four years earlier, since Vasu... Mr Gupta, had attended the same school as his uncle, and the job as assistant in the shop in England was thought of as a rare opportunity indeed.

Chandu walked to the back of the storeroom, but instead of going to the tiny kitchen area, with its single camping gas ring and battered aluminium kettle, he turned left to the shelves where the nails and screws were kept. Putting his hand into a large brown box of one-inch flathead nails, he pulled out a handful and moved them around his palm. 'One nail, two nails – which shall it be? Two I think – two nails today.' He slipped them into his trouser pocket and went to make the tea, drinking his as quickly as he could without burning his throat, then going back out into the store with Mr Gupta's – a bucket of soapy water in his other hand. Every morning he washed the entire floor area with an old string mop, often egged on by his employer's comments.

'Put your back into it, boy, scrub harder,' which was quite unnecessary since Chandu liked washing the floor... He liked the damp, faintly perfumed smell and the dark red colour that the tiles went before slowly drying out again.

Halfway through, he heard the door open at the bottom of the stairs that led to the flat. He turned to see Mrs Gupta, her beige rainmac tightly buttoned up to her neck, and her hair twisted on top of her head in a tall bun made from winding the long plait. Her legs were uncovered to the knee and were encased in shiny stockings, her feet clad in equally shiny platform shoes which made her much taller than she normally was. Her face was made up like a model in a magazine, and a large straw shopping bag hung over her arm.

Chandu gawped, unable to understand why such a fine-

7

looking lady would dress herself like this… like a western woman. Actually, this wasn't true. He knew exactly why she dressed herself like this. He had heard Mr Gupta shouting at her, especially in the early mornings when he arrived at the store, often well before the shop opened. Chandu had a key to the rear entrance and usually crept in as silently as possible in order to not disturb them, and also perhaps to listen to their arguing. This was so different from the conversations he had with his own wife, Babita, whom he loved very much. He rarely used her full name, more often referring to her by the childhood family nickname of 'Babi.'

'Stop staring, Chandu,' Meera said, her face flushed with embarrassment. 'I am going to see your wife. Is there any message you wish to give?'

He thought for a moment. 'Yes, Mrs Gupta, please can you say that her husband requests more chilli in the chicken curry, and only two-three chapati. I am not a horse.' He moved his head in a loose undulating fashion then raised his eyes and smiled.

Mrs Gupta smiled back at him. How she wished that she too could move her head in response and engage in teasing, telling him that his wife spoilt him, and how grateful he should be.

'Don't delay, Mrs Gupta, the rain will be coming. Do you have your umbrella?' her husband asked, ushering her to the door.

'How could I forget it in this godforsaken country?' she replied bitterly, pulling the door firmly behind her – the bell tinkling loudly.

***

Meera walked quickly along the street, her eyes cast downwards towards the pavement. It had started to spit with rain but she hurried on, suddenly turning into the public toilets a few hundred yards from the hardware store. She emerged some ten minutes later dressed in a sari of bright orange silk, its black border gleaming with gold thread, and a sheer chiffon headscarf over her beautiful coiled-plait bun. Her shoes were the same platforms, which she liked, but her eyes were now heavily lined with black kohl, and a bright red bindi had been placed at the centre of her forehead. She looked like an exotic flower against the drab, dull backdrop of the street, and heads turned as she walked, one man so mesmerised that he crossed the road without looking, causing a driver to beep his horn loudly.

The Crimplene suit was neatly folded at the bottom of the shopping bag underneath the Jalebi – the rainmac still on, although now unbuttoned and draped loosely over her shoulders. The rain had stopped, and quite unaware of the stir she had caused Meera proudly continued walking, her head held high, looking and feeling like the beautiful Indian lady she had been before arriving in England, and before her husband had taken on his mission to be more English than the English and restricting her life so badly.

She arrived at the Kumars' fifteen minutes later, and pressed the bell on the dusty front door. They had lived here ever since their move to England six years ago. The rent like everywhere in London seemed expensive, but they had found nothing better, and the other tenants were not unfriendly to immigrants which was most certainly not always the case. The door swung open and Babita ushered her in, her tiny figure dwarfed by an overly-large sari of bright pink and gold. It was one that Meera had given her, and she always wore it on these visits to show her appreciation of the gift, and how much the friendship meant.

'Come, come, I have been waiting for you. You are late. How beautiful you are in that sari! He did not try to stop you this time? Your husband… Mr Gupta?'

As Meera walked in she inhaled deeply, the heady fragrance from a sandalwood joss-stick doing little to mask the smell of strongly flavoured curry.

'Do please sit,' continued Babita. 'I have made something very special for you! Such a treat you do not often have. I know how things are. You want the bathroom?'

Meera shook her head. 'I need to wash my hands, though.'

'Already I thought this. Here is a bowl. Let me hold for you.' She held out a plastic washing up bowl half-filled with warm water – a few rose petals floating on the surface. A bar of soap was lying at its bottom and, quite used to this ritual, Meera washed her hands, then took the proffered towel and dried them carefully.

Whilst Babita emptied the bowl, Meera glanced around her. The room was large, about sixteen feet by twelve and L-shaped, with two sash windows overlooking the tatty garden at the rear of the house. There was a tiny kitchenette in one corner comprising of a white enamel sink with a gas water-heater over it, a few cupboards, and a small Baby Belling oven with a two-ring electric hob on its top.

The Kumars had little by way of possessions; a table and chairs, one armchair, an old-fashioned sideboard and a double bed. On the wall above the tiled fireplace was a large glittering picture of the Taj Mahal which Meera had given them as a gift when they first arrived in England, with nothing but a suitcase of clothes between them. A small shrine had been made on the mantelpiece under the picture, with a brass statue of the Hindu elephant god, Ganesh, a few family photos, and two rosebuds picked from the garden, all carefully grouped together. The room was sparse in comparison to the Guptas' home, but even so, something appeared to be different.

'Ah, I have made change. Do you see?' asked Babita, her eyes shining with excitement. Her English was less good than Meera's, and less good than her husband's too, although she had learned very quickly after she arrived, speaking almost no English at all back then. Enchanted by her prettiness, the other ladies who lived in the house made it their mission to teach her, and had been successful with their willing pupil. Often, Meera and Babita chattered away in their native Hindi, but Babita still wanted to perfect her English and Meera would correct her as they talked. She scanned the room again, still unsure of the change that had been made.

'The bed is moved. You see it? I am thinking that it might also change the luck in that way.' Babita peeped shyly from under her eyelashes at Meera, who nodded, understanding perfectly that she was referring to her desire for a child. Neither of the ladies had been successful in that department, and whilst Meera had long ago given up any hope, her friend had not.

'May you be blessed,' she muttered, 'blessed with many children.'

'Let it be so,' replied Babita. 'Now I must feed you. You will see what I have made.'

Meera had already smelt the chicken curry that Chandu had mentioned when she first arrived, and her mouth watered. She passed on his message and they both laughed.

'I am still not understanding why Mr Gupta will not allow in his house. This is our food.'

Meera nodded her head sadly. 'I don't understand it either. He wants to be an Englishman. Sometimes he thinks he is one, the fool.' The ladies glanced at each other and began to laugh again.

'Then you must come here more often,' said Babita. 'I will feed you. You are my good friend and it is my duty!' She looked as ferocious as her tiny person would allow and stamped her equally small foot, like a child having a tantrum. The name Babita in Hindi meant 'small child,' and Meera thought it most appropriate to the person standing in front of her.

'Now you will eat,' Babita continued, bustling around and placing dishes on the table, finally bringing a plate of warm chapatis covered with a lace-edged cloth.

They ate in silence, both munching on dried chillies which left their mouths burning with pleasure, reminding them of their homes in India and the places and people that had been left behind. Finishing their meal with the Jalebi, and coffee drunk, they lay on the bed – full to bursting and weighed down by the heavy food.

'You must tell me everything about your husband. He has hurt you again?' asked Babita. Meera once told her friend that Vasu had slapped her after an argument, and this had not been forgotten.

'No, not again. Just that once. I told him that I will go to the police and that they will send him back to India. That stopped it, you see. He is an English lord now, and to go back is no longer an option. For me, yes – for him, no.'

Babita sat up, crossing her legs under her. 'You would go without him?'

'I might. It is what I want. This life has little pleasure for me, you know that. I am planning my escape, but not to worry, my dear. It won't be for some time, so I can still be auntie to your many children.' They both giggled and Meera sat up too, smoothing the creases from her sari with her hand – a large diamond ring flashing with multi-coloured fire as she did so. 'Please pass me my bag. I have something for you.' She tipped its contents out onto the bed, quickly pushing the hated Crimplene suit to one side, cursing it under her breath for all that it represented. She carefully picked up a bright-pink net drawstring bag and held it out to Babita, her eyes now shining almost as brightly as the ring. 'For you, Babi. He gave it to stop me telling the police but I have no need for it. I have so much already – enough to last for years.' Pulling open the top, she pulled out, piece by piece, a matching toiletry set of talcum powder, soap, cologne and bubble bath.

Babita gasped. She had no spare money for luxuries, and to have a set like this was beyond her imagination. She began to thank her friend.

Meera raised her hand. 'No, no thank you needed. Without you I don't know what I would do. But you must make me a promise?'

'Yes. Anything.'

'You must use it everyday. No bottom drawer, no childrens' dowry – showri or saving for the future. The future may never come, and I want you to smell like the angel you already are. You understand? It might help you and Chandu... you know?' Babita nodded and smiled.

'Every day, I will use it. Tonight is my turn for the bath. I will smell like a princess.'

'Good. Now I must brush my teeth and go. She picked up the toothbrush and paste that had been in the bag and within minutes was standing at the door. They embraced.

'No need to come down, Babi. I know the way by now. Same day next week?'

'Of course. I will have something so very special for you. You will see.'

'My mouth is already watering,' replied Meera. Within half an hour she was back in her Crimplene suit and walking through the door of Mr Gupta's hardware store. Both men were serving customers and she slipped upstairs, barely noticed. After changing into loose cotton pyjamas and making a cup of tea, she sat in her chair by the window, allowing the hypnotic hum from the street below to gently sooth her vexed spirit.

Reliving the past few hours, she thought about Babita and her desperate desire for children. Would it ever happen, she wondered? She tried to raise images in her mind of their smiling faces, even their crying, but none would come. She thought about going back to India alone, leaving Mr Gupta in his shop checking the stock and counting his money. Would he even miss her at all, or would he enjoy the peace without her unhappy complaining voice and their large wedding bed, half empty? She sadly shook her head. How would it all end?

The ornate black clock on the wall ticked away time and Meera closed her eyes, now almost asleep – but not quite – lingering for a moment in that in-between place of nothingness, claimed neither by reality nor dreams. It was here that Mr Gupta found her a few minutes later and, silently fetching a chair, he watched as she slept, both tormentor and guardian angel in one.

CHAPTER
THREE

It was nearly seven by the time Chandu got back home because Mr Gupta had insisted on him washing and sweeping the pavement in front of the shop. This was a job usually reserved for Monday morning, but he had been particularly peeved that afternoon when he discovered that someone had vomited right outside the door, and that a customer had trodden in it, bringing it into the hardware store on the bottom of his shoe.

'No worries – no worries at all,' he said. 'Mr Kumar, please wash Mr Davis's shoes for him.' Chandu did as he was told and the customer left, happy and pleased with shoes now far cleaner than they had ever been since they were new.

As he entered the hallway Chandu smelt his dinner and sighed contentedly. It was far stronger than the other food smells that often hung around for days of meat pies, cabbage, and gravy. He twisted his face in disgust.

'You are late,' scolded Babita, her hands on her hips, waiting in the open doorway of their room. 'What problems this time? Mr Gupta was wanting you to wash his face for him? This would not surprise me!'

'A face wash would have been better, believe me – a shave, also! I was engaged in the cleaning of vomit, and then the washing of the shoes which stood in the vomit.'

'What?' she shouted. 'You are now working as a street cleaner? I shall speak to him myself!'

'Calm yourself, Babi. It is of no matter, and to argue with him is pointless. Now, where is my food? I am half starved!'

After washing his hands he sat down at the table, where a plate and cutlery were already set for him. Babita brought him the chicken curry she had made earlier, with several smaller dishes of potatoes and green beans, both liberally showered with chilli flakes. She hovered as he ate, responding immediately to his demand for lime pickle and more water. When he had finished he let out a loud burp.

'Ah, Babi, that is better now. I was thinking I might faint with hunger,' he teased.

'Then you must take more tiffin with you tomorrow. I will make sure that there is more in the tin. It is true that you are so thin, but always you have been like this.'

'Did you have a nice time with Meera?' he asked.

'Oh yes. She loved the food and gave me a gift of soap and bubble bath.'

'How kind she is.' He turned to look at the glinting picture of the Taj Mahal on the wall. 'Has he struck her again?' he asked, just the idea of this causing his already wrinkled brow to crease further with alarm. He liked Meera very much and thought her a true lady, far better than any other he knew, apart from Babita, of course.

'She says no. She threatened him with the police, and this has stopped him, but she says she will be going back to India in the future. I shall miss her so much.' She paused for a moment. 'But maybe she won't go? He still makes her wear English clothes. She hates it, and she hates him, also.'

'Yes, I saw her today. What a fool he is – sometimes I can barely silence myself. One day I will tell him to keep his job. I will tell him to go to hell!' This was a common theme for Chandu, who would often fantasise for hours about what he would say to Mr Gupta when he finally got another job and handed in his notice. 'I will tell him to stick it when there is no sun shining!'

Babita laughed loudly. 'I think you are meaning to say, "Mr Gupta, you can stick your job where the sun does not shine."' She laughed again, soon to be joined by her husband. They were standing in a queue at the local grocers when they first heard this phrase as part of a discussion between two men who were stood in front of them.

'Oh, how I wait for this day,' he continued. 'Finding another job is not easy, but I am searching all the time.' He put his hand in his pocket, pulling out the two nails taken from the storeroom earlier and dropping them down onto the table. 'Two nails today, although perhaps it should be two-thousand nails.'

Babita picked them up and examined them for a moment. 'Or even two-million? You are treated like a slave, but...' She paused, discomfort showing on her face before speaking again. 'I am still not quite liking the nails. Every day the nails.' She always said this when he handed them over, her belief in honesty at all times at odds with the abusive treatment of her husband, by Mr Gupta.

'It is symbolic, you know that,' Chandu replied. 'Each nail is a symbol of my suffering at his hands. It is not theft, Babi. More it is a marker of time for our lives here in England, and of my life in Mr Gupta's hardware store.'

She nodded, and letting out a sigh went over to the cupboard under the stairs in the far corner of the room. She disappeared inside, dropped the two nails into the large tin at the back, and came out again – smoothing her sari to brush away any cobwebs.

In bed that night they made love, Babita imagining throughout the large happy family she hoped to have. Later, she told Chandu about Meera wanting to be auntie to their children. 'How wonderful this would be. She would be the best auntie in the world, and my children I will share with her.'

He let her chatter away, making small gestures to let her know he was listening – a pat on the back or a tighter hug, or replying on several occasions with, 'Yes, what fun we shall have.' In his mind and what he didn't say was that it seemed most likely that there would be no children. About a year after they first came to England, Babita had been taken to hospital with pains in her stomach. They were told she had benign cysts on her ovaries, but one was particularly large and the whole ovary would need to be removed. The doctor said that there should be no problem in conceiving with just the one which appeared to be working normally. Chandu remained unconvinced,

19

and as the childless years went by no longer placed any faith at all in the doctor's words.

Eventually Babita fell asleep, but for Chandu sleep didn't come for at least another hour. Mr Gupta's shiny face and his false reassurances to the customer – the smell of vomit and the safety of the dark storeroom all replayed themselves. Turning over again, he thumped his pillow and tried to relax, remembering the frequently used words of his long-dead mother when faced with adversity of any kind.

'What can you do?' she would ask. 'This is life!' With a shrug of her shoulders she would carry on with whatever she was doing, the problem pushed away by simple acceptance of misfortune and hopeless circumstance. Without doubt she had been a strong and wise woman. Her pragmatic approach to life had seen her through many difficulties, and repeating the words to himself like a mantra, Chandu finally slept.

CHAPTER
FOUR

1974

Babita left the doctors surgery in a daze, and carefully tried to organise her jumbled thoughts in order to go over and take in the conversation she had just had.

'Mrs Kumar, I am pleased to tell you that you are pregnant. Our little experiment has worked this time.' He leaned across the desk and held out his hand, shaking her tiny one with such gusto that she gave a small yelp.

'About twelve weeks I would say – but it's early days and you will need to take great care. I want you to rest every afternoon, do absolutely no heavy lifting – not even bags of shopping and no heavy housework.'

Babita nodded.

'And good food, Mrs Kumar: milk, eggs, fish, meat, fruit and vegetables. I'll give you a vitamin supplement too.

I shall see you again in a few weeks to check how things are, and we'll need to talk about the possibility of a scan after that. As I told you, when you take fertility drugs there is always a chance of more than one baby and we shall need to know what we are dealing with, especially because you are so small. Make an appointment as you go out, perhaps for a time when your husband can come with you?'

'Yes, Doctor, thank you. I will do what you say.' She hesitated for a moment. 'But Doctor, do you think everything will be alright? After all these years, and I am thirty-eight now – an old lady to be having a baby.' She smiled at him, then peered anxiously into his eyes waiting for a reply.

Dr Greene sat back in his chair to think for a moment. He had become very fond of Babita Kumar over the years. She was unfailingly polite, gracious, extremely pretty and dressed in a peach chiffon Sari, looked quite good enough to eat. Mr Kumar was a very lucky man. He smiled back at her, then spoke as gently and thoughtfully as he could.

'Mrs Kumar, it's impossible to say for sure. So far everything seems fine and you're in good health, but with your past history there can be no guarantees. There have been two miscarriages so far?'

She nodded her head.

'Yes, I think the most important thing to do is to follow my earlier instructions. If we have to take you into hospital for bed rest, then we will. You must take what I've said very seriously – about no lifting and housework?'

Babita let out a big sigh. 'Yes, Doctor, I promise I will… and I shall hope and pray. Thank you.' Walking home through the park and with plenty of time, she sat on her favourite bench that looked over the lake. The view never failed to calm her, especially if the swans were there. She gazed around, taking deep aromatic breaths of air, marvelling at her good fortune, yet fearful, knowing full well through experience how quickly tides could turn and joy be replaced with misery. The sun shone on her face and she closed her eyes, deciding to enjoy the moment no matter what the future might bring.

***

Chandu would be home late tonight because he and Mr Gupta were stocktaking. He was paid no overtime for these extra hours, and his one attempt to ask for payment about a year ago, was met with a verbal assault of such force that he had come home in tears, refusing to ever go to the store again. Meera arrived some forty minutes later, having heard the row from the flat upstairs. Her face was red and swollen, and Babita could make out the print of a large hand across her right cheek. She reached into her bag and pulled out a handful of pound notes, pushing them across the table.

'He has struck you again? Is this so, Meera? I can see it. Oh, I shall speak with him, and I shall go to the police myself if you will not. How could he do this thing? He is a bully. April, the school teacher from upstairs has taught me this word, and this is what he is. I shall slap his face!' She jumped up from the chair and went to pull on her coat.

'No, no, there is no need,' Meera replied. 'I shall be writing to my brother tomorrow to make arrangements for my return home to India. I wanted Chandu to have the money he is owed for so many extra hours over the years. I opened the till and took it. Vasu tried to stop me and I slammed the drawer on his hand. He still has his fingers, but only just!' She looked across at her friend, watching the indignation slowly disappear to be replaced by the corners of her pretty pink lips beginning to curl upwards. Within seconds they were both leaning on the table shaking with laughter, which is where Chandu found them when he came back in from using the bathroom out in the hall.

'You say he still has fingers?' asked Babita. 'This is a great shame. Far better the fingers had dropped off into the till.' This set them off again, and quickly working out what had happened, Chandu soon joined in. Meera spent that night with the Kumars, sleeping in the bed with Babita. Chandu dragged the armchair to the far corner of the room and, unseen from the bed area, spent the night there.

They both walked Meera home the following morning, Chandu waiting outside whilst Babita went in with her friend. They ignored the ashen-faced man standing by the till, his fingers heavily bandaged. After settling Meera in the flat, Babita came back downstairs, quietly closing the door behind her. Mr Gupta kept his back to her, and made no move to face the little lady behind him.

'Vasu! Turn around, you fat oaf. Have you no manners left at all?' she cried, appalled to be treated in this way.

He slowly turned to face her, his mouth slightly ajar and dark circles under his eyes revealing a lack of sleep from the previous night.

'You would strike my friend?' continued Babita, her temper growing. 'A beautiful lady? The best lady in London? You are a mean bully and a common wife-beater! From here I will go to the police. Chandu is outside and he is taking holiday for one week, holiday which you have never given. He will be paid for this and will have an increase in his wages from this time. You hear me, Vasu?' By now she was almost shouting, and he nodded, his eyes cast downwards.

'Good!' She began to walk towards the door then, thinking better of it turned back again, stood on her tip-toes, and as quick as a lightning strike raised her right hand and caught him with a hard, sharp slap across the face. Hand stinging she marched out of the shop, slamming the door behind her and the bells jangling wildly. She smiled as she remembered then got up from the bench to continue the journey home, pulling the end of her sari a little further over her head to protect it from the sun. Although Chandu still wasn't paid for the overtime, Meera made a point of buying them something for their room each time, taking the money from the till in full view of Mr Gupta.

***

Chandu had just left the store and was walking home, in his pocket the two nails taken from the box earlier. He had initially taken only one, but by early evening Mr Gupta's vicious temper began to show, and Chandu had gone back into dark storeroom behind the till and taken another. He knew that Babita did not entirely understand, but the taking of nails was, as he so often said, symbolic of his suffering at the hands of his employer. It was a way of standing up to him – of silent defiance and bold-faced retaliation toward the older, stronger and more powerful man.

As he walked, he wondered what would happen if Gupta ever found out about the nails? He had done a rough calculation the other day of how many he now had, and arrived at a figure of somewhere in the region of three thousand, six hundred. There were three containers almost full, and if his life must be valued by the acquisition of nails, then he was satisfied.

When he reached the boarding house, he stopped for a moment to gaze at it bathed in the late evening sun. At the centre of a tall and very long row of Victorian redbrick properties, it had a small garden to the front, always overgrown but none the less attractive for that. Now mid-summer it was a jungle of flowers: roses, honeysuckle, jasmine, and many more that he didn't know the names of. The backdrop to this bright show was a spread of Virginia Creeper reaching halfway up the front of the house, the low garden wall and part of the broken gate densely covered with dark-green ivy. He closed his eyes for a moment, revelling in the warmth of the sun on his back before opening them again.

In that moment, for the first time ever in his life, he was struck by a profound sense and acknowledgement of beauty. It was like he had never opened his eyes before, or had been previously blinded to it. But here in England? Surely the knowledge of beauty would have been first seen in his home country – India? He shook his head slightly in wonder. How very strange. Then he shivered, suddenly

26

chilled as though a dark cloud had come over him. He looked upwards seeing nothing but bright blue sky, then heard a noise. The front door of the house had opened, and a name was called, his reverie now broken.

'Chandu, what are you doing here staring at the sky? I was about to search for you thinking that Gupta had weighed you down with a ball and chain. I was to slap him again!'

'Yes, my Babi, you are the master of slaps. This is why I am always so obedient. I am terrified of receiving the gift of one myself!' He held his hands up over his face in mock defence at this possibility.

'Come husband… I have made such a dinner for you that you will not believe it. Even stuffed paratha I have made – your favourite!'

'But wife, to what do I owe this most special of dishes which makes so rare an appearance, that I have almost forgotten its taste?'

'Not true! I made it for your birthday, but come inside and I will tell you what it is that we are celebrating.'

***

He followed her up the stairs, hearing both a television and then a radio in neighbouring rooms. Babita often listened to the radio when he was out, saying it helped her English, which was undoubtedly true. April from upstairs continued to give her lessons, as did an older lady who lived on the ground floor called Miss Grant. She had once been a governess in India and told them many wonderful stories from her past – sometimes using such appalling

27

Hindi that neither of them understood more than two words out of ten. Too polite to say, they would both smile and laugh in what appeared to be the most appropriate places, and so far had caused no offence.

As usual, the table was laid for one, Babita keeping the tradition she had been taught of serving her husband before eating herself.

'Why can we not eat together? It would be the English way, and I want it!' demanded Chandu, lightly thumping the table with his fist in a mock display of authority.

'You think you are Mr Gupta?' replied Babita, indignantly. 'Soon I shall have to call you Mr Kumar, and you will strike me and leave your mark on my cheek? I am an Indian lady, and this way I shall remain! Now sit and eat your dinner.'

With a sigh, Chandu did as he was told. When he had finished, and the two nails were put in the almost-full third tin, Babita demanded that he sit in the armchair.

'Sit, Mr Kumar,' she said, teasing him. Then more seriously... 'Sit down, Chandu, I want to tell you something.'

He sat, and Babita gracefully knelt down on the rug in front of him, bought by Mrs Gupta after Chandu had been forced to work for a whole Sunday to mop up a leak. Taking his hand in hers she looked down for a moment, then up and into his dark brown anxious eyes.

'I went to see Dr Greene today,' she said quietly.

'You are not ill?' He gripped her hand more tightly, suddenly upright and tense, his forehead furrowed with concern.

'No, I am very well. Be quiet, and I will tell you.' She began her story about the fertility treatment.

'Babi, you told me you had stopped this after the last two failures. You said that enough was enough. You lied to me?'

'Not lied, husband, more an omittance. I was going to stop – I meant it at the time, but then I thought again that at my age there would not be much more time left for me to try for a baby.'

'But why did you not tell me? You think I would have stopped you? Never! Never would I have done that!' He was now feeling quite cross… Perhaps he was so intimidating as a man that his wife felt the need to keep secrets from him?

Babita sighed. 'You are the most wonderful of husbands, and I do trust you. It was just that I felt like I had failed you, and did not want to fail you further – so best that I did not say and then there is no upset.'

'You have never failed me, never. But tell me, why did you go to the doctor today?'

'I am pregnant, Chandu. About twelve weeks, the doctor said. He also says I must rest every afternoon; must do no lifting, not even shopping, and must eat good food. He says I may need to have special scans because multiple babies are not unusual when these drugs are used, and because of my size.' She waited for a moment, watching for any signs of how he might be feeling – for approval or disapproval. 'Well… Chandu? Please say something.'

'I think you must lie down now – you have been cooking for hours. What a selfish woman you are, harming yourself in this way.' He stood up and held out his hand to pull her from the floor.

'I do not want to lie down. I feel quite well, not even sick in the mornings. It is like a miracle!' Still protesting, he led her across the room to the bed, where he made her lie back against the pillows.

'Tea or coffee, madam? I am your servant, and every demand shall be met.' He flung a tea towel over his arm, pretending to write on an imaginary pad of paper, as a waiter might do.

'Very well,' replied Babita, relieved to be spared any more questioning, and to see her husband joking and fooling around as he so often did. 'If you wish to wait upon me, then let it be so. I shall have tea, please. Weak, with milk and no sugar.'

Later that night, unable to sleep, Chandu got up to drink a glass of water. He looked at his sleeping wife, then silently began to cry. He wanted a child, of course he did. What man in his position wouldn't? But Babita was so small, and she had lost two babies that he knew of with this treatment. It wouldn't surprise him if there had been more. What if something went wrong? What if she lost the baby again, or worse, if she died? He stopped himself. No, she wouldn't die. This was England after all. But the disappointment for her if things went wrong – he couldn't bear it, really he couldn't.

Quietly pulling out a chair he sat at the table, every now and then looking across to the bed and his wife in it. The duality of his situation bore no resemblance to that of Mr Gupta, despite the similarity of both holding a night-time vigil. Chandu had not a tormentous bone in his body, nor could he think of himself as a guardian of any kind, having little belief in his physical or emotional prowess. He knew he was a good man, no question, yet felt so constrained by the absurdity of his situation as a skivvy and second-class citizen, that he no longer even knew where to look for the qualities that he felt Babita so deserved in a husband.

A bright moon shone through the window behind him, casting his shadow across the room and to the wall opposite. He looked huge – like a giant, and to any wise observer there was an analogy to be made here, that within the smallness of Chandu's body, lay a man of such immensity that a room was filled with his presence. All that was needed was the belief within the man that it could be so. It had become second nature for Chandu to perceive only the inadequacy that he felt, and despite being directly faced with his other self, he saw it not.

An hour later he crept over to the armchair, and pulling a blanket over himself fell into a restless sleep. Taking its turn, the picture of the Taj Mahal now directly faced with the bright beams of the moon, glinted and flashed its brilliance upon him, revealing yet again the dormant potential that lay within, and offering a blessing of light at the same time. The small statue of Ganesh glowed, and the moon continued its journey, finally plunging the room into darkness.

CHAPTER
FIVE

'Mrs Gupta? Where are you?' Mr Gupta walked into the sitting room but not seeing his wife nor hearing a reply, opened the door to the bedroom where she was sitting at the small desk in the corner, writing a letter.

'I am here, as you can see. What is it?'

'I was thinking. It has been almost ten years since we took over the store, did you know this?'

She paused for a moment to reflect. 'Yes, I do believe you are right. What of it? Are you going to give Chandu a raise in salary as a celebration, Mr Gupta?' Since he hit her for the second time, and Babita had come in and taken him to task, Meera ceased to call him 'Mr Gupta' unless through sarcasm – then saying it constantly in order to mock. At first he objected, saying that she would lose the formality for which the English were renowned. She had marched up to him as close as she could get, presented her face, and with as much menace as she could muster, spat out her words.

'Perhaps you would care to strike me again, husband? Please do, and the chief constable at the police station will come and arrest you. As you know, I have spoken to him and I only have to say one word and you will be behind bars.' This wasn't actually true since she had not been to the police station at all. Her husband suspected this, but not being entirely sure, refrained from any further assaults and a truce had been drawn.

He pretended that he hadn't heard her question about the raise in salary, and carried on. 'Ten years, Mrs Gupta – this is a long and most auspicious amount of time. I have been thinking that we should celebrate.'

Meera stared at him with wonder. 'You surprise me, Mr Gupta. I would have thought that spending your profits would be the last thing you would be considering.'

'Who said anything about profit-spending? I was thinking we should hold a special sale. Buy cheap things from the wholesaler and mark up the price. We could offer English food to our customers, sandwiches and sausage rolls – you know these things that they like?'

Meera screwed up her face in disgust. 'Why can you not offer Indian food? Many English people do like it, you know?'

'Never! This is England, and we are living amongst the English. We must do as they do. We must fit in.'

Meera had heard this statement a thousand times, and sighed. He had never shifted from his stance despite the furious arguments that they had, as well as more amenable discussions, attempting to convince him that he need not entirely eradicate who he was in order be accepted. He refused to waiver his view, and she continued to go to Babita once a week for proper Indian food. Each time, she took a gift of some sort – often groceries or something else that she thought they might need, including several good quality saris for her and shirts for Chandu. Their rent had gone up four times since they had lived in the boarding house, and she knew how they struggled each month to keep up with the payments on Gupta's paltry salary.

'Do what you will. The bakery on the corner will make things for you, and no doubt you will fill the till with your sales. I shall need money for my ticket to India. I am arranging things with my brother, Manju. Everyone wants to see me, and I shall go for six months at least, maybe more than this. Maybe I shall not come back at all, Mr Gupta.'

Hearing this, he took a few steps back before sitting on the edge of the bed. 'But you are my wife, Mrs Gupta. Your position is by my side. You must stay with your husband.' He said this without raising his voice, sounding only quietly indignant – shocked even.

'There is no "must" Vasu. I am not a prisoner here. My brother knows what you have been doing to me, and the circumstances in which I am forced to live. He and I will discuss further when I am there, and we shall see. Perhaps you should start to care for your wife more. Maybe it is too late?'

'But you have everything you need here; the best clothes, furniture, hairdressers every week. What is it that you are saying to me?'

'I have nothing. These things you mention mean nothing to me. There is no love between us, and without that my life is empty. My only attachment to this place is Babita. Be grateful that there is at least one thing to return for. Without her, I would have left you a long time ago. I have a letter to post.' She stood up, straightened her sari, and walked towards the door.

Unable to help himself, he tried to stop her. 'Mrs Gupta, you shall not go out in these clothes. When will you learn?'

She stopped in the doorway, her back facing him – her body perfectly still and as taut as a stretched wire. 'Mr Gupta – you are the one who is refusing to learn. From this moment on, I shall wear what I wish. I shall not walk the streets dressed like a woman of the night. I shall cover my body and my legs. I shall cover my head if I wish. I shall paint my face in a fashion of my choosing. I shall wear bindi, kohl and sandalwood fragrance. I have told my brother what you have been forcing me to do. He has said that if you continue, he will come here and kill you.'

She waited for a response, but he was silent; his mouth open and jaw hanging down from his startled face. Meera's brother held a high government position and had powerful contacts. The fact that they would hold no jurisdiction in England had not occurred to him. Power was power, and there would always be a way.

'Did you hear me, Mr Gupta?'

He nodded, the 'yes' barely audible.

'Good!' And with that, she carried on walking, slamming the bedroom door behind her. She was shaking all over, but triumphant.

'Worms will turn, Mrs Gupta,' she said aloud, 'and this worm has just turned into a cobra!'

CHAPTER
SIX

M r Gupta continued with his plans for the anniversary celebration. Several posters were placed in the shop windows and on the door, and each customer that came into the store was handed a flyer to use as an invitation.

He had given an order to the bakery across the road to make an English buffet, and argued the price down as best he could. The manager stood her ground, eventually agreeing to ten-percent off the normal cost, providing they were all invited, and that his wife would be there. All the staff waved to her throughout the day as she sat observing the street from the first-floor window, and she usually popped in for a quick chat if she was out. She was very popular with them, and on numerous occasions had brought over Indian cakes for them to try, the smell of which offended her husband less than a good, strong curried dish which she herself favoured.

He had been to the wholesalers twice leaving Chandu in charge, and there had been two deliveries of goods. Chandu was given the job of sorting it all out; cleaning up the old stock that his boss had bought, and fixing sale stickers on the items which were worth far less than the prices asked. At least he was able to be in the storeroom whilst doing these tasks. As well as this unexpected pleasure he was also mostly undisturbed, since it had been a busy week and Mr Gupta was rushed off his feet.

He squatted on the floor, just as he had done in his uncle's furniture workshop, wiping dirt and dust from out-of-date paint tins. He hummed softly to himself, thinking about his wife, and the chance they had been given to have a child. He hadn't told Mr Gupta, quite simply because he didn't want to. He didn't want any type of intimacy with the man for whom he had so little respect, and anyway, Babita wanted to tell Meera first which would be that very afternoon. When it was nearly six, he got up from the floor and went to the sink to wash his hands, moving automatically from there to the boxes of nails. 'One nail today,' he said to himself, slipping it into his pocket then walking back through to the shop.

'Ah, there you are. Have you finished cleaning everything ready for Saturday?' asked Mr Gupta. 'It has been very busy, and so many people say they will be coming to the celebration.'

'Almost finished. I just need to wipe the oil from the boxes of tools, put on the price tickets, and then it will all be done.'

Gupta opened his mouth as though he was about to comment, then perhaps thinking better of it remained silent, and started to count the notes in the till to take to the bank the following morning.

Chandu said no more and slipped through the door to begin his walk home.

***

That afternoon, after Babita had fed her friend and cleared the plates, they both lay on the bed to rest and talk – just as they would have done in India, with a fan spinning slowly on the ceiling. There was no fan on the ceiling in England, although it was certainly hot enough for one.

'I think you have something to tell me,' said Meera. 'You have been nervous all afternoon so far, and I am now beginning to worry. What is it? You didn't like the fruit and vegetables I brought? You would prefer something else next week? What is it – please tell me.' Babita propped herself up on one arm, and Meera did the same, both now facing each other.

'You are right – there is something. Last week I went to the doctor and…'

'You are sick? Is that it? I will help! I will pay for any treatment you need,' Meera broke in, her face now showing concern, and her hand holding tightly onto Babita's arm.

'No, no, nothing like that. You are like Chandu, always thinking the worst thing. Let me speak and you shall know everything.'

Meera nodded, letting out a long garlic-scented breath.

'I have been trying the fertility treatment again.'

'But I thought you decided to stop after the losses. You changed your mind without telling me?'

'Yes – that is so,' said Babita firmly. 'I did not tell Chandu either, so you have no need to feel bad. I did not want to disappoint anyone further, so made a decision to carry on alone.'

'Hmmm, so headstrong for such a small person. You were thinking you could not count on the support of your old friend? Ay, ay, this is a bad thing. No trust.'

Babita chose not to enter into a discussion about trust and carried on with what she had to say. 'So, I have been taking the medication for a while and nothing. Then last week I find I am having a baby. It is about thirteen weeks now.' She smiled, pulling her arm out from under Meera's hand then holding onto it tightly.

'Oh Babita, at last we have a baby!' Meera jumped up, and started to pace around the bed. 'I shall be auntie as we have discussed. Oh, what joy... what fun we shall have; you, me and another Babi.'

Babita smiled at her excited friend whilst thinking to herself – if only, if only, please let it be... please. 'We must stay calm. It is very early days, and you know what happened the last two times, although a little earlier than this, it is true. I am told I must rest and do nothing that would strain me. Chandu is doing the housework, and the shopping also. I will have tests in case of problems, and the doctor says he will put me in hospital if I do not listen to his advice.'

'Oh Babita, you naughty, naughty girl! And you cook for me? You stand for hours to chop and peel, and also wash dishes?'

'But I enjoy it. I cannot lie on the bed all day!'

'From now on I shall cook for you! I shall come here earlier and cook, and you shall sit and be served. I shall be like your maid – you shall command and I shall do. There! This is how it will be. You will not dare to argue with me or you will meet your match, you will see!' Meera wagged her finger ferociously at her friend, then wiped a few tears away. 'I shall pray every day,' she added.

'I do this also,' Babita solemnly replied.

***

When Chandu walked in that evening the table was set as usual – the room fresh with the scent of lavender furniture polish. The floor had been swept and the sheets on the bed changed, taken home by Meera to wash and bring back again. Babita was lying down reading a magazine, feeling content and happy.

'Ah, husband... here you are at last. Everything is ready, and I will serve if you wash your hands.'

'I can do it myself. No need to get up, Babi – stay and rest.'

For the first time in her married life Babita did just that, stretching out like a pampered cat and revelling in the luxury of it all.

CHAPTER
SEVEN

The preparations for the anniversary celebration continued apace, and by Friday evening everything was ready. Even Meera had taken the trouble to come down and check the table where the food was to be displayed, spreading out one of her own tablecloths brought over from India. She smoothed the creases from the fine linen, remembering how she had hoped to entertain and have wonderful dinner parties using this and her other wedding gifts, but it had never happened. How disappointing it had all been, her life with Vasuman Gupta. So many dreams, so many hopes, and now nothing to show for it.

Then she remembered. The baby – Babita's baby, and how she would become an auntie. It would be an answer to many years-worth of prayers – all unheard – or if heard, ignored entirely by all the gods and deities that she knew of. Things could always be worse, she knew that, but comparing oneself to those less fortunate was not always helpful. This was the life she had been given, and how she felt about it was her prerogative. If there were more lives after this one, then who knew what they would be?

'Are you sure you want to come tomorrow?' Chandu asked Babita when he got home that evening. 'You might find it very tiring, and the walk is quite a long one, twenty minutes at least.'

'I take a walk at least that long every day. Staying shut up in here would drive me crazy. The doctor said no heavy work, not no walking at all. Gentle exercise is good, so I will come. Two o clock, isn't it?'

'Yes, and I shall make sure that there is a chair for you. Maybe we shall get a cab to take you home? The money is not important, but you are.'

'Very well, if you insist, but let us see how I am feeling and then decide.' She was due to see the doctor the following week. Apart from a few twinges she felt fine, and was tentatively beginning to allow herself to feel more hopeful of things turning out well.

***

At the hardware store, Meera had received a letter from her brother agreeing to the date she suggested for her arrival in India, in a few weeks' time. She hadn't yet told Mr Gupta, thinking it best to let him have his special day tomorrow, and tell him on Sunday. She would buy a one-way ticket which would allow her to decide when to return. Because of Babita and the baby she knew she would be coming back, but she certainly wasn't going to

43

tell her husband this. It would do him good to be kept wondering. Since she had involved her brother, and put her foot down about the clothes, she had begun to feel a little better. The future seemed more positive all round, and she was glad of it.

Mr Gupta stayed in the shop until late that evening, eating only a quick meal before going back down again. 'Everything must be perfect, Mrs Gupta. Tomorrow is a very important day. We have become a part of this community and I, at least, am very proud of it.'

'I don't know what you mean when you say this, "part of the community," rubbish. You have a store in their community which they tolerate because it is of use to them, but that is all. When are we invited into their homes, or their family celebrations? I will tell you the answer. Never! We will never fully be a part and that is all there is to it! I accept this, but you do not.'

'It is all a question of attitude,' replied Mr Gupta. 'Treat people with respect, and then you will get it back. This is my belief.'

'And is this how you treat Chandu... with respect? You pay him a salary so small that the rent can barely be paid.'

Looking very uncomfortable he stood up from the table, pushing his empty plate towards her. 'I treat him well. The store cannot pay out large sums of money, and anyway, you give to them all the time!'

'I give very little! And you have seen the signs, *No Irish, No Blacks, No Dogs*, Mr Gupta? At least heard of this even if you have not seen it, since you rarely go out anywhere at all. We foreigners are likened to dogs. You keep your eyes closed to the truth, and with you it has always been this way.'

'Perhaps it would be better if you closed your eyes a little more to the truth, if things are as you say they are. Then you would suffer less!' He stomped loudly back down the stairs, slamming the door so hard that the cutlery rattled on his plate.

Meera felt her blood pressure rise, and went to sit in the chair by the window to calm herself. A small fan was blowing cool air from a side table which she always found soothing, and she began to unwind her long plait in order to massage her aching head. 'We are like two cats, Mr Gupta and I, always fighting and spitting at each other,' she said quietly – and then in a much louder voice, 'The man who drew the horoscopes for our match needs to be flogged!'

She carried on rubbing and ruminating on her marriage before quickly clearing up and making a cup of tea which she took to the bedroom. She was soon asleep, and if her husband came up from the store at all, he had slept on the sofa. She remained undisturbed for the whole night, dreaming about the family house in her home town, and the servant they had who would massage her scalp for her.

CHAPTER
EIGHT

Saturday turned out to be bright and sunny, and by eight Mr Gupta was down in his beloved store, polishing the wooden counter with wax. He skipped breakfast, but had brought down a large cup of black coffee which he sipped as he worked. The previous night had been spent on the sofa, feeling too peeved with his wife to share their bed. He too had been thinking about their marriage and how he ended up with Meera, when he would have much preferred a more docile and less argumentative wife.

He had been let down very badly, but it was the dowry that turned their heads. His family were certainly not poor, and they came from similar backgrounds, although his family were academics – mostly teachers and headmasters. Why, he even had a bachelor's degree in English! Meera's family had only in the last few generations considered university education to be of value, but held posts in very high places, mostly in government office. In India, this held much kudos, which was also why Meera had been considered such a good match.

He let out a long sigh. He did love her, far more than she loved him, that much was clear. If only she would… At this moment his thoughts were interrupted by Chandu coming through from the storeroom. 'Late, ten minutes,' he barked, not even turning around.

'Not late at all,' replied Chandu, equally as curt. 'If you remember, you asked me to stop to get flowers for the celebration, and the flower shop does not open until eight.' He placed the flowers on the counter; a mixed bunch of roses and lilies in bright red and orange.

'Not there – I have just waxed it. Put them in the sink at the back, and I will call Mrs Gupta to arrange them in a vase.'

It was a busy morning, and both men worked flat-out. In between serving, Chandu mopped the floor and ran a duster over the piles of sale goods around the store. Everyone was very jolly, and many said they would be back later that day. The food arrived, and Meera came down to check it was laid out correctly and arrange the flowers.

'What have we here, Mr Gupta – your favourite sausage rolls? I know how much you love them, and shall keep some aside for your meal this evening. With salad and potatoes? Yes, it will be no problem, no problem at all.' She smiled to herself, knowing full well that he had never eaten pork in his life. In fact, he rarely ate any meat at all, and if he did, it would usually be chicken, or sometimes fish.

He looked at her, his face perplexed, and Meera turned away. She had gone too far and knew it. Smiling brightly, she faced him again. 'All done, Mr Gupta. How else can I be of assistance? Ah, I know! I have paper serviettes upstairs. They will be perfect. One moment.' She disappeared through the door to the flat.

Chandu had been watching this interaction with interest. When she taunted him with the sausage rolls, Mr Gupta seemed genuinely hurt. He had never seen this before. Anger, yes, but not hurt. Perhaps he had feelings after all, and wasn't just the miserly old scrooge that he thought? Chandu quickly dismissed this idea.

'Stop gawping, you fool! I don't pay you to stand around doing nothing!'

Chandu gave his employer a glare of utter contempt, so much so, that Gupta widened his eyes as if he hadn't seen correctly the first time. Chandu then turned and walked into the storeroom, going straight over to the boxes of nails and putting two in his pocket. He momentarily thought about taking three, but that would be wrong. One or two nails, that was his choice, not more. He washed his hands, taking his time to do a very thorough job. Babita would soon be here, and he didn't want her to see him looking like a sweeper-man from the back-streets of Delhi. Changing his dirty overall for a clean one, he smoothed his black hair, took a deep breath, and went back out into the shop.

***

Babita had arrived, and was sitting in the chair that had been put out for her earlier. She was wearing the same peach-coloured sari that Dr Greene found so attractive, and Chandu's heart melted at the sight of her.

48

'You have arrived,' he said, moving over to stand by her.

'As you see,' she replied. 'Could you get me a glass of water, please? I had not realised how hot it was today.'

He poured her one from the jug on the table that Meera had brought down, ice cubes chinking pleasantly. 'Are you alright? You should have stayed at home and rested.'

'Really, I am fine – nothing to worry about. I shall sit here and not move, then you can relax!'

Mr Gupta was serving a customer when Meera emerged from the door to their flat, a pile of paper serviettes in her hand. She looked quite stunning, her bright green and silver sari set off perfectly against her clear, dark skin – the plaited hair as usual piled upon her head like a coiled snake. Even Gupta watched as she moved quickly over to her friend, kissing her on both cheeks, then holding her hands as though she hadn't seen her for an age, instead of just a few days ago.

'You are looking tired. Stay seated, and we will bring anything that you need.' Babita sipped her iced water, small beads of sweat now forming on her forehead and upper lip. Meera took one of the serviettes and began to gently dab at her friend's face. Babita quickly snatched it away to do the job for herself.

'I am not entirely helpless, both of you, but I shall certainly allow you to serve me for the whole afternoon. And Chandu? When I am tired, I shall take up the offer of a cab. It really is too hot to walk.' She sat back in her chair, beginning to feel better. 'I shall observe everything and watch for thieves!' she laughed, the sparkle quickly returning to her eyes. Mr Gupta's customer had now gone, promising to be back in half an hour. He came over to the seated Babita, and putting aside the slap she had given him – or perhaps because of it, he too held both her hands.

'So long since I have seen you, my dear. You should call in more often. Here, let me refill your glass. You would prefer squash?'

'Thank you, just water, please.' Meera continued to watch this exchange with interest. This was the old Vasu. The one she had known in India, who was full of charm and thoughtfulness. Coming to England and taking over the hardware store had been the ruination of him and their relationship. Her thoughts were interrupted by several customers coming into the shop. Mr Gupta welcomed them, offered drinks and food, and continued with his charm offensive.

'Please do walk around. There are many bargains at reduced prices everywhere just for today, to mark the ten-year anniversary of my taking over the store.' This was repeated as more customers came in, and Chandu found himself permanently at the till, Mr Gupta's beloved pile of notes growing rapidly under their clip. Gupta was in his element, and the event certainly seemed to be a success with at least two dozen people standing around, eating, drinking and generally appearing to have a pleasant time.

Babita gazed through the window to check if the cab had arrived, quickly becoming absorbed in watching the people walking by, and the never-ending stream of cars and buses. Her thoughts drifting, she began to fantasise about where they might all be going... Suddenly, there was a screech of car brakes and angry shouting voices.

This was followed by a smashing of glass and a scream from Meera, who raced to the front of the shop to protect her seated friend, closely followed by Chandu. A brick lay on the floor in front of Babita's feet, and there was glass from the shattered shop window everywhere.

'Oh my god, what has happened? Are you alright? A brick has been thrown through the window? I knew it, I knew something like this would happen one day.' Meera glared at her husband hoping to catch his eye, but he was engaged in reassuring the remaining customers.

'Nothing to worry about, just a stupid prank,' he said. 'Just children playing silly games.'

'Not a game, Vasu! Someone could have been killed.' Meera turned to Babita who appeared calmer than everyone else, and was engaged in brushing the shards of glass from her lap – assisted by her husband.

'Did you see who it was?' she asked.

Babita thought for a moment. 'It was a white car with young men inside. Skinheads I think they are called? I see them in the park sometimes. They shouted very rude things, and then threw the brick.'

Mr Gupta called the police whilst this exchange was going on, then showed the remaining customers out of the store. 'Business as usual on Monday. Thank you so much for coming. It has been a such a pleasure.' He came over to listen to the description of what Babita had seen. 'What rude things?' he asked. 'Can you tell us, please?'

Babita beckoned to Meera who moved closer to her, putting an arm around her shoulders. Leaning over, Babita cupped her hand to whisper the things to her friend that she felt unable to say out loud.

Meera gasped, her hand raised to her mouth in shock. 'Just as I thought, Mr Gupta. This is the racism that you said did not exist. Respect others and they will respect you? Hah! We are not exempt. This will never be our home. Never! I want to go back to my real home – to India.' Before she could say anymore a horn beeped outside, and Chandu and Meera escorted Babita to the cab, giving the driver instructions. Just as it drove off the police arrived, lights flashing but with no sirens at all.

'As Indians we are not worth the sirens, is this it?' Meera shouted as the officers walked in, then repeating it to her husband.

'My dear, do try to stay calm. I shall talk to the police if both of you could clear the glass? Chandu, first you can call Mr Patel, the carpenter? His number is under the counter. We shall need his assistance to board up the window until the glass can be replaced.'

The police stayed for about half an hour. Meera hovered close by, keenly listening to what they were saying, and every now and then chipping in with a few comments.

'I do understand your distress, Mrs Gupta. This sort of thing is very upsetting. Unfortunately, there is little we can do to prevent these attacks since they are so random. We'll ask around and see if anyone else saw anything from outside. If we could get a car registration number or even just the make and model, that would be a great help. We know it was white, which is a start. And don't worry about your friend. We won't call on her unless it becomes absolutely necessary. You have told us exactly what she said, so that should be enough for now. If there are any other concerns do phone us. We'll be in touch soon to let you know how the investigation is going.'

They left, and Meera went upstairs. Chandu finished clearing up and Mr Gupta began to take the cash from the till. Despite the upset, he smiled as he did this, putting the notes into the bank deposit bag.

'A sad end to a very good day. You say Mr Patel will be here in half an hour?' Chandu nodded, walking past to put the broom and dustpan back into the storeroom.

'The takings are six-times the normal amount for a Saturday. Six-times!' He waited for a reply from his employee, but there was none. The rear door of the shop slammed, and Chandu began his walk home, anxious to check that Babita was alright.

'Just hooligans,' Gupta said to himself, 'and we have insurance,' he added, continuing to sort the cash, then tidy the store. A short while later he heard a banging on the shop door, and with a contented sigh went to let the carpenter in.

CHAPTER
NINE

Babita was lying on the bed propped up by pillows, a cup of tea in her hand, and the events of the afternoon running through her head. She had felt surprisingly calm when the brick smashed through the window. Of course she was startled, but it wasn't the brick that had been most disturbing – it was the words that were thrown with it. To some extent, she was used to hearing bad language and swearing. She heard it in the park all the time, and it was one of the things about England that she disliked the most. Gangs of youths would have almost entire conversations made up of foul language, much of which she didn't know the meaning of. She had never been abused directly because she always moved away from them immediately. There was no equivalent to this type of behaviour in India, not that she had ever seen, anyway.

India… It had been on her mind quite a bit lately, perhaps because of the baby. She knew how keen Meera was to go home, but she had little doubt that she would come back. It was easy enough to imagine that everything was perfect elsewhere when you were having troubles, but she knew that this was rarely true. How was it said in English? 'The grass is always greener.' April from upstairs said it a lot when she was talking about her job as a teacher, and the possibility of changing schools. Yes, in one's head the grass was greener, but in reality – not. India had many troubles and problems that England did not, but overall, she wasn't sorry that they had come here. If she was lucky enough to have a baby, then England was certainly a better place to be. At this point the door opened and Chandu walked in looking hot and tired.

After he had put two nails in the tin and had a wash, he lay on the bed with her, letting out a huge sigh. 'What a day. Are you sure you are OK? I have been worried all afternoon. You must take extra care, you know that, or I shall make sure you do go to hospital like the doctor said.'

'No need. Really, I feel fine.' She went on to explain her thoughts before he had come home. 'It wasn't the brick or the noise that disturbed me, it was the hatred and anger in the voices. Why would anyone hate another in this way? And without reason?'

'Meera told me what they said, and so ignorant too in assuming that we are all from Pakistan. If you are going to abuse, then at least get the nationality correct.'

'We are foreign, Chandu. Dark skinned and foreign,

55

and given the way they behave, I think that accuracy with regard to our home country is of no interest to them. April was coming in when I got back and made me some tea. She said the black children at her school are often abused and called names by the white ones. They are even struck! Can you believe this? Little children?'

Chandu nodded. 'It is hard to believe, but you are right. And not everyone feels this hatred. April likes us very much, despite our race.'

'April is a highly educated woman,' replied Babita. 'She does not need prejudice. If we are lucky enough to have this baby, then we will need to take great care to choose schools with a good reputation.'

'But with regard to the baby, what are you feeling? Does all seem well? I was worried that the incident would have frightened you so much that the baby might be affected.'

'No – not the case. I have had twinges of pain this week, just a few, and only seconds at a time. That is all, and I will talk to the doctor about this when I see him in a few days. I remind myself all the time not to raise my hopes too high. I have never got this far in the pregnancy, this is true, but we must be realistic and stay calm.' She looked at him, silently asking for his support to ease the fear of loss that she really felt but was unable to express. He understood perfectly and squeezed her hand.

'Babi, whatever happens we shall cope. We have each other, and if that is all we have then it must be enough! Now – food. Something different, I think? Madam likes fish, does she not?'

'Yes, she does! I know what you are thinking. Fish and chips… yes? A special English treat which we deserve.'

He smiled and jumped up from the bed, happy to be pleasing her and relieved to keep her lying down for a while longer, with no cooking to do.

CHAPTER
TEN

On Monday afternoon, Meera arrived at the boarding house, her bag bulging with things she thought her friend might like. She had also been worried about Babita's reaction to the incident on Saturday, and was greatly relieved to find her looking relaxed and well. She herself was more shaken than she had shown; the fears that were so often thrown at Mr Gupta suddenly becoming a reality, and not just another way of venting her anger at him. She had been tearful since then and unable to hide this from her husband who, to give him his due, had done his best to reassure her.

'I know you are frightened of such things,' he said. 'But if you take an overview, we have been very lucky. Nothing like this has happened before, and the business does well. We must rise above it, must we not?' He said this gently, and quite unlike the direct, matter of fact way that he had adopted since their arrival in England, thinking it very correct and appropriate to the country he now lived in.

How complex everything was, she thought. Really, it was far easier to hate her husband, than find him endearing and comforting. If he were to be this way all the time, then who knows? Maybe things would be clearer after her trip back to India? She hoped so. Sitting down at the table with Babita opposite her, she began to pull things out of the large straw bag that she always brought on her visits. 'I have bought you a new salwar kameez and dupatta to go with it, all matching. This is a child's size, but should be perfect for you, I think.' She stood up and held the trouser suit with marching scarf in front of her, admiring her choice. 'Do you want to try it on now, and then I can take it back if it is no good?'

'There is no need to buy gifts, you know that. Seeing you is gift enough, but thank you. Yes, let me try it now.' Going to a corner where she would not be seen, she picked up the suit and quickly changed her clothes, discarding the overlarge sari that she had been wearing.

'Oh Meera,' she exclaimed, 'it is perfect!' The blue silk was printed all over with tiny, multicoloured flowers, and the effect was both young and fresh. 'How can I thank you? You are so good to me. Without you, my life here would be so different.'

'For me, also. Without you, my life here would be intolerable. I think I would have left a long time ago. I am booking a ticket this week to go and see my family. Most likely I shall stay for two, maybe three months, and then I will be back. Plenty of time to care for you as baby grows.'

She paused for a moment, then spoke again, this time her voice full of doubt. 'Now I am thinking that I should not go. I should stay here in case I am needed.'

'No, there is no need. You must have your holiday. I have Chandu, and the doctor. There is a phone in the hall, and I always have money on the shelf to use for emergencies. April is upstairs and Miss Grant downstairs. I know you will come back, so there is no problem. Anyway, I think it might help you and Vasuman to have a break from each other?'

'Maybe.' Meera told her about the kind comment he made after the incident, and how he had been when they were first married. 'It was all so hopeful then, but he has changed so much.'

'I think he wants to show you how successful he can be – you and your family. He wants you to be proud of him but does not seem to understand how to do this. Being in England has confused everything, so that he now has no idea how to behave at all. Truthfully, it is confusing for us all, and for all immigrants, I imagine. I am not unhappy here, but sometimes I feel like I am in a holding place? How can I explain? It is like I am waiting for something – as if I am living my life in an airport lounge, or train station. I don't belong here, but I don't know where to go anymore to feel the belonging. I don't think India would make me happy for long. You will see this when you go back.'

Meera had never heard her friend speak in this way before, and felt quite in awe of the accuracy and astuteness of the dear lady sitting opposite her, who had the appearance of a pretty child, but the wisdom of an old woman.

Babita continued. 'Once a foreigner, then always one – and after a few years, even in the place of birth – still a foreigner. We become homeless, belong nowhere, are not fixed to the soil, even though we live in one place. Once a carrot is pulled from the ground, it can never be put back in to grow – not in any ground – nor any country. Do you see? I have given this much thought and have decided that it is the truth!'

Meera began to cry, her head cradled in her arms on the table. She had been unhappy for so long and only now did she fully understand why. The pain and sadness, the longing and loneliness, even when she was with her husband or Babita, now made sense, and the dam she had surrounded herself with broke at last.

Gently stroking Meera's back, Babita waited until the sobs calmed, then going to the sink she held a clean muslin cloth under the cold tap – finally splashing it with several drops of rose-water. She held this to her friend's ravaged face, gently patting and wiping, both silent – neither having any more to add to what had already been said. Within ten minutes Meera was being driven home in a cab, feeling too tired to walk. Her husband was with a customer when she arrived back at the store, allowing her to slip upstairs without revealing her distress.

She was lying on the bed when he came up later and, pleading a headache, he brought her a cup of tea and left her to rest. The tea cooled on the bedside table as she fell into a deep sleep, finally waking at almost nine the following morning, feeling exhausted but calmer than she had ever been in her entire adult life.

The bubble had burst, and an enormous shift had

taken place within her. How this would affect her from now on, she did not know. What she did know was that nothing would be the same, and she determined to face the future with new knowledge, and to do all she could to emulate the strength and courage that filled her tiny friend, Babita.

CHAPTER
ELEVEN

The hardware store was soon back to normal, and the broken glass was replaced on Wednesday. At the beginning of the week Mr Gupta's mood was still up, and he was much more pleasant to Chandu, even complimenting him after the floor had been washed.

'You do a good job of the floor. I like the smell – wet and fresh, a bit like after heavy rain in India before the bad smells come back out, you know?'

Chandu did know, and had often thought similar things as he swished his mop back and forth. His favourite and frequent memory when floor washing, was when he used to sit on the covered verandah of his childhood home during the monsoon – the rain falling heavily, and he protected and safe under the sturdy roof, yet still outside to enjoy it all and breathe fresh, clean air. Mistrustful of his employer most of the time, he nodded. 'Yes, I also think this,' he added, and carried on with his task. It was after the window had been replaced by Mr Patel that things returned to normal, and the insults, bad temper and general criticism of his employee and the customers after they had left the store, started up again.

On thinking about it, and when choosing two nails that evening before leaving through the usual back door, he realised that it was the window that had done it. Whilst it was still boarded up, Mr Gupta was continually reminded of what had happened last Saturday – of the brick, and the hatred from the skinheads outside. With the board, he was forced to accept the truth of his own vulnerability, and the fact that pretending to be the Englishman that he had invented in his head, was no protection against negative forces such as this.

Once the board was gone and the window replaced, it was like the incident had not happened, and 'Gupta the Hun' returned to his old self. Chandu had re-named him this after struggling to read a library book about the ruthless leader, and now namesake, Attila. He had found similarities between the men and smiled each time he applied the name to his employer. These small things helped him to get through his working day, although throughout the years of working at the hardware store, two nails were the main rebellion against the abuse, acting almost like a talisman against any permanent emotional damage.

***

When he arrived back home after fetching groceries, Babita had been talking to Miss Grant, and they walked up the stairs together. Everything stored away, and the nails put in the fourth tin, Chandu ate his dinner whilst his wife told him about her appointment with the doctor that afternoon.

'I told him I was having some twinges of pain, and I am now waiting for an appointment at the hospital to give me a scan. Dr Greene said he would make sure this was soon, most probably next week. He said many women had twinges and they amounted to nothing, but under the circumstances he wanted to take no chances.'

'Very wise. I do worry, though. Not about the baby, although you know how much I want one – no, I worry about you. The loss of an unborn baby I could cope with, but not the loss of you.' He stopped eating, his eyes cast down to his plate and fork held in mid-air.

'Chandu, please do not worry like this. I think it will all be fine. Apart from the twinges I feel well, and the doctor said I was in good health overall. You can come to the scan with me. Gupta can go to hell if he thinks he cannot allow this. Anyway, Meera will make it OK with him.'

Chandu raised his head, feeling relieved that he would be there to support her. 'Yes, of course. He will do nothing if Meera tells him so. Then, with the scan, at least we will know what we are dealing with. We can face what we know – that's right, is it not, Babi?'

They listened to the radio for a while and Chandu attempted to read more of the library book, eventually slamming it shut with frustration. They were soon in bed, Chandu snoring gently, but thirty minutes later Babita was still awake. She had felt more twinges and was trying to breathe deeply in the hope that they would pass. Eventually, they did, and she fell asleep to dream that she was in an airport lounge, waiting for a plane that was repeatedly delayed. She became increasingly anxious, as did the other passengers, until she woke with a start, sitting upright and holding her stomach to try to soothe the increasingly gripping pain. She groaned, and suddenly woken by the noise, Chandu leapt out of bed as though he had received an electric shock.

'No,' Babita shouted, then groaned again, bending forward so that her head was almost in her lap. The sound was like that of a wild animal – an unearthly choked howl of pain, fear and extreme distress. 'No... No, this must not happen! Help me Chandu, do something!'

'Babita, what is it? The baby? You are losing the baby? What can I do? Tell me, what can I do?' he shouted back, so panicked by what was happening that he was almost hysterical. From above he heard footsteps, and ran to open the door to let April in. She had been sitting at her desk marking the children's homework, and had heard the commotion in the room below. Guessing what might be happening, she ran down the stairs and through the unlocked door into the Kumars' room.

She quickly took in the scene and went over to the bed, pulling back the sheets. Babita was now lying on her side, holding her knees to her chest in an attempt to stop the pain. She was no longer screaming, but silent sobs shook her body; a small pool of blood spreading out over the white nightdress and the sheet behind her.

'Ambulance, Chandu. Hurry, and tell them to be quick.'

He nodded, and unsure if they would be needed, reached for the coins that were always ready on the shelf, then fled through the still open door and down the stairs. Miss Grant, hearing the commotion and the urgent telephone call, was standing by her own door, as were two other residents. 'Go back to bed. April is with us, and help will soon be here. Mrs Kumar is unwell, but don't worry, all is under control.' He certainly didn't feel that anything was under control as he dashed back upstairs, but there was no point in creating more panic than there already was.

Back in their room, he quickly pulled on the clothes he had been wearing that day, whilst April attended to his wife. Grabbing a small bag, he flung in a few of the things he thought she might need at the hospital, then went downstairs to wait for the ambulance. As he pulled open the front door, he was struck by the strong fragrance of honeysuckle and jasmine that grew in the garden. In that moment, he knew he would never smell these flowers again without being brought back to this terrible night. The noise of sirens was getting closer, and he went out into the street to flag the ambulance down.

'Indians do get sirens in England,' he said, his voice now calm and steady. 'Indians do get sirens in England, Meera,' he repeated, just as the vehicle slammed on its brakes – blue lights flashing wildly. Two men jumped out, and armed with their medical bags and considerable urgency, they followed him back up the stairs.

Ten minutes later Babita was carried into the ambulance on a stretcher, Chandu holding her hand and April following closely behind, having decided to go to the hospital with them. With lights flashing and sirens blaring, the race to the hospital began – the boarding house slipping back into the dark, scented, and silent night, as they sped away.

CHAPTER
TWELVE

Chandu sat in the dim corridor, alone apart from the occasional doctor or nurse that hurried by. April stayed with him for a few hours, but eventually went home, having commitments for the next day. He had been told nothing, and each time he heard footsteps he looked up hopefully, desperate for news about Babita and the baby.

His thoughts leapt about wildly from one scenario to the next. Babita was dead and they had forgotten to tell him, she had lost the baby and was dying alone in a room somewhere, she was in surgery and they were trying to save her life, and the worst one of all – she was lost. They had sent her to another hospital and he would be unable to find her. This scared him the most, and the thought raised such a panic inside his chest that he thought it might burst.

He was thirsty, but had only one coin in his pocket which he would need to call Meera when he knew what the situation was. He knew she would be furious if she wasn't told, and he had thought of calling her, but feared the wrath of Mr Gupta and any cutting remarks that might come his way about the disruption of sleep. He had already decided he would take two nails when next in the store. Two nails because he was too scared to phone Meera and ask for help. He heard footsteps and looked up as a nurse passed by, leaving the smell of disinfectant in her wake. It reminded him of his childhood home which was washed weekly with something similar, and he wished his mother was here now to take charge and make sure Babita was safe.

'Mr Kumar?' Chandu jumped to his feet, a white-coated young doctor standing in front of him.

'Yes, I am Mr Kumar,' he whispered, in a voice quite unlike his own. 'My wife, Babita, how is she? She is not…'

'Please don't worry. Your wife is fine. Come and sit over here and I'll explain.' The doctor led him to a small alcove at the top of the corridor, enclosed on three sides with glass screens. They sat down, Chandu's hands held tightly together, his knuckles showing white through his dark skin. Unable to look at the doctor's face, he kept his head bowed. 'Stupid, stupid, stupid,' he thought – 'you are a mouse that you cannot raise your head?'

'Mr Kumar…? Mr Kumar?' The doctor gently touched Chandu's shoulder, and he slowly looked up and into the bright blue eyes that were gazing at him with concern.

'It's alright – your wife is fine. There's no danger at all, do you understand?' Chandu nodded. 'I do have to tell you that she lost the baby – I'm so sorry. It wouldn't have survived so it was for the best, but I'm sure that's no help right now. There doesn't appear to be any reason why you both can't try again in a few months' time. She's resting and can probably go home later today or tomorrow. She's asking for you. Would you like to see her?'

Once again, Chandu nodded. 'Speak, you fool, speak,' he berated himself. 'Your tongue has not been cut out, what is wrong with you?' He finally spoke, his dry throat making the words sound gruff; the suppressed emotion constricting his voice to that of a child. 'Thank you, Doctor – thank you. I would like to see her, please.' He followed him to a small side room where Babita lay in a narrow bed, a white sheet pulled up under her chin; her eyes shut, and her body perfectly still. The door closed behind him leaving them alone, and he sat in the plastic chair by the side of the bed, carefully reaching his hand out to touch Babita's, under the sheet.

He stayed like this for some time – half an hour at least until he felt a movement, very slight at first, then becoming greater; Babita shaking with trying to hold back huge sobs that threatened to wrack her entire being. Eventually they escaped, and she cried as never before, repeating over and over. 'Chandu, Chandu, the baby is gone – the baby is gone.'

Once again, he found himself with no adequate response and held her hand tightly, his own tears slipping silently down his cheeks and onto his shirt. An hour later she was calm again and sat up, allowing Chandu to wipe her face with a cool flannel and smooth back her hair.

'That will be the last time, Chandu – the very last time.'

He nodded. 'Just us now, Babi. No more upset like this. No more hormone treatment.' It was a statement, not

71

a question, and Babita looked straight ahead at the bare, empty wall in front of her.

'Can you call Meera? They should be up by now, and you will need to go to work.'

'No, I shall stay here with you.'

'No need. Meera can come, and I shall be home later today – she will be with me. I want to see her,' she said, her eyes filling with tears again. He felt for the coin in his pocket and went out into the corridor to make the call.

***

Meera was still in bed when the phone rang, although she was awake, and had heard her husband's disgruntled voice before he came back into the bedroom.

'Take the call. Chandu is going to be late and wants to talk to you. This is too bad, being late when he knows how much there is to do. There was a big delivery yesterday…'

'Oh, shut up!' Meera interrupted. 'There must be a reason. When was he ever late? Get out of my way. I hope it is not Babita – please, not that.' She leapt out of bed, a thin cotton night-sari loosely draped over her voluptuous figure. Since her rebellion, gone were the thick flannelette nightdresses that she detested in favour of more traditional Indian sleepwear. 'And stop looking at me like that. Go downstairs and leave me alone.' She pushed him away from the door, attending to the slipped sari at the same time. Gupta continued to stare, only moving when she picked up the phone; deliberately slamming the door that led down to the shop as he left.

'Chandu, tell me – what is it? Babita? Tell me.' She

listened carefully to the barely audible voice, finally replying. 'I am on my way. Tell her I will soon be there.' Banging down the phone, she rushed back into the bedroom to change. Ten minutes later, she called back to Gupta, who was coming out of the storeroom just as she hurried through the shop door.

'Vasu, I am going to the hospital. Chandu is there with Babita. I shall see you later.'

'What time is he arriving at work?' he shouted back to her. 'What about my lunch?' If Meera heard either of these questions then she made no reply, deciding to slam the door instead, setting the bells jangling ferociously. For the first time in several years he swore in Hindi, throwing a box of hinges onto the counter in temper. He immediately opened the box to check that the contents weren't damaged before putting them back on the shelf.

'This is what they have married me to,' he said aloud. 'A woman who sleeps naked and abandons her husband for the slightest thing! Where is the respect, where is the loyalty?' He thought of her dishevelled figure from that morning, and the long plait unravelling itself over her uncovered shoulder. The door bells began to jangle again and, letting out a sigh, Mr Gupta went to greet the first customer of the day, all thoughts of Meera quickly disappearing with the anticipation of a good sale.

CHAPTER
THIRTEEN

'Lie down, Babita, and I will make you tea,' said Meera, placing the small kettle on the stove. They had just arrived back at the boarding house, Chandu going straight to the store. He was exhausted but thought that it would be best to leave the two ladies alone. The doctor had advised that Babita stay in overnight, but she had refused, and it was now four in the afternoon.

'I have no need to lie down because there is nothing wrong with me. Neither is there need to be careful, since there is no baby.' She put her hand to her stomach and rubbed it gently. 'There is nothing there now, nothing at all, and never will be. You will never be auntie and I shall never be mother. There it is – the truth!'

'But you can try again,' Meera replied. 'That is what the doctor said.' She lifted the kettle with shaking hands, the steam almost burning her fingers as she poured it into the pot. When she arrived at the hospital Babita had been calm, although by the look of her swollen face, had clearly been crying. Outwardly, Meera was more distressed than her friend, and could barely contain her upset and disappointment. However, she knew that the matter of fact speech hid a depth of feeling that way surpassed her own, and this concerned her greatly.

'My dear, please talk about how you are feeling,' she said gently. 'I understand that you are wanting to deny, but this will harm you in the end – please trust me.' She sat down on the bed, Babita now with her feet up and the pillows piled behind her head. Facing each other, both exposed and unable to hide their grief from the other, Meera leaned forward to pull her friend close, holding her tightly until the tea was cold... and the tears had run dry.

***

Chandu arrived at the store just after one. He was hungry and dishevelled, and still wearing yesterday's clothes he went into the storeroom to put on the overall he kept there. Standing at the sink, he cupped his hands under the tap and drank deeply, before going over to the nail boxes to select the two he would be taking home. Mr Gupta was serving a customer, and Chandu started to unpack the delivery that had been left there since yesterday. He began to stick on price labels, and was soon lost in his task until Gupta came in, looming over him as he squatted on the floor.

'Half the day is gone already,' he barked. 'This will be deducted from your salary, of course.'

Chandu looked up at him, not surprised by this reaction but disturbed, none the less. He studied Gupta's face noting the light sheen of sweat on his forehead, the large nose with open pores across it, and the shiny, raven black hair, looking like it was one solid lump of glistening coal rather than a multitude of individual hairs. His moustache had quite a few grey strands in it, and in the gloom of the storeroom his eyes looked as dark as his hair – almost like black holes in fact.

He shivered, goosebumps coming up on his arms despite the warmth of the day. There were many things he might have wished to say to retaliate – to match spite for spite and hurt the man who shamed and belittled him at almost every opportunity. He could plead with Gupta to find some empathy for the suffering he had undergone over the past night; for the child who no longer existed, and for his wife who might never fully recover from her loss. He put his hand in his pocket and felt for the two sharp nails he had put there. If his suffering were to be marked, then let it be marked with nails; that was what he had said. Mr Gupta would suffer too, there could be no doubt.

Chandu stood up, brushing the dust from his knees. 'Would you like a cup of tea? You must be thirsty here on your own all morning.' He moved his head from side to side; so very Indian, so very him.

Clearly uncomfortable and unable to hold his gaze any longer, Gupta looked away, stepping back toward the door. 'Yes, tea, of course… thank you. Black today, and not too weak.'

Tea made, Chandu continued with his task, now feeling light-headed and his stomach grumbling loudly.

Eventually hearing his employer lock the shop door and take the cash from the till, he checked his watch, and at six precisely quickly hung up his overall and left, desperate to get back home.

***

Babita took a bath, taking the opportunity to do so when most of the other residents were out. In her absence, Meera packed the laundry to take with her, tidied everywhere, and opened the windows wide to let fresh air into the room. She then went to the local store, coming back with two large bags of shopping and to find Babita dressed in the flowery salwar kameez she had so recently bought for her. Her long curly hair had been left loose to dry, her face was pale and her eyes still red from the recent bout of crying. She is a child and a woman in one, thought Meera – inseparable, yet two, none the less.

At the same time Babita watched her friend as she moved around the room; tall, dark and strong in appearance like a beautiful, female warrior – but what depth was inside, like a pool with no bottom. Did Vasu really not see who she was or how honoured he should be to have her for a wife? Maybe he did – maybe it was this that made him behave so badly? He feared for her loss and sought to control.

'Chicken and spinach tonight, with cashew? Not so hot, but I might be able to persuade Vasu to eat some!'

'Perfect,' replied Babita. 'We can eat together and then phone a cab to take you home.' She paused for a moment… 'How do I thank you for being here? What can I say? What

77

can I do?' Her eyes filled up again, her face contorted with trying to prevent another flow of tears.

'You...? Thank me? You have no idea, and that is your beauty. We need each other. Let us leave it at that!'

Everything was ready for when Chandu got home. He looked awful; tired and thin and his clothes dirty and crumpled. He washed his hands at the sink, and for the first time ever they sat at the table together, helping themselves to what they wanted.

'You must eat more, Chandu,' said Meera. 'You look like a stick of sugar cane.'

'Yes, already I have decided to send more food with him to work. He has always been like this, but no more. Soon you will be fat, because I am going to get a job and there will be more money to buy food... Chocolate, I shall buy, and chips every day.'

Chandu groaned. He felt better for eating, and although he was still worried about his wife, the relief to see her in front of him like this was immense.

'I hate chocolate, but chips I will eat and with you sat beside me.'

'Just this once, husband, just this once.'

'Job, Babita? What job are you thinking of? You know how hard it is for immigrants to get work here.' Meera stopped eating, her usually smooth brow now furrowed with concern.

'Just wait and you will see... I will show you that I can also work.'

Ten minutes later Babita was lying on the bed while Chandu went downstairs with Meera, carrying her bag and the dish of chicken and spinach for Mr Gupta.

'Don't worry,' he said. 'We will be fine. Have your holiday in India – you deserve this.' He waved as the cab drove away, and hurried back upstairs to find that Babita had fallen asleep. He was glad, she needed to rest. He went over to the armchair, pulling the blanket that was draped loosely on the arm over himself. Within minutes he fell into a deep sleep of his own. He dreamed of the doctor at the hospital gently touching his shoulder and looking at him; not with his blue English eyes, but with eyes like the black holes of Mr Gupta in the storeroom that afternoon – empty, hollow, and revealing nothing.

CHAPTER
FOURTEEN

Meera let herself into the now closed shop. She rarely came down at this hour and found it slightly eerie in the fading light, with no Mr Gupta behind the counter and no customers walking up and down the aisles. She paused for a moment to take it all in, breathing deeply and inhaling the quintessential smell of paint and polish that she knew was there, but had never registered in her mind. Then she heard her name being called, and the door at the bottom of the stairs opened to reveal her husband.

'At last, you have decided to come to your own home. Where have you been all this time? I was thinking to call the police.' He took the heavy shopping bag, and she followed him back up the steep stairs.

'You know where I have been. Babita has lost the baby and I was at the hospital with her.' She looked at him, wanting to see if any emotion showed on his face or if there was any reaction at all to what she had said. What she saw was a slight raising of his thick dark brows, just for a second – so brief that a blink of the eye would have missed it. He said nothing.

'She is home now, and I cooked for them,' she added.

'You cooked for them, but not me, your husband.'

'For you too! It is here, in this box.' She went through to the kitchen and began to heat the chicken and spinach made at the Kumars earlier.

'I made it with little chilli for my English husband who does not like the heat! Odd really, Mr Gupta, since you look very much like an Indian man to me. I remember at my wedding the Indian man I married who ate whole dried chilli peppers like sweets. Where has he gone?'

'He is right here, Mrs Gupta, but circumstances change, and I no longer wish to smell of garlic and chilli and breathe this all over my English customers.'

'What, you fear they will faint with the smell? You do not see the English going to Indian restaurants, coming out themselves smelling like an Indian and breathing fumes all over each other? Sit down and eat, and if I faint with your breath then leave me there until the morning!' She placed the food in front of him and he picked up his fork, gingerly tasting it as though it were laced with poison.

'I hope you were not rude to poor Chandu? And you will pay his salary in full, or I will pay it myself!' She went to the bathroom, and when she came out half an hour later, saw her husband's empty plate in the kitchen sink. 'Yes,' she said to herself, 'he still likes it, the fool.' Later, in bed, she heard the door open.

'Meera,' came a whisper, 'Meera – are you awake?' He paused, waiting for a response. Hearing nothing, he sighed, and quietly closed the door, leaving his wife alone in the large bed to contemplate the future and whether it included her husband – Mr Vasuman Gupta.

***

A few days later she went down to the shop to ask Chandu how Babita was.

'She is OK I think, and talking about jobs.'

'Still? You think she is serious? Who will employ her?'

'I don't know, but Meera, if the job is suitable I am not against it. She needs to be busy now there is no baby, and now there will be no more thoughts of one. On her own all day is not a good thing. Let us wait and see, then worry if we do not agree with her choice.'

'Yes, I suppose so.' Meera was not convinced, but the next few days were busy ones, preparing for her trip, shopping for gifts for all her family, and filling the freezer with meals for her husband which he could easily heat himself.

The day before Meera left, the two ladies spent an afternoon together in the flat above the store. Helping her friend to pack and neatly fill the two large suitcases, Babita spoke a little more about the job that she hoped to find.

'I am looking in the newspapers every day. I know you think this is a mistake, but you are wrong. You must not worry about me – I shall be careful and will choose wisely. Many women work in England, immigrants also. Even ones of small size, like me!' She laughed as she said this, and Meera couldn't help but join her. They sat on the edge of the bed, still smiling at each other and surrounded by brightly coloured clothes and packages.

'Here, Babita of small size, this is for you. A small size going-away present.' She handed a parcel to her friend, wrapped in bright pink paper and tied with multi-coloured ribbons.

'No, not more. I have told you, there is no need to give like this. To be with you is all the gift I need.'

'Stop that! If not to you, then to who can I give presents? Open it,' Meera demanded, watching as Babita tugged at the ribbons and tore away the paper. She pulled out a small box and began to read the label.

'French Almond perfume? It smells of almonds?' Babita looked confused.

'Not really. Open and spray – you will see. It is the best, and very fashionable.' Seeing her friend fumble with the lid, she grabbed it from her and liberally sprayed them both; the sweet, musky scent quickly filling the room. 'You like it?'

'I love it – thank you!'

'Then you must wear it every day. Who will not give you a job when you smell like this?' Remembering her concern for an unprotected Babita out in the harsh world of work, she gripped her hand and held it tight. 'You will be careful? Trust no one and be safe?'

'Yes – and you must trust me and not worry.'

***

Once again, Meera spent the night before her departure alone. Gupta had said nothing, and her suitcases stood by the door at the top of the stairs, ready to be carried down. She couldn't sleep and lay in the dark room, the sounds of an equally restless London outside, humming unceasingly.

She longed for silence and to sleep on the verandah with her family, the row of charpoys always ready for the night to come. There would be chatter, of course there would. However, this would slowly fade, and they would become enveloped in the black, black night, without blankets yet draped with a covering of epic universal proportions; the cloak of the sky, studded with sparkling jewels. Lying there, she would be a princess, and master of her own destiny.

With her family beside her, she would be safe. She was a part of them, and they her; they were one. And here – what was she? She didn't know. Sometimes it felt like she was nothing; she was a ghost, barely able to see herself or be seen... except through the eyes of Babita. Babita saw her, and through this medium alone, she saw herself.

***

When she got up the following morning, the suitcases were gone. For a moment, Meera wondered if her husband had destroyed them in order to prevent her leaving, and she went downstairs, finding him in his usual place behind the till.

'Where are the suitcases? They are gone.' He nodded towards the door. Turning, she saw them stood neatly together, as though waiting for their departure with some impatience. 'The taxi will be here at eleven,' she continued, waiting for a response – for him to say anything, even if it was laced with sarcasm. He made no reply and continued with the morning ritual of polishing the counter. Meera went back upstairs. How childish that he should sulk in this way. Why could he not behave normally, like any other man might whose wife was about to depart and not be seen for several months, or maybe never again? She finished tidying up, and just before eleven heard Chandu's voice call up the stairwell.

'Mrs Gupta? The taxi is here.'

'I am coming,' she shouted, and picking up her bag walked to the door, stopping for a moment to take a last look at the flat before going downstairs. Mr Gupta was nowhere to be seen. Was it to be like this, then – not even there to say goodbye?

'He is outside waiting for you,' said Chandu. 'I will look after the shop until he returns. Babita says to trust no one and be careful and safe.' He smiled, and remembering the instruction that she had given to her friend the previous day, Meera smiled back.

'Thank you, Chandu. Please tell her also to do the same.'

Seeing her come out of the store, Gupta opened the door of the cab and she got inside, still unsure if he was coming with her. He hesitated for a moment, then got in, slamming the door behind him.

***

Arriving at the airport, he wheeled her bags to the check-in desk, then walked with her to passport control and where he could go no further. He had been silent for the entire trip and, standing before her husband now, she too struggled to find the words that she wanted to say.

'Vasu – please look after yourself and eat hot food each evening.' She shook her head. 'Why are you talking about food?' she asked herself. 'Here is your husband before you, and you are about to fly away from him, like a bird in the sky.'

'You are coming back, Mrs Gupta?' he asked, stepping back a little to see her more clearly. He looked puzzled and studied her face intensely as though in it, like a book, lay the answers that he now sought.

Unable to be scrutinized in this way, Meera opened her bag and took out a tissue, pretending to mop her brow of moisture that was not there. Feeling more composed, she met his gaze and took in the emotion that she so rarely saw. Still not answering the question, she brushed a few flecks of dust from his shirt, then raised her hand to gently touch his face. 'I will send postcards for you,' she said, her eyes filling with tears. 'And you can telephone, but you must remember the different time in India?' He nodded, and she leant forward, kissing each of his cheeks in turn.

To him, her lips were like butterflies fluttering across his face. They were like angels' wings, and he brought up his hand to touch the place where they had been, then held it out in front of him, as though unwilling to lose the residue that was now on his fingers.

A tannoy sounded in the distance calling for all passengers on Meera's flight, and she slowly turned to walk away, now separated from Mr Gupta by a metal gate as well as the words that she could not find. 'Do not look back, Meera,' she thought, 'do not look back,' but she did. She looked back to see her husband still standing in exactly the same place; the same puzzled expression on his face – his eyes shining, and butterfly-kissed fingers now held to his lips.

Sick to the heart, she moved with the crowd all around her – and then was gone.

CHAPTER
FIFTEEN

Babita sat in the waiting room of Dr Greene's surgery. There were several other patients there, including a mother with a small child, and she turned away, sitting sideways on so that she couldn't see them. It was nearly two weeks since she lost the baby, and although she was doing well, seeing things like this still made her feel raw inside, and overcome with a sense of longing for that which she would never have. She tried to concentrate on the magazine she had picked up, but then her name was called, and she thankfully placed it back on the pile and hurried down the corridor to the doctor's room.

He stood up as she came in, shaking her hand with the usual firmness that squashed the rings on her fingers painfully into her flesh. 'Mrs Kumar, thank you for coming. The hospital sent me details about what happened, and I wanted to know how you were? I'm so sorry about the miscarriage. I had hoped that this time it might be different…'

'Yes, Doctor, we were also hoping this time…' She massaged the crushed hand, then began to twist the silver rings around as she spoke. 'We don't want to try any more. No more hormones – no more disappointments. We have had enough of this, you see, and Chandu, particularly, cannot cope with the upset.'

'I understand how you feel. The option is open however if you change your minds.'

'We won't,' she replied firmly. 'I am looking for a job to help with expenses, and with this I must be satisfied.'

Dr Greene's immediate reaction was similar to Meera's. He felt concern for the lady in front of him; concern about how she would survive in a world that was often so hostile and brutal to immigrants, and how she would cope in a work environment, away from the safety of her home.

'I can see you are thinking that I will not be suitable for work, is that not so? But you are wrong; I can work, and I will work.' She felt cross that once again she was seen as weak and frail, when truthfully she was neither of those things.

'Just because a person is small and an Indian does not mean that they are useless, Doctor, not at all.' She quickly stood up, wanting to get away from anything or anyone that might attempt to crush her already fragile spirit. She liked Dr Greene very much and knew that his intentions were good, but what she needed now was support and encouragement, not another setback.

'Please, Mrs Kumar, I'm sorry. You are absolutely right, of course. Do sit down and tell me what type of work you would like to do. I see a lot of people each week and maybe I can help?'

Babita sighed, but did as he asked. 'I have been looking in the newspaper every day, Doctor, and so far there is nothing. I do not know what type of job would suit me, but things like working in a bar and cleaning toilets, I will not do. We are Hindus, and although you do not have the caste system here in England, my husband will not allow this. Already his job is less than it should be, but there was no work for him in India and a choice had to be made.'

'Yes, I see that.' He thought for a moment, rubbing his chin as he did so. 'Hmmmm, I wonder... what do you feel about working with children, Mrs Kumar? Would that be too distressing for you under the current circumstances?'

Babita also thought for a moment, continuing to twist her rings. 'I think I might enjoy that very much. I have always liked children; their chatter – their play. I think it would not distress me, perhaps the opposite of this. It is a very good idea. Thank you, Doctor. You have been very helpful.' She stood up, and keeping her bruised hand to herself began to walk to the door.

'Wait... I have something in mind, which was why I asked. It's for a friend of my wife. Her nanny has left and she herself may be leaving the country soon, but she works and needs help with childcare. Her name is Stella; she's Italian, and the children are five and three. They don't live far away – I have her number here.' He fumbled about in a drawer, eventually pulling out a small notebook, then copying the number onto a scrap of paper which he pushed across the desk towards her. 'Give it a go, you never know… It might suit you very well.'

Babita picked up the piece of paper, her hand trembling slightly as she studied it. 'Yes, I will call and see. Thank you again – you are always very kind to me.'

He got up to open the door for her, and watched as she walked down the long corridor. Always observant, he had seen her eyes brim with tears and the trembling hands. She had been deeply affected by the recent loss, but he admired her courage greatly and hoped she would phone Stella. He went back into his room and called for the next patient. He could do no more.

***

Babita took her favourite route home through the park, stopping for a moment to sit on a bench that was by the side of a small lake. Several children were throwing bread to the ducks and, seeing their frenzy, two regal swans slowly made their way across; four grey cygnets almost as large as their parents following closely behind.

In Hindu culture, swans were revered as having an ability to be in the world but to maintain non-attachment. Deemed to have superior knowledge, it was also believed that they would know the difference between good and evil – the transient and the everlasting. She had been taught this at school, as well as the fact that they mated for life. Approving whole heartedly of this sentiment, she pondered on the rest, particularly the concepts of that which lasted for eternity and that which did not.

Was her baby gone for ever, like a wisp of smoke to be seen no more? Or would the fact that it had existed once, mean that it would continue to exist, even though it was now dead? Surely as long as she could remember it, then it would live? A wisp of smoke from a fire might be remembered for a few days for its form or scent, but then another image would replace it and it would be gone for good. The two were different, she was sure of it.

Her thoughts were broken by a scream from one of the children in front of her, scared by a swan that had come too close – hissing in order to protect its young. She got up and walked home, stopping in the hallway by the telephone and searching in her bag for the number given to her by Dr Greene. She would 'give it a go' as he had said. Seeing the swans today had given her much food for thought, as well as comfort, and with this in mind she lifted the receiver and began to dial.

***

Chandu came home that evening to a smiling wife. Whilst she served his dinner, she told him about her visit to the doctor and the suggestion that was made.

'He asked me what job I wished to do, and I was unable to say.'

Chandu stopped eating for a moment, to listen to the story that would give an explanation as to why his wife was so cheerful.

'Then he asked me if working with children would cause upset given recent events, and I thought about this and decided no – it would not cause upset. The effect

92

would be the opposite of this. I would be happy.'

'Yes, this is true. You have always loved to be with children, and they with you.' Privately, he thought that her doll-like attributes might account for some of this, but remained silent, not wanting to deflate her in any way.

'What else were you going to say?'

He started to eat again, waving his fork to indicate a full mouth and an inability to speak.

'Yes, well, it is very good for you to have not said it, or dinner tomorrow would be meat pie and cabbage. You know how much love you have for this.'

He smiled apologetically, cheeks bulging.

'He gave me the number for a friend of his wife,' she continued. 'Her name is Stella and she comes from Italy. She has two children and is needing help, so I called her on the telephone and we are to meet tomorrow. The house is on the other side of the park, and to walk there is not a problem.'

Chandu stopped eating and got up. He grabbed his wife around the waist and swung her up as high as he could, then span her round and around until they both fell onto the bed, laughing and gasping for breath.

'And all the while I knew that to marry you would make for an easy life. Babi can work and I can retire from slavery. This is good sense and perhaps you can work at Gupta's, also. He will not bully you in the same way, fearful of a smacked face or worse! Maybe even a beating with a stick?' They laughed again, Babita struggling to get up and straighten her sari.

'The job is not mine yet, Chandu. We shall see, and yet to work with Gupta is a pleasing thought. Maybe I will try this, and you can stay here to cook and clean and wash the clothes.'

'One day, Babi, one day I shall be a housewife, and will show you how the work is done!' he replied. Oh how he loved to tease her like this, and so soon after the loss. He could hardly believe it, and quickly gave thanks to whichever god might be listening, Indian or English, for his good fortune to have married a woman such as she. He got up from the bed and put the kettle on the stove. 'You will not walk in the park at night, I insist upon this. I will meet you, or you will not go at all.'

'Ah, the master speaks, and the frightened wife must obey. Very well; I will concede. But be warned, husband. More demands like this and the stick will be brought down on your own back, not Gupta's!'

Chandu nodded. 'Deal!' he said. 'We are in agreement.'

'Deal!' replied Babita. 'Now, make my tea, housewife. It is time you learned your trade.'

CHAPTER
SIXTEEN

M r Gupta locked the door of the shop and turned the sign to 'closed.' As usual, Chandu had left without saying a word, slipping out from the back entrance for fear of being given more work to do. He would have been given more tasks, it was true; probably enough to have added on at least another hour to the working day before he was allowed to escape. Whether this was fair or not was another matter entirely. Given the way things were, if Chandu had stayed in India his life would undoubtedly have been much worse, but even knowing this, at times Gupta did feel some guilt and at other times – not.

He had no idea what made him behave in this way, yet felt pulled backwards and forwards by a force that held him in a vice-like grip. He knew it created a barrier between himself and Meera, and that did matter – it mattered very much. When on his own in the store, as he was now, this was far easier to admit to than when she was with him, or in the flat upstairs. He remembered her walking away from him at the airport, and for the umpteenth time he touched his cheek where she had kissed him. He shook his head as if to toss away the memory and went over to the till, taking out the larger notes to pay into the bank tomorrow.

In the two weeks since Meera left, he had tidied the storeroom and reduced the prices of old stock, washing the shelves at the same time. Of course, it was Chandu that performed these tasks with Gupta watching over him, criticising and changing his mind constantly. At one point, Chandu had flung his soapy rag into the bucket with such force that the water splashed all over his employer's shiny shoes. He then stomped through to the storeroom to choose the two nails that would account for the day's suffering. Nothing was said when he emerged, and he continued to wash the shelves with no more interruptions.

When Gupta came down into the store that morning, a large dish covered in tinfoil had been placed on the counter full of a spicy, chicken curry; fried onion bhagi to one side and folded naan on the other. The wonderful smell made his mouth water, and he picked it up to put in the fridge for later. 'Thank Mrs Kumar for me, won't you?' he said, avoiding Chandu's gaze.

'Of course. It is my favourite and I also will be eating this tonight,' replied Chandu, head wobbling and a broad grin on his face.

Sitting alone at the table later that evening, Gupta consumed the whole lot, wiping the bowl with the naan so that it was entirely clean. He burped loudly, then cupped his hands over his mouth and nose, inhaling deeply to smell his breath. 'Garlic and chilli, cardamom too,' he said out loud, and hurried to the bathroom to brush his teeth.

That night, in the large bed, he stretched out like a starfish then quickly curled up again, moving over to one side to take up as little room as possible. In his mind, to leave the larger space for Meera meant that she might come back to take up her position again. A space filled left no possibilities – an empty one, many. If he held on to this belief, then maybe it would come true.

Wound around his neck, the end held tightly in his hand, was Meera's night-time sari. It smelt of her perfume; a residue of heavy sandalwood mixed with something else. It reminded him of the almond cakes that his grandmother used to make, and taking some comfort from this thought, he fell asleep.

CHAPTER
SEVENTEEN

Meera arrived at New Delhi airport in the early hours of the following morning. A few hours into the flight the man she was sitting next to lit a cigarette, great plumes of pungent smoke soon hovering in the air around him. She flapped her hands in an attempt to disperse it, hoping he would see her discomfort and stop. Instead, he turned his head to the window, and puffed even harder. Now becoming angry at the man's ignorance and lack of consideration, she tapped him on the shoulder.

'Excuse me,' she said, 'but your smoke is making me feel sick. Please can you stop.'

He turned to look at her, his eyes bold and unrepentant. 'I booked a smoking seat because I smoke. Perhaps you should move if you don't like it?'

Meera had not expected such a forthright response and drew in her breath which made her cough. 'You are a very rude man, with no respect,' she replied. 'Clearly your mother taught you no manners!' The man made no further response and turned away, continuing to smoke and ignoring her objection entirely. She grabbed her bag and stood up, scanning the rows of seats nearby for one which was empty and smoke-free. At the far side of the central aisle, and the only person in the row, sat a nun, who appeared to be asleep. Meera walked to the aisle on the opposite side and, careful not to wake her, quietly sat down. About half an hour later the woman opened her eyes, and seeing Meera sat beside her in the previously empty seat, smiled.

'I hope I have not disturbed you?' Meera asked, reaching out to gently touch the nun's arm. 'But you see, the man I was sitting next to was smoking, and I cannot bear the smell. I thought I would be sick!'

'Then perhaps he might have moved to save you the trouble, and received appropriate punishment for such lack of consideration,' the nun replied. 'Also, this would have provided others who have been troubled by the smell, much amusement.'

'Yes! You are right! Perhaps I should go back to complete this task of correction?'

'Remember it for next time. Stay with me, my dear, I think we have much to discuss of mutual benefit.'

'I knew it as soon as I saw you! I am Meera – Meera Gupta.' She held out her hand and the nun took it, but to Meera's surprise, instead of shaking it, she raised it to her lips and gently kissed it. It was the most humble and respectful of gestures, and one which Meera had never experienced before. With the distress of parting from her husband at the airport and all that led up to it, she felt herself suddenly overwhelmed, and tears came to her eyes which she hastily tried to wipe away.

'Sister Maria Benedicta, at your service. You have suffered much, I can see this. I too. Perhaps we should thank the man for our meeting instead of chastising him with your vomit? No matter… You are going home? To Delhi?'

'Yes, to my family just outside the city. My father is there and my brother, Manju, and his wife and children. I have missed them all so much.'

'My home is in the old city. I did visit a year ago, but the pull to return has become so strong of late that I could resist it no longer. I will stay this time, maybe even for good. My family run a home for young girls with babies, and for now I shall work there with them.'

'Ah, that is a very good cause. You have my admiration. So many girls suffer at the hands of men, is this not so? I too understand the pull you speak of. I have left my husband behind – that is how strong it was for me,' replied Meera, gazing into the strange, sparkling silver eyes of the nun sitting beside her. Set against dark skin they glistened as though lit from within, and in an instant she had the strangest sense of hearing her own voice as though from another place, like an echo, or a reverberation from another time altogether.

'They do indeed suffer at the hands of men,' the nun replied, 'and most likely always will. Tell me, my dear, you are having problems?' she asked. 'He is a good husband to you?'

'Problems? Yes, there are problems. We are always on the opposite side of each other, never the same one. We are like two halves of a different fruit.'

'But do you love him?' persisted the nun.

Meera thought for a moment. 'I don't know. He is not always an easy man to love. We have a shop – no, he has a shop – a hardware store. It means everything to him. He pretends to be an Englishman and I cannot bear it. I am not wanting to be his English wife, and here is our problem. I am an Indian and this is all I can ever be.'

The nun grasped Meera's hand and held it tightly, the large wooden crucifix that was dangling from her waist, held in the other. 'You must be who you are. We both know this, or we would not be responding to the call from our homeland. None the less, can some compromise not be found? A middle ground? Some kind of sanctuary for you both?'

Meera shook her head sadly. 'Once again, I don't know. When I left him at the airport and saw his sad face, then yes. This man I could love and share the middle ground, but he is not always this way. He can be spiteful, and sometimes cruel. He has slapped me twice, and this I cannot tolerate, husband or not!'

'Agreed. He sounds like a child – a man-boy. So many of them are like this, which is why I have chosen to marry the one who is without flesh.'

Meera wasn't sure what her new friend was saying. 'I don't understand you… oh, I see,' she laughed. 'You mean Jesus – the man with no flesh – yes, you are the clever one to have avoided such problems. But you share him with so many and don't mind?' Now she was curious, all thoughts of her husband and marriage set to one side.

It was Sister Maria Benedicta's turn to laugh; a deep, rumbling sound – earthy, and so very fitting to their native land where all things were louder, brighter, hotter and more extreme in every possible way.

'Yes, I am the most-clever of women. And you? You, Meera Gupta, are the most beautiful. This is a single truth, and one that you must carry with you, no matter where you go.' She let go of Meera's hand as though her job was done. 'Ah, look, food is coming. Let us enjoy our dinner, or breakfast – I am not sure which it is. Who knows if we shall ever sit together like this again?'

Meera, still slightly stunned by the words she had just heard, nodded in agreement. That they would sit together like this again was most unlikely. 'Then let us make the most of it!' she said. 'We should celebrate our meeting! I shall never forget you, Sister Maria Benedicta. You will always hold a place here.' She placed her hand over her heart, and the nun smiled.

'And you, here,' she replied, kissing her carved figure of Jesus.

'Perhaps we could meet once more, whilst I am in Delhi?' Meera asked, tentatively. 'Would this be possible? Now we have met, I find myself unwilling to let you go.'

'Of course,' she replied. 'Come to my home. I shall look forward to it.'

***

Landing about two hours later, the new friends parted and hurried to collect their bags. Meera walked through the brightly lit corridors, and out into a sea of expectant Indian faces. The heat was intense, and for a moment she found it hard to catch her breath. She had forgotten what it was like to be amongst so many people of her own race, and feeling bewildered, paused to examine the crowd and search for her brother. Unable to see him she continued to walk, hearing shouts and cries all around her, yet recognising none of the voices.

'Meera, Meera, here – over here...' She looked frantically from side to side, then suddenly there he was, hurrying towards her with his arms held wide.

'At last, you have arrived!' he said, and as if from nowhere, his wife and children appeared, and she was surrounded by her family.

Her niece and nephews had been little more than children when she last saw them, and now four teenagers stood in front of her; the girl, fifteen, and the three boys ranging in age from sixteen to nearly twenty-one. She pinched their cheeks, and flung an arm around Delilah, her niece. The boys were all tall with dark complexions like their father, each showing the promise of becoming very handsome men – the eldest already having achieved this. Someone appeared to have brought a band with them, and the traditional Indian wedding music added to the vast amount of noise already present.

Manju's wife, Suvi, stood behind the boys. She had always been shy, and her relationship with her bolder and brighter sister-in-law had not always been an easy one. Meera moved to embrace her, wanting no ill feeling or upset throughout her stay.

'Come on, let's get out of here,' said Manju, taking her trolley and pushing it in front of him. Meera held on tightly to Delilah and Suvi – one to either side, as they pushed through the crowds, the boys trailing behind. The busy London streets were nothing compared to this. How could she have forgotten?

'Are you OK?' asked Manju. 'It is a bit overwhelming, but don't worry. The driver is waiting and you will soon be home.'

Home. The words of Babita echoed through her head. At this moment, home was in the flat above the hardware store. And yet, when she was there, home was here, in the place of her childhood. Her head was throbbing, and she was very thirsty. She turned to her niece.

'You have some water for auntie?' Delilah handed over her plastic bottle of water, and Meera drank it as they walked until it was all gone. The car was waiting near the front of the building, and they were soon speeding through the streets; empty in comparison to their daytime chaos. Thirty minutes later, and on the outskirts of the city, the roads became narrower as they made their way to the town north of Delhi, where she and her brother had been born.

Now an old man, her father would be waiting, and in her mind's eye, she could visualise him standing on the front porch. He was smoking a bidi and looking up the street. His eyes were misty, his thin body utterly still apart from the slight movement of his hand to hold the cigarette, and the grey smoke drifting above his head and out into the still air. The dawn had slowly begun; the dark, star-strewn sky seeming to lighten with every minute that passed. Meera gazed out of the window watching it, too tired to talk.

Their family home was on the far edge of the town. Originally the old quarter, new development had taken place everywhere but here, the land being owned by the original settlers, all of whom refused to sell. It was a bungalow, although this was far too modest a description for the large old house. It had been added to over the years, and now comprised of some ten rooms, with a large verandah that ran around all four sides. The garden was large, and densely planted with trees and shrubs, hiding from view two small houses which were lived in by servants. This hardly seemed the right name for them, since they had been with the family for as long as Meera could remember, and were as much a part of it as she was.

A few minutes later, the car pulled up outside and she got out, walking slowly towards her father and embracing him. This was met with little response, and she was soon pulled away by her sister-in-law.

'Come, come inside. You must be exhausted.' Suvi took her arm, leading her to a room at the back of the house. It had been carefully prepared, with jasmine flowers wound around the tall mirror, and the sheets turned down on the huge wooden bed. Manju brought in her suitcases, and Suvi came back with a tray which held a glass of iced water and a tumbler of camomile tea.

'Can I get you anything else? You are hungry?'

'No,' replied Meera. 'I think I will sleep, and tomorrow we can talk. I have brought many presents and have much to say.' The children and her father were nowhere to be seen, presumably having gone to bed themselves. When the door was finally closed, she went to the bathroom to wash her hands and face, then pulled off her grubby, travel-stained clothes and climbed into bed – instantly falling into a jasmine-scented and dreamless sleep.

***

Three hours away, in the centre of Delhi, Sister Maria Benedicta knelt down and gave thanks to her Lord Jesus for the day she had just spent. She prayed for the nuns in England with whom she used to live; for the tramp who died under the railway bridge near the convent, and for Meera Gupta, her man-boy husband, and the finding of the middle ground in which they could live in peace.

CHAPTER
EIGHTEEN

Babita had prepared herself carefully for the interview with Stella. She was wearing one of the saris that Meera bought her; a dark, ochre-yellow silk, with a velvet border in a soft forest green. She knew that it must have been costly, and although Meera insisted it was nylon and was bought from a market stall, she knew that this wasn't the case. She had been thinking of a way to repay her generous friend, but as yet had come up with nothing. She certainly intended to send Gupta food several times a week, knowing full well that he would eat it, spicy or not. It was the least she could do.

In her bag was a small, linen pouch tied with red string. Inside it, were five tiny finger puppets brought with her from India and made by a cousin as a wedding present. Most of Babita's family were dead, and the two wrote to each other occasionally, sharing their news and comparing their lives. She thought that the children might enjoy them, and hoped to impress her prospective employer with her ability to entertain.

Once again, the day was warm, and she enjoyed the walk across the park, coming out on to a wide, tree-lined street, the houses grand and beautifully maintained. She walked in the dappled shade, counting the numbers until she reached fifty-two. 52 Park View. This was the address she had been given, and she stood at the bottom of the stone steps that led to the red front door. 'Wish me luck,' she whispered, although she had no idea from whom the luck might come. Earlier that morning, Chandu firmly stated that Stella would be mad not to employ her, although Babita did not share his confidence. She pressed the brass bell, and within a few seconds the door was flung open.

'You must be Babita – do come in. I'm Stella. Andy has told me all about you, and I'm so glad you're here.'

***

Later than evening whilst Chandu was eating his dinner, she recounted the events of the morning and the interview that had taken place. 'The house, Chandu, oh, the house. Never have I seen anything like it! So big – and the furniture? Like a magazine, it was... like a Habitat shop, do you remember when we once went in one?'

He did remember. He remembered feeling like a complete fool walking around a London furniture store with less than a pound in his pocket, watching whilst Babita sat on the chairs and stroked the fine fabrics and rugs. It was excruciating, and whilst he was glad that she had enjoyed it so much, it was an experience that he did not intend to undertake again – not ever!

'And she was so beautiful. I told you Stella is Italian?' She didn't wait for a reply and chattered on, excited by her experience and the things she had seen. 'She is small, perhaps not quite like me, but small and dressed like a model. The Italian women are very stylish, everyone knows this.'

Chandu did not know it, nor did he believe that this Stella was any more stylish or beautiful than his own Babi. 'She cannot be more beautiful than you!' he stated, banging his hand on the table. 'This I refuse to believe.'

'If you saw her, then you would believe. And the children, so sweet. The little boy, he is not quite three and has curly hair the colour of straw. He is called Peter, and Sasha, the girl, is nearly five. Her hair is dark like her mother's, and long. I shall brush it every day, for this is how to make it strong and thick.'

'Am I to assume that you have been given the job? If you are planning the brushing of hair, then I am thinking that this must be so.'

'Be quiet, and I will tell you! We talked, and she told me that she works for a fashion company designing clothes for the very rich and famous. Think of that, Chandu? Her husband works abroad a lot, even in India, she told me. In the future they may return to Italy, but not this year.'

'Good. To start a job just as they are leaving would not be sensible.'

She tutted at the interruption, and picked up his plate, despite there still being some food remaining on it.

'Give this back,' he demanded. 'I have not finished, and you know that there is a fattening process to be attended to.'

She put it back down with a clatter, and her husband continued to eat, intent on the expansion of his skinny person, even if she was not.

'I got out the puppets that Shushila made for me, and you should have seen how much they laughed – Stella too. Many more questions were asked and then she said; "Babita, we would so love to have you here to help."' Trying to imitate her new employers voice, she used her very best English, but her accent was still quite heavy and Chandu hoped it would stay that way. He liked it, and had no intention of trying to erase the Indian in his wife like Gupta was so determined to do.

'We have agreed the salary, which is good – better than Gupta pays, and I am to go there for three mornings and two afternoons whilst she is working. On the afternoons, I will pick up Sasha from school, taking Peter with me.' She let out a big breath, finally running out of steam and things to say.

'Then congratulations are to be given. Congratulations, wife, you are now a working woman and I am very proud.' He repeated his sentiment. 'Very proud, indeed. Soon we will have a house like the Italians, and wear the clothes of the rich and famous.'

Babita picked up a tea towel and flung it at him, he catching it in mid-air before it hit him on the head.

'Always joking, Chandu. Perhaps you should have been a comedian, not a shop worker,' she teased, laughing with happiness and excitement of a future now filled with hope.

'Find me the job of comedian, Babita, and I will take it. Then, always I can play the fool, rather than to be the fool – the fool who works for Vasuman Gupta at the hardware store. Here is the only true joke in my life – of this I have no doubt.'

***

When he arrived at the store the following morning, his first interaction with Mr Gupta did not bode well for the day ahead.

'Late, fifteen minutes,' his employer barked. 'Salary to be deducted.'

'Not late,' responded Chandu, equally curt. 'Groceries bought for you, as requested. Two pounds and thirty pence to be added to salary!' Gupta said nothing and made no attempt at an apology.

Chandu placed the bags on the counter, and went to the storeroom to collect the two nails that he would take home that evening. Lately, he tried to not react to his employer's spiteful temper finding that it distressed him less. The work became more pleasant when he was not angry or upset, and on quite a few occasions he had succeeded with this new philosophy. 'Gupta the Hun' as he still sometimes thought of him, appeared confused by the non-reactive responses, and this also added to the feeling of being more in control, allowing him to get on with his tasks – many of which he quite enjoyed.

Today he was going to wash down the tins of paint. Although this was satisfying when finished with the tins gleaming like new, the task itself was dirty and the tins, heavy. He usually ending up with backache, bruised knuckles and filthy hands and face; which was far from pleasing. He went to the sink and filled the kettle to get hot water. This made the cleaning easier, and five minutes later he had a bucketful of steaming soapy water, with several rags floating around inside.

Once out in the shop, he began to take the large tins from the shelves, stacking them neatly to one side. The shelves themselves where cleaned not long ago, but he gave each one a quick wipe before starting on the tins themselves. He found the names of the colours fascinating and automatically began to rename some of them, particularly the ones that did not appear to suit the actual colour sample on the tin. For example, a bright yellow had been named 'Biscuit', which seemed somewhat inaccurate, and in his head the colour was relabelled as 'Sunshine'. Gupta was serving and there were quite a few people milling around, asking questions now and again, before taking their purchases to the wooden counter.

Mr Jackson, of drooping, cigarette-ash fame, was looking at a colour chart, intending to paint his kitchen later that day. 'Yellow,' he said in response to Chandu's question about what he was looking for. 'A bright, sunshine yellow. That's what the wife wants, and she that demands must be obeyed!' he joked, shaking with mirth and depositing an inch of ash into the soapy bucket.

'Ah, yes. I know just the colour that will suit and please the lady,' Chandu replied. He leaned across to the stack he had made and firmly grasped the plastic handle of a large tin. 'I have renamed this colour the exact same name that you have asked for – Sunshine. What do you think?' He held up the tin so that Mr Jackson could see the sample sticker on its front. It was then that it happened... The plastic strap snapped, and the tin fell from Chandu's hand, landing on its bottom edge and exploding like a colour-bomb at Holi. On many occasions over the years he had arrived home late at night, splashed from head to foot in a multitude of vivid colours, as did most of the people who attended the traditional spring festival.

The paint appeared to fly from the tin in slow motion and he stood watching, transfixed, as it covered Mr Jackson from head to foot with a force that was quite incredible to behold. The cigarette had stayed in Mr Jacksons mouth, but was now dripping like a tap pouring custard, and his eyes, thankfully obscured with glasses, were totally obliterated, as was his hair and virtually every other part of him.

He couldn't help it, he told Babita later that evening, but had burst out laughing like he hadn't done since he was a child. Within a few seconds he was bent double, almost choking with trying to catch his breath, – convulsed with laughter. Mr Jackson, to give him his due, wiped a channel across his mouth, as well as one on the fronts of his glasses, and was grinning from ear to ear, chuckling; his breath coming out as chesty, nicotine-lunged wheezing.

Mr Gupta flew across the store, his face so enraged that Chandu thought he might have a heart attack, and this caused another round of helpless laughter from both himself and the wheezing Mr Jackson. Looking down at his employer's feet, he could see that Gupta was standing in a pool of 'sunshine.' The irony was not lost on him, and he fought to gain control whilst fully expecting to be ordered to leave the store for good.

'Please, Mr Gupta,' said Mr Jackson, gasping as he continued to laugh. 'Don't tell him off. It was an accident and couldn't have been helped. The handle came off... No harm done.' He reached for the yellow cigarette still wedged in his mouth and lobbed it into the paint splattered bucket. 'It's one way to stop a bloke from smoking, that's for sure. These are my old painting clothes, and there are plenty more where they came from.'

'Are you sure you are alright?' asked Mr Gupta. 'Can I lend you some clothes to go home in?'

'No need. No need at all. I've not had so much fun in years. I'll go and change, and then come back for the paint.' He looked at Chandu, still smiling. 'Thanks, mate. I shall be telling this story for years. You've done me the world of good!' and with that, he marched from the store, leaving yellow footprints behind him with each step.

Gupta turned to look at Chandu, his face now undecipherable. Chandu swallowed and waited for the worst.

'Paint, two pounds. To be deducted from your salary.' He walked to the door that led to the flat above, slipped off his shoes and went upstairs, closing the door behind him.

A massive clean-up operation began which took the rest of the afternoon, and the recounting of the tale added to the general joviality of his conversation with Babita that evening. A clean Mr Jackson, fresh cigarette between his lips, came back in to get the paint. Refusing to be given it for free, he repeated his words to Chandu, making sure that Mr Gupta was within earshot.

'I'll say it again, mate, that's the best laugh I can remember, and the lads down the pub will crack up when I tell them. I reckon your sales will increase over the next few weeks, in fact, I'm sure of it!'

Gupta had said no more, and the event would remain in Chandu's mind for a very long time, even without any mates from the pub to remind him.

CHAPTER
NINETEEN

As usual, Mr Gupta spent that evening alone, he too going over the events of the afternoon. What he recalled the most, and the memory that was most vivid, was the laughter between the two men; a sense of the ridiculous which they shared, and the bonding that appeared to have been achieved because of it. As he sat in Meera's armchair looking down at the busy street below, he failed to remember a single moment in his own life that had created anything remotely like what he had observed today. Should he have laughed with them? Could he? And one final question – how?

He came from a serious family. A family that spent their evenings discussing politics, or reading stiff, academic tomes covered in dust and so boring that once, he fell asleep, and had received a thump to the side of his head that rendered him deaf for a whole week. But, he pondered, he had gone to school with other boys, and they played and laughed and teased each other like all children did. Had he not been a part of that? He had most certainly been there... Once again, he tried to slip backwards through the years to the playground of his old school, and the children that he had grown up with.

Attempting to reflect in this way was not easy for him, and he struggled to access the moments that he sought to remember – the moments that might make him like the other children, or like Chandu and Mr Jackson, helpless with laughter and covered in yellow paint. He felt like he was fumbling around in a dark cupboard; one with no doors in its walls, or windows to give a chink of light that might show him the way.

At that moment, something in the street caught his eye, and he sharpened his gaze to see the lady who owned the cake shop across the road, waving at him in the same way that she did to Meera. He raised his hand to wave back, and she smiled before walking away, presumably to her husband and home. He wondered what Meera was doing. He had received a card from her today; the second she had sent and showing a picture of the Red Fort in Agra. They had taken the train, and were to spend the night in an expensive tourist hotel. She wrote that her brother sent his love. Remembering her previous comment that Manju wanted to kill him, he thought that the love sentiment was most unlikely, and that she had made it up. He wondered if she had told him more things about her bad husband, and if divorce had been discussed? He didn't want to be divorced from Meera. What would he do with no wife? What would be the point of having a shop, or a home above it? What would be the point in anything?

***

Meera had been back from Agra for more than a week and was sitting on the verandah at the front of the house; her niece, Delilah, sat on a cushion at her feet. Her official name was Deepti, meaning bright flame, which had been Meera's mother's name. The name Delilah, which had firmly stuck, was given later as a nickname because of Manju's obsession with the British singer, Tom Jones. His songs were played on many evenings, sending her nephews scurrying back to their rooms to listen to the Beatles, the Rolling Stones and various other bands that Meera had never heard of. She thought it odd that they craved the music of the west so much, but still brought over several LP's from England, prewarned by Manju of their musical tastes.

She was engaged in plaiting Delilah's hair and had completed this task several times already, only to be told to undo it and start again, not because of flaws in the plait, but because her niece enjoyed it. She had hoped that Vasu would telephone, but he hadn't, and once again she was spun into a minefield of opposing thoughts and possible beliefs that she and her husband were indeed two halves of a different fruit.

'Auntie?' her niece asked, 'Why did not Uncle Vasu come to India with you?'

'He has the store to run. It is very busy, and he needs to be there.'

'But you are here. If I marry, I will want my husband to be with me when I am on holiday.'

'Then I am sure that this is what will happen,' answered Meera, smiling to herself at the simplicity of a child's mind and the thoughts that came from it.

'Mummy says you might live with us for ever. Is that so? Will Uncle Vasu come then?'

'I am sure he would come if I was to stay for good. Why would he not?' Why indeed? She was unwilling to answer this question honestly, fearing the answer, which might be that he preferred his hardware store to her, and that his choice had, in fact, already been made.

Later that evening, Meera lay under the black night sky, her family all around her just as she had dreamed in her London bed. She looked up at the stars, wondering about their names and who had given them. Delilah was asleep, but her nephews were still talking with subdued voices, until Suvi demanded silence. The following year, Devi, the eldest, was going to university in England, and she thought that perhaps if she were his mother she would want to hear his voice all the more, in preparation for the parting that would take place. Oxford was not so far from London. Hopefully, she would be able to see him much more often than she did now, and this thought pleased her greatly. If Delilah also came to England to study, which she knew Manju wanted, then perhaps her life with Mr Gupta might be made more bearable with visits from her lively niece and nephew?

It was very hot and although a soft breeze was blowing, it too was warm, and the word 'Zephyr' came to mind. Meera loved its sound and had been taught it by her father when she was a child. Special candles had been lit to keep the mosquitos away, and lying on the string cot, surrounded, and yet alone, she heard the howls of the jackals from the huge plains that lay beyond the house. How plaintive and sad was the sound, as though their hearts were breaking, or that they were somehow in great pain. In packs, it was as though they had formed a choir, and Meera smiled at the thought of a large group of jackals lined up neatly together in organised song.

She heard other noises too; rustlings in the grass, and small squeaks from tiny mammals searching for their food. Once, when she was about Delilah's age and during the monsoon, she remembered her now-dead mother finding a large cobra curled up inside the house. She had run screaming into the street, refusing to go back in for three days, even though the snake had been removed. Meera was sent to stay with an aunt, but her mother never forgot the event becoming anxious and permanently worried, eventually dying from cancer when Meera was seventeen.

Her father lay at the end of the row and was silent. He rarely spoke, ate little, and appeared to live in a world of his own. He spent much of his day lying on a mattress on the verandah, the plume of bidi smoke acting as a beacon to let his family know that he was still alive. With the choir of jackals singing, and her bejewelled blanket of stars, she switched her thoughts to Mr Gupta in his hardware store on a dusty London street, and to Babita, her dear friend, both so very far away. She prayed for their safety and happiness, before turning over to seek the solace of sleep.

CHAPTER
TWENTY

It was three months since Meera left, and Mr Gupta felt himself sinking like a stone to the bottom of the sea. He had run out of meals from the freezer, and although Babita cooked for him twice weekly, he knew this was done out of love for Meera, not himself. He lost weight but had no worries about that since he was too fat before. He rather liked his new svelte appearance, and if she came back, hoped that his wife would approve.

Last night, he gave Chandu a list of groceries to fetch for the morning, and hearing him moving around in the shop below, he made his way to the stairs to fetch the shopping and open the store. Chandu, somewhat amused by this new role as housekeeper to his employer, opened the door to the flat. He was about to call up the dark stairwell to announce the food delivery, when he heard an almighty crashing sound with repeated heavy bumps.

When it stopped, he looked down to find Mr Gupta kneeling at his feet, in a once-in-a-lifetime posture of either adoration or prayer.

Leaning forward even further, the almost prostrate man began to moan, slowly increasing its intensity to little short of a scream. 'Ow, ow, ow... Chandu, do something, you fool. Do something.'

Chandu leaned over to touch Gupta's back, more in a sign of acknowledgement of his plight than actual assistance. 'Are you alright?' he asked.

'Of course not, you idiot.' He swore in Hindi using the most colourful of expressions that the language could offer. Chandu had heard nothing like it since he left India, and his admiration for the man at his feet grew considerably. He could not wait to tell Babita what he had heard later than evening.

'Don't just stand there gawping, moorkh, help me up.' He raised his head, let out another howl, then held out his hand to Chandu who, taking it gently, attempted to heave Gupta from the floor. Letting out another blast of shrieks and swearing he tore his hand away, then began to slowly turn himself over so that he was now on his hands and knees; head facing up the stairs, his bottom towards Chandu.

Another once-only position, thought Chandu, smiling broadly, the habitual head wobble going into overdrive as the image of him raising his heavy shoe to Gupta's rear end presented itself in his mind. Moorkh was moron in Hindi, and Chandu let out a muffled snort, almost helpless with suppressed amusement. Pulling himself together, he cleared his throat. 'You must lie down on the bed. Can you make your way back up the stairs in this position?'

Gupta didn't reply, but slowly and with frequent yelps of pain, climbed the steep stairs to the flat above, his assistant following close behind. Once at the top, Chandu jumped in front of him and opened the door to the bedroom to make an easy passage for the injured man. He watched the painful journey, attempting to assist the particularly difficult ascent from floor to bed, tears rolling down Gupta's face. Now lying flat, he began to relax, and Chandu's moment of dominance began to fade as Gupta made to reclaim his authority.

'Call the doctor, fetch me water, and open the store,' he demanded. 'The number is in the book by the telephone.'

Chandu did as he was asked and, chores done, went downstairs to unlock the door and prepare for business. He looked around him, noting the full shelves and everything clean and tidy – made so by his own efforts. He drew in a long breath, holding it for a moment before slowly letting it go with the acknowledgement that, even if only for a short time, he was in charge. Chandu Kumar was in charge of Mr Gupta's hardware store.

***

An hour later, a very attractive lady came through the door, the bells announcing her arrival in an afterthought of metallic jangling. She held a large, leather bag and marching up to the counter, banged it down before announcing herself.

'Dr Shaw,' she said, 'Lucy Shaw – I take it you're not the patient, or I will have wasted my time in coming out.'

'Chandu Kumar – most definitely not the patient. He is upstairs lying on the bed. One moment, please.' He went to lock the door, turning the sign before showing the doctor up the stairs and leading her to the bedroom. Gupta looked pale, with a faint sheen of cold sweat across his forehead. He had spilled some of the water that Chandu brought him, the splashes showing on his shirt and on the table by the side of the bed.

'He fell down the stairs when I brought him the groceries. He has injured his back, I think.'

'I see – and was he able to stand?' she asked.

'No, not at all. He crawled like a baby across the floor,' replied Chandu, smiling at the memory then quickly straightening his face, not wanting her to think him heartless.

The sharp-eyed doctor saw the smile and turned to Gupta, who had opened his eyes to see the young and attractive lady in front of him, struggling to believe that she was a doctor at all and not a cosmetics representative.

'You are the doctor?' he asked.

'Indeed I am,' she replied, 'so no jokes please – I've heard them all, and like the good Queen Victoria, I am not amused.'

Neither Chandu nor Gupta had any idea what she was talking about. What had Queen Victoria to do with broken backs? Seeing their confusion, she shook her head and proceeded to question her patient, asking Chandu to make tea before getting back to his work. Coming down to the store some ten minutes later, she waited until he had finished serving, then gave him the news.

'Mr Gupta has injured a disc, no doubt about it. He will need bed rest for at least four weeks, maybe more. If he can make it to the bathroom, then fine, but nothing else. I've given him a shot, so he should sleep for a while, and here's a prescription for strong painkillers. I'll come in again next week to see how he's getting on. Any problems, do ring the surgery. Has he a wife?'

Chandu nodded. 'Yes, she is visiting family in India.'

'Hmmm, well, she might want to come home. This could be a long job. Lucky that he has you, isn't it?' she smiled, revealing her small, white teeth.

'If only he knew it,' replied Chandu, as she left, slamming the door again, leaving a flurry of bell-noise in her wake. He was kept busy for the rest of the morning with a constant stream of customers; some, friends of Mr Jackson, wanting to see the man who had dropped sunshine on their friend, buying a few things whilst they were there. Chandu enjoyed the gentle teasing. It reminded him of the friends he had left behind in India, and of the easy relationship of men, bound together by their gender and the desire to make fun.

'Watch him, mate,' said one man to a new customer who was coming through the door. 'He chucks a tin of paint on your head if he doesn't like you.' He then left, laughing loudly and leaving the bemused incomer to wonder on the comment, smiling all the same.

***

At lunch time, Chandu slipped quietly upstairs to find Mr Gupta still asleep and snoring gently. He pulled a blanket over him and, as gently as he could, tugged off his shoes, both still showing a few small splashes of yellow paint on the black cotton laces. How were things going to work, he wondered, with this situation? He could not be upstairs and down. He could not run the store, cook and clean, get prescriptions, do laundry, and keep the shelves in the shop full.

Here was a problem, and in this moment he could think of only one answer; his wife, Babita. Their joke about her working in the store may have been a prophetic one, and he was soon to find out. Going into the small hall where the telephone was, he lifted the receiver and dialled the number of the boarding house, waiting for some minutes until it was eventually answered.

'Yes?' he heard, recognising the voice immediately. 'Miss Cordelia Grant speaking, how may I assist?' She always answered the phone with it being right outside her door, and her formal style made the house sound like it was in Mayfair, rather than a Victorian backstreet in a tatty London suburb.

'Miss Grant, it is Chandu here. I wonder if you would be kind enough to call for my wife? I need to talk to her, please.'

'Of course, my dear. How nice to speak to you, you should telephone more often.'

What an odd thing to say, he thought, as though he didn't actually live in the same house as she, and was a visitor of some kind? However, she was elderly, nearly eighty she once said, and perhaps she was becoming confused? He then heard a very loud calling of his wife's name. She certainly had power in her voice, most likely from when she was a governess in India and had to shout for naughty children. Babita then picked up the phone.

'Why are you calling from the store?' she asked. 'This is very unusual, and if you are wanting to place an order for your dinner then you will be unsuccessful, since the decision has already been made!'

'Yes, I am calling to make an order, but of a different kind.' He explained what had happened, and how he wondered if she might perhaps be able to assist in between the hours of her new childcare job, which was to start next week.

'Hmmm, well, it would seem there is little choice, but I do this for Meera, not for him. Tell me again, what was his position at the bottom of the stairs?' They both began to laugh, Chandu ending the call before he became weak again. He had also remembered that the door to the shop was locked, and as temporary manager he should behave in a more responsible way. An image of Mr Gupta's backside poised perfectly to receive a good kick came into his mind, and he once again felt a bubbling of mirth rise inside him. Taking a deep breath, he pushed the image away. His management style would be a different one from Mr Gupta's, he decided, and confidence growing, he went down to the store to let his customers in.

CHAPTER
TWENTY-ONE

Babita arrived some forty minutes later. She had packed a large basket with food for the evening, some clothes in case they ended up having to stay the night, and a simple, pink cotton overall, bought yesterday to protect herself from splashes when she was painting pictures with Stella's children. If there were other things they needed, then Gupta would have to pay for a taxi! She was not going to exhaust herself on his account, but she would do anything for Meera, which was why she was here.

Chandu was surrounded with customers, and she went straight up to the flat to address what awaited her there. Putting down her basket, she peeked through the open door of the bedroom to see Gupta awake and staring up at the ceiling. He turned his head when he saw her, then looked away again to continue the ceiling observation.

'How are you?' she asked quietly, carefully sitting down on the edge of the bed. 'You are in pain?'

'Some,' he said, his voice subdued and slow. 'The doctor gave me a painkilling injection, but this is beginning to wear off. I am hoping to be back in the store very soon, though, very soon...'

'Vasu,' she replied, gently touching the top of his hand. 'There will be no shop for you for a while. You must accept this truth and rest. Only then will you become well again. I have come to assist, and your need to worry is over.'

'You have come for Meera's sake, I know this is the case.'

'Maybe,' she said, 'maybe, but to help her is to help you, is that not so? Accept and trust, and all will be well. You wish me to telephone her? She should know and will want to come home.'

'No!' he almost shouted. Then more gently, 'No, my dear. When she comes back then it must be because she desires it, not because her fool of a husband fell down the stairs to land on his knees, as if to pray to Krishna.'

Babita looked into his almost black eyes, confused for a moment, taking in what he had said. He knows, she thought, he knows that his behaviour is often so bad that others mock him, and yet, if this is so, why does he not change it? She had no answer to give herself, and noticing the time on the bedside clock, she stood up, smoothed back her unruly hair, and straightened her sari. 'Right, first job is to feed the patient. A sandwich? Cheese with lettuce, or chicken well sprinkled with hot chilli? I believe this is your favourite?' She smiled, and watched as the corners of his mouth begin to rise, the lines to the sides of his eyes responding in turn.

'Cheese, Babita, we can save the chilli for later, no?' he answered, and Babita agreed.

So, she acknowledged, as she left the room, a new order had begun, brought about by misfortune and pain. And might happiness also spring from this? If she were to believe in Hindu philosophy, then she must accept that it could well be the case. Its teaching said that each could not exist without the other; its twin – its other half.

'We shall see,' she said aloud, washing her hands in Meera's kitchen. 'We shall see. One must desire the change in order for it to take place.'

***

Chandu ate his lunch in the storeroom, the door left open to see if any customers needed attention. He began to wonder how Babita was getting on upstairs, and if the patient might sustain another injury from his wife if he didn't behave. As if in response to this thought, the stair door opened and his wife came out – pink overall on and her hair fastened neatly at the back of her head.

'He is asleep again but ate a cheese sandwich. I have to go to the chemist now and get his tablets. The meal for tonight is already prepared, so I can help you in the shop. If you wish to throw paint, then make sure it is a colour that suits me. Red, I like, and orange.'

'All morning I have had jokes about paint. I am famous in the district with this one act.'

'Yes, soon you will be on television with your fame, but we do not have one, so you will miss your own show. At least your head will not swell, which is a good thing.

'Now,' she said, walking towards the door. 'More nursing duties, then we shall see how the shop is to be run.' She then left to collect the painkillers for her patient who was lying upstairs in agony.

'The woman is a marvel,' thought Chandu. 'There is nothing she cannot do, and maybe soon she will be the manager, and I shall be the assistant again.' He didn't care – let her manage, and he, the faithful servant, would oblige in any way he could.

When she came back he taught her how to use the till, and in between customers she went upstairs to check on Gupta. Later that evening after they had eaten – Vasu balancing the plate on his chest and wincing each time he moved in the wrong way, Chandu and Babita went into his bedroom to try to sort out the management of the shop and the care that he would need.

'We cannot pretend that you will be working in a week. The doctor told you it would be a long time, and even using the bathroom is very difficult. To leave you alone in the flat at night is also impossible. Facts must be faced.' Babita stood by the side of the bed, Chandu leaning against the door frame, uncomfortable with the exchange and such frank speaking.

'Thank you for helping me. I know I am... well...' Mr Gupta wrung the cotton sheet in his hands, his awkwardness and desperation at the situation he found himself in also showing by the worried, even frightened, look in his eyes. He had never been helpless like this before, never been so out of control, nor dependant on someone else to look after his beloved store.

'What can I do?' he asked, 'what can I do? I can

barely move!' He tried to get up, grabbing the top of the wooden headboard in an attempt to heave himself into a sitting position. He screamed with pain and Babita peeled his fingers from the bar, helping him to find a more comfortable position, totally flat with his arms by his side.

'Exactly!' she said. 'You see? We need a plan. Three heads together, and we will find a way.'

'Three heads together,' echoed Chandu.

'I shall speak to the surgery,' continued Babita. 'You need assistance in the mornings to wash and change your clothes. I do not have the strength for this, and also I think you would not wish me to see you in this way?'

Chandu stared at his wife – gawping, a facial expression he had so often been accused of; just that morning, in fact. So bold, he thought, she is like a man! She speaks so strongly to the bad-tempered Gupta, and he does not abuse her like he does to me or even his wife? If he, Chandu, had attempted this discussion, he would be insulted by the disabled Gupta, bedridden or not. Why only this morning he had been called a fool, an idiot, and moorkh – moron. He was abused so often that the names went over his head; they meant nothing apart from their amusement factor, especially 'moorkh' because it had been said in Hindi.

Gupta shook his head. 'No, not you. I will agree to help from the surgery.'

'Good. Food and laundry, I can do. Meera has a machine which will make for easy work, and Chandu can dry it in the launderette across the road.'

'Yes, I am always in the launderette. It is one of my many tasks as a housewife. I am well known for my drying of sheets.'

Babita turned her head to look at her husband. 'Shut up!' she said, and Chandu grinned, head wobbling from side to side meaning, in that moment, so many things; his great amusement at what was playing out before him? Definitely! His acceptance of the greater force of his wife? Absolutely, but rather more than that, not just acceptance, but a total surrender. So be it, it meant. And just one more thing. It said without words... 'I, Chandu the clown, love you, Babita the Queen.'

'I shall help in the shop when I can. I have learned the use of the till. Paint colours I can choose, perhaps better than any man, but I will use the chart. Holi is an Indian festival, and there it can stay.' Amazingly, Gupta smiled – a proper full smile that neither she nor Chandu had ever seen before.

'We will have to sleep here. Backwards and forwards is no good. I have already made the bed in the spare room and will fetch more things from home tomorrow. You know that I start a job next week?'

'No,' replied Mr Gupta, his smile now gone.

'You men don't talk?' asked Babita. 'How sad. To talk is the great art of a human being! I have a job, three mornings and two afternoons, looking after children. The pay is good, better than the store. The walk from here will be a long one.'

'Taxi. Taxi each way – I will pay. I know the man to do this, a good driver. Give him your times and he will collect you from both places – I shall pay him direct.'

'Yes, a good idea. Very well,' Babita agreed.

'Chandu,' Gupta continued, 'I will match your own salary to this children's job, and Babita will earn the same whilst she is here.'

My wife is incredible, thought Chandu. What a politician she would make, like Indira Gandhi, the prime minister of India. Given the opportunity, how far Babita could go, tiny in size but with the force of a jet engine.

'No! I want no salary when I am here. Your wife is everything to me, everything. That is enough. Taxi and expenses, this is all I will take.'

Humbled in a way he had never experienced before, Gupta held out his hand, and she took it, continuing to talk.

'One final thing, Vasu,' Babita lowered her voice and sat on edge of the bed, Gupta wincing at the shifting of the mattress. 'I understand the reason for you not wanting Meera to return out of pity. This is honourable, and I am pleased to hear it. Maybe there is feeling in you after all.'

Chandu gasped. She was going too far. Soon he would call her a moorkh, and she would smack him on the face and then how much bigger the problem would be.

'But you must understand that the position these circumstances place me in is not a good one. How can I not tell my dear friend that her husband is crippled and cannot move from the bed, to be washed by another woman; his sheets dried by a man?' This aside was for Chandu's benefit, although she kept an entirely straight face, bringing more admiration from her husband.

'So, this is the proposal I have for you. One month, only. If you recover in this time, then what you tell Meera is up to you. If not, and you are still lying in bed, then I will tell her. If Chandu was sick and I was away, I would expect to be told.'

'I am in no position to refuse,' he replied. 'I thank you from the heart. I do have one, you know?'

'Then show it! Now, there is much to do. I will bring a bowl, and you must wash as best you can. Call if you need help and Chandu will come.' She squeezed his hand to show she meant only good, and left the room, Chandu following closely behind.

CHAPTER
TWENTY-TWO

It was raining heavily, and Meera sat on the verandah; a cup of steaming tea in her hand. Her niece and companion was back at school, and she missed her comforting presence and constant questioning, so very much like Meera had been when she was that age. The rainy season had been late in coming, and now in September it hit with a force. It cooled the air considerably, although when it stopped, especially if the sun came out, the steam rose from the ground leaving her feeling like she was in a sauna. That people in England would pay for this luxury was quite bizarre, and when the humidity became too much, she would lie on her bed in a blouse and petticoat, the fan on the ceiling switched to full speed.

The heavy saris she brought with her from England were swapped for much thinner cotton ones, and like all the other ladies, a cool evening meant a shawl being thrown around her shoulders. She had bought several of these in the market, thinking how useful they might be for sitting in her chair by the window if she returned to England. If, she thought, if. A particularly beautiful example made of fine pashmina wool and threaded with real silver and gold was bought for her by her brother. He bought one for his wife too; always careful to show no favour to his sister, wanting no ill feeling to raise its ugly head.

Meera went back to the market the following day and bought another one; dark red in colour and threaded with gold, for Babita. For Suvi, her sister in law, she bought a wonderful parasol made of silk and hand painted with birds of paradise. There was a picture similar to this in the hall which she knew Suvi loved, and when she presented it to her later that day, her pleasure seemed genuine and her thanks profuse. There was no shortage of money in the household. Within reason, anything could be bought if desired, but like everywhere she supposed, the thought was much valued, and the giving of gifts, or 'Dana,' was seen as an essential part of Hindu life.

Her father lay behind her, the plume of dark smoke ever present, and earlier she had put a blanket over him, fearful that he might catch cold in the damp air. Looking back she could see that he had pushed it off, and she sighed, frustrated that he refused to speak or communicate in any way. At that moment a car pulled up outside and Delilah jumped out. With her raincoat over her head she was soon under the porch, her satchel carelessly thrown to the floor.

'Your mummy is visiting your uncle and said she might be late. Come, let us find you some buttermilk and a biscuit.' They both walked into the house and sat at the kitchen table; Meera with more tea, and her niece munching peanut biscuits, a frothy line of buttermilk on her upper lip.

'Today, we have been talking about careers,' stated Delilah. 'I want to be an archaeologist and dig things from the ground. The teacher said to be a doctor or a social worker, but no, I don't want any of these.'

Since she had been a small child, Delilah had been obsessed with all things ancient, demanding to be taken to museums and forts, or anywhere old and historic. At six she started to dig small holes in the garden, and at one time it was littered with these pits. After several accidents with both her family and the servants falling in them, they were all filled in, and the hole digging was now banned.

In one of her excavations she had found a small golden ring, at first thought to be brass with a blue glass stone. However, further examination revealed it to be more than four hundred years old, and the stone was a sapphire of intense colour and vivacity. Delilah's obsession grew, and was one which she refused to give up.

'What did they say when you insisted?' asked Meera.

'They said I might have to go to a university in England.'

From a very young age Delilah had shown herself to be extremely bright, and Manju insisted on sending her to a school that excelled in academic achievement. Suvi disagreed, still thinking that a good marriage was enough, but appalled at this backward view Manju ignored her. If she wanted to marry, then she could do so. There would be no more arranged marriages like he and Meera had been forced into. Never!

'Then you would be wise to perfect your English. It is true that England has many excellent universities. You must follow your dreams, Delilah.'

'Daddy says that. I will, no one will stop me.'

Meera smiled at the fortitude of her niece. She would need it if she was to succeed in a world where digging holes and scraping the ground was a main part of the work. What would she have done, she wondered, if a marriage had not been arranged for her? She had still heard nothing from Vasu. Part of her was enraged by this, and the other, curious. What was he doing, the silly man, stuck in his store day and night, alone. Was he eating, or would she find him looking like a skeleton if she returned?

'What are you thinking, Auntie? You are smiling like this.' Delilah twisted her face into a leer, and Meera laughed.

'Go and get changed from your school uniform. Your father will be home soon, and tonight we are meeting with his friends. Your other auntie is coming to stay with you.'

Delilah groaned. 'Oh no, not her. She is an idiot, Daddy says so.'

'No, Delilah, you must not say things like this. Maybe she thinks in a different way, but that is not always bad. Come, I will help you to choose your clothes, and you can help me to choose mine.'

***

Manju's friends lived in an enormous white house, with a domed roof and round towers at all four corners. It reminded Meera a little of the Taj Mahal, not in size, of course, but in style. She and Vasu had gone there for

139

their honeymoon, and Meera had bought a small replica of the building that was then converted into a lamp. It still sat in the sitting room in England, although usually remained unlit. Perhaps it was symbolic of her marriage, she thought – still standing, but with no light inside? She smiled at the asperity of her own description; sharp to the point of painful.

The evening passed in a daze, and it was only when the musicians started to play that Meera began to come alive. People stood around the edges of the room, but some were sitting on the thick rugs that were placed at the front in a traditional manner. Meera moved forward and sat, tucking her legs beneath her like she sometimes did when on the bed with Babita. Soon she was swaying back and forth, completely lost and almost in a trance, until Manju came to tell her they were going home. Reluctantly, she allowed herself to be led away, the music still ringing in her ears.

That night she couldn't sleep, and eventually went out to the verandah at the back of the house. The rain had stopped, and the night was warm and very dark. The moon and stars were hidden behind the clouds, and she felt as though she was swimming in ink, her head spinning slightly with the lack of visibility. Unable to see a single light or the outline of another building, even sound seemed to be muffled, and the jackals were silent; their choir gone into hiding perhaps for fear of attack in the darkness.

I want to go home, she thought – the other home, not this one; to the hardware store, and Babita, and the brown-skinned man who kept her kisses on his fingertips.

CHAPTER
TWENTY-THREE

A new routine was now established in the hardware store and, so far, things were going well. Spending the night there saved much time, and Chandu was able to complete the orders and take in the early morning deliveries with little difficulty.

Babita started her new job, coming back each day full of excitement and news about the family for whom she worked, and the children who were under her charge. They had all entered a new phase and felt the better for it, except perhaps for Mr Gupta, who felt trapped, moving only to use the bathroom after taking his painkillers fifteen minutes before.

One afternoon, when Babita was in the store, Chandu went upstairs to make him a cup of tea and felt a pity that he never thought he would feel for the man who lay on the bed, day after day. 'Gupta the Hun' had temporarily disappeared, to be re-christened with the new name of 'Krishna Gupta.' Babita told him what Mr Gupta had said about finding himself on his knees in front of Chandu as though he was praying, and he thought the name most appropriate and fitting to a man who wanted to become a better person. Also, as the god of love, what better a name for someone who desired to lure his wife back into the home? His new role away from the sarcasm and put-downs gave him a confidence that he never thought to own, and he carried the tea to his employer in the plastic beaker that the nurse had brought so that he could drink without spillage.

'I was wondering,' he said hesitantly, putting the beaker in Gupta's hand and watching the man drink for a moment.

'Yes, you were wondering what? If you are wanting to change the design of the store, then no. I am not ready to give this much power, when already you have so much. Soon you will be crazed with it, and then we shall see the true Kumar – then we shall see him.' In such a delicate position Gupta had taken to toying with Chandu, leaving him unsure if he was being chastised or teased.

Chandu cleared his throat, deciding to continue. 'Yes, I was wondering if to have a television in your room would be a good time-pass for you, especially if the disc takes much longer to heal. Babita thought it a good idea, and I have proposed it to you to think over.' The name of 'Saint' Babita was usually brought in if there was any doubt about Gupta's reaction to something, she now holding a status in Gupta's eyes that could not be surpassed.

142

Taking another long drink of his tea, Mr Gupta thought about Chandu's proposal. He and Meera, like the Kumars, had never owned a television, although not through lack of funds. Meera had broached the subject a few times, and maybe it would be a good idea, especially if she came back to find it here, ready and waiting to be used for the many women's programmes that he knew were shown.

'Maybe this idea from your wife is not such a bad one.'

Chandu opened his mouth to say that the idea had been his, not his wife's, but then thought better of it. 'Yes, she is always full of good ideas. You are in agreement, then? I was thinking that if the chest of drawers was moved to here,' he pointed to the wall opposite the bed, 'then you would have a very good view without having to twist yourself and injure your back further.' He scrutinised Gupta's face, looking for any signs that he was happy with the positioning that Chandu had given so much thought to.

'Very well, go ahead and order. Around the corner, the electrical shop has many televisions. Please choose a large one. An aerial will also be needed, so you must tell him to do it all, and for a good price.'

Chandu nodded, although he knew that there would be no bargaining done. The prices were fixed, but Gupta would pay without fuss – he would make sure of it. He went back down to the store, and seeing Babita happily helping a female customer to choose paint from the chart, he slipped through the door to buy the television that would amuse Krishna Gupta as he lay, trapped by the misfortune to have fallen at his assistant's feet.

The next few days were busy ones, and the flat above the store became a hive of activity, with holes being drilled and wires fixed to the walls. The workmen had already been on the roof, and a new aerial stood proudly from the disused chimney stack. The first viewing was an exciting moment for Chandu and Babita, and the store was closed for five minutes whilst they witnessed the switching on of Mr Gupta's 'time-pass.' He seemed genuinely animated and held the remote control tightly in his hand, trying to find a programme that he liked. Chandu wanted nothing more than to stay and watch 'Columbo,' an American detective show, but he had not been asked, and anyway, Babita had to go to her job and the store needed him. Reluctantly, he dragged himself away.

That evening, after dinner, Babita went downstairs to look for old paint charts that she knew were in the storeroom, thinking that Peter and Sasha would enjoy cutting them up and making pictures with the pieces. Walking to the back of the dark, poorly-lit room, she saw the many boxes of nails on the shelves to the side of the sink. She put her hand in one of them, pulling out a dozen of the pointed, metal spikes, exactly like those Chandu had brought home for so many years. There were thousands of them in the cupboard under the stairs of their boarding house room, and the number of tins had grown each year.

She slowly curled her fingers, squeezing on the sharp points until they began to pierce her palm, then quickly opening her hand again. Two pinpricks of blood were visible, and throwing the nails back into their box, she brought the injured hand to her mouth to suck at the wounds like she had been taught to do as a child.

That her husband should gauge his working life by these barbs hurt her greatly. His constant joking went some way to hide the sensitive man, but not quite. Not quite, and she determined to protect him from future harm by any means she could. Her husband was the finest of men, and Gupta, even in the position of praying to Krishna at Chandu's feet, would never even begin to attain the pureness of spirit that lived within the man she had married.

Their new working situation did at least mean that no nails had been added to the pile for several weeks, and for this, she was relieved. If only the new, more harmonious relationship with Gupta could be maintained after he recovered from his injury. How likely was it? Chandu was so much happier, and so was she, especially in her job with the children. Shaking her head, the bleeding now stopped, she found the paint charts and walked back up the stairs. It seemed to be very noisy, far more than the television usually made, and she walked closer to the source of the sound, Gupta's room, and peered through the crack of the door left slightly ajar.

What she saw was her husband sprawled on the bed, his employer by his side. Both men were laughing loudly, Krishna Gupta holding his sides to prevent the body-shaking humour from damaging his healing back. Morecombe and Wise, a comedy duo, were acting out a scene which clearly appealed greatly to the sense of humour of the two men. How very strange to see them in this way, like friends… There were further shrieks of laughter and Babita smiled, then turned away to attend to the sorting of charts for Stella's children.

CHAPTER
TWENTY-FOUR

Delilah stood by her aunt's bed, fiddling with the handle of the suitcase that lay open on top of it. Tears dripped steadily down her face, and grabbing the tissues that she had handed her earlier, Meera reached out to gently hold her niece by the chin and attend to the mopping herself. Bending down to give her a kiss on the top of her head, she then proceeded to fold clothes and lay them carefully in piles, ready for packing.

'I don't want you to go. Mummy said you might stay for ever, but you are going back? Why? Uncle Vasu can come to live here. He can have a shop in the town if he likes it so much! Why not, Auntie, why not? Even a house can be built, daddy said this; the land is ours, yours too, and the jackals can howl their songs every night, just to please you. Please Auntie, please stay!'

'Come,' said Meera, 'sit here with me, and I will explain.

It is true that I had thoughts to stay. I still do, but I have other thoughts to go back to England. Vasu is there, and the future is unclear. He loves his shop, and we have much to discuss, but this cannot be done by letter or telephone. Do you understand?'

Delilah nodded her head, now looking down into her lap, more tissues screwed up in her hands.

'I have been talking to your father. If you wish it, when you are sixteen you can come to England to stay with me and Uncle Vasu for the summer. I will show you London, and if your final decision is to study archaeology at university, then maybe London will be the place to do so. That is all in the future and many things can change, but there is much to look forward to, no?' Delilah nodded again. Privately, Meera thought that her return to India might not be too far away, since her father would not last more than another year, she was sure of it.

'I shall talk to daddy about what you have said. I think London will be the right place to study, and me and Pritti are going to the library to do research on the many universities of the world. Her brother is in America, and she will probably go there to live with him. You will write often? And telephone?'

'Of course. Nothing will stop me,' promised her aunt.

'And you will send a Laura Ashley dress and Afghan coat? Pritti has English magazines and says that these fashions are everywhere.'

'Don't worry. As soon as I am back I shall send them. You will be the most fashionable girl in the district.'

'Very well, then, Auntie. I shall allow you to go,' and with this announcement she left the room to phone her friend, and make arrangements for the library trip that would dictate her future.

***

Later that day, she sat with Manju in the swing seat on the verandah, drinking iced mango juice from tall glasses. Suvi was visiting her mother, and Meera had come to realise that her brother's marriage was not an altogether happy one. She broached the subject, and he answered honestly.

'We have little in common, it's true. She would be happy to pick the insects from rice all day long, read fortunes from shells, and henna her hands and feet.'

'Yes,' replied Meera. 'She cast the cowrie shells to read my fortune just this afternoon.' She shuddered at the remembrance, feeling instantly uneasy.

'You see?' Manju sighed. 'And I suppose you shall meet a tall, dark stranger and live a happy life?'

'I am already married to a tall, dark man, and at times, he is indeed a stranger!' replied Meera. In truth, she had been shaken by the experience. As requested, she had cast a handful of small shells across the table, expecting as Manju just said a frivolous and fairground-style response. Instead, Suvi carefully examined the shells, then looked at her sister-in-law for a few moments, her strange pale green eyes glinting.

'What is it?' Meera asked, beginning to feel afraid. 'What do you see?'

Suvi quickly gathered up the shells and dropped them into the glass jar where they were stored. 'Nothing,' she replied. 'It is just a silly game. Come Sister, let us have tea, and then I must visit my mother.'

Meera followed her into the kitchen but didn't believe that Suvi had seen nothing. She suspected that it was quite the opposite, and something bad had been shown to her – something that she didn't want to reveal for fear of causing upset.

Oblivious to Meera's discomfort, Manju let out a sigh. 'Don't misunderstand me, there is nothing wrong with these things and Suvi is not a bad woman, not at all, but she is uneducated, and our views on life are out of sync. Our own upbringing took us beyond the desire for these simple comforts. Although I would not wish my mind to be different, I acknowledge that I am somewhat displaced. You also feel some discomfort, Meera. I recognise it in you because I have it within me. We are out of step with our own selves, and herein lies the problem.'

Maybe he was right, thought Meera, his comments bringing her back into the moment, and her unease subsiding. Their father was educated abroad and had a mind like that of a sponge. He sought information on everything, gaining as much from a discussion with a beggar as one with the likes of Nehru and Gandhi, both of whom he had spoken with on many occasions. At one time he even took to spinning the wool for his own clothes, on the very same spot where she was now sat. Her strongest image of him was one of a slim, clean shaven and very handsome man, beautifully dressed in a Saville Row suit, a handmade silk shirt, and smelling of spicy cedar and sandalwood.

Meera shared her memories with Manju and he smiled, both looking behind them to see the same man dressed in a dhoti and thin woollen shawl; flat on his back on the hard, teak floor and the smoke rising to declare that life still existed within him – for now, at least.

'He and Mother were mismatched, without doubt,' continued Manju, 'which is why I absolutely refuse to countenance any such nonsense with my family. Aunt Nalini ruined everything. Left to him alone, and with Mother dead, we would have been free.'

'Agreed, but in truth my needs are much simpler than yours. For me, a happy marriage would be enough. I had this before I went to England and then everything changed. If I could have it back I would want for nothing else, but people are different. Can you imagine Delilah being forced into a marriage with a man not of her choosing?' Meera laughed, and Manju joined her.

'She is destined for fine things, our girl,' Meera continued, 'and the boys too; they are all so like you, and that makes me very happy. I have been thinking of late about Vasu's childhood. As you know, he has much intelligence but there was little warmth in his family, only books, and a problem was created for him.'

'He can learn to be different! If he wants it, he can learn. You must tell me if he ever hits you again. I shall come over and give him such a thump that his head will spin for a week. How dare he...' Manju became agitated, and Meera placed her hand on his arm to calm him.

'Don't upset yourself, Brother. Once more, and I myself shall hit him back with one of his own shovels, and then we shall see.' She told him about Babita and the slap that Vasu had received from her.

Manju laughed. 'Ah, this sort of wife would suit me

better. I like a feisty woman, one with character and strength of mind.'

'She is all of those things, it is true. I cannot wait to see her again.'

'Are you still not going to let Vasu know that you're coming back?'

'No, I shall not tell him. I will just turn up and see how he reacts.'

'I wish I was there to see it all. A fly on the wall.' Manju sighed, and leant further back in his chair.

'Your English is so much better than mine, even though I am the one living there!' complained Meera, 'and as for you being a fly on the wall, remember the slapping habits of Mr Gupta. Quite likely you would end up flat, squashed like a chapati, never to move again!'

They both burst out laughing, children once more, sharing a joke as though no time at all had passed.

'Silence,' came a deep voice from behind them, and they turned to stare at their father; eyes closed, smoke rising, no movement to be seen.

'He spoke?' they asked each other, simultaneously.

The brother and sister laughed again. Their father had spoken, and now anything was possible.

CHAPTER
TWENTY-FIVE

Once again, Meera arrived in the early hours, blinking in the bright lights of the airport as she waited for her luggage. The taxi driver stowed her cases in the boot, and sat at the back, she watched the beginnings of dawn creeping slowly into the dark sky. She felt calm, her fate to be decided by Gupta's behaviour, and her ability to love the man that he once was, and could again become.

When the cab pulled up outside the door of Mr Gupta's Hardware Store, she paused before getting out to take in the scene before her. She felt like she had been away for ever, yet knew well enough that once inside, her stay in India would begin to slip from reality to become just a memory. Such tricks were played by time, and all without any possibility of outside control. Puppets only, thought Meera, eventually opening the cab door and climbing out. Puppets only, but this puppet would tug at its strings, and she hoped that her husband would do the same.

She watched as the taxi drove away, then took another look up and down the street; lights everywhere and cars slipping by in a never-ending stream. Did these people never sleep, she wondered? The hum of London had not stopped in her absence, of course not, but if she were able to choose, she would have the howl of the jackals around her at night. No question. She smiled to herself as she turned the key, opening the door as gently as she could to not awaken the wild bells strung upon it. Jackals on the streets of London would create quite a stir, and leaving this thought on the pavement, she crept inside, pulling her cases carefully to minimise noise. Then the smell was upon her; the heady fragrance of paint, oil and polish and, just as she had thought – as she breathed it in, it was like she had never left at all.

If she dragged her bags upstairs she would undoubtedly wake Mr Gupta. Suddenly shy of seeing him, she unzipped one of the cases, fumbling around for a while in the half-light to eventually pull out a thin, kaftan-style nightdress that had been made for her in the markets of Agra. Quickly taking off a jacket, she unwound her sari and pulled off her blouse. Then, petticoat removed, the kaftan was pulled over her head, and she bent over to pick up the clothes she had removed, flinging them over the shiny wooden counter.

A passer-by looking into the store would have seen a statuesque woman, her clothes dropping to the floor around her; the dark skin making her look like a shadow that had a life of its own, with no host needed. Meera may well have thought of herself as a puppet, but the observer would have seen something altogether different. He would have seen her as a mirage; a fragment of an imagination that hailed from another time, a queen from the Mogul empire, or a princess from a Maharaja's palace.

Quite unaware of these potential images, Meera gently pulled open the door at the bottom of the stairs. Shy as a new bride, she crept up, deciding to sleep in the spare room and greet her husband in the morning. The door to the room was slightly ajar, and unbeknown to Meera was kept that way in order to hear any calls of distress from Krishna Gupta, her newly christened husband.

She heard a gentle snoring from within, and suddenly confused, took one more step forward. In the permanent glow from the street outside she saw the face of Babita, dark curls spread about her on the pillow. By her side lay Chandu, the owner of the snores. Why were they here, she wondered? Had the boarding house burned down? Had they been made homeless and were desperate enough to come and live with Vasu at the store?

Silently retreating, she entered her own bedroom, the door also slightly ajar; her husband lying stiffly and over to one side. Quite unlike his normal sleeping style, he was on his back, a black object with buttons held tightly in his hand. She could see that the furniture had been moved, and peering around the walls, she eventually saw the large television at the foot of the bed. A television instead of a wife, she thought, and what other changes had been made in her absence? Why, for two rupees she would shake him awake and demand answers!

Calm yourself, she thought, remembering her feelings

of shyness after being apart from him for so long. Walking silently to the other side of the bed, she lifted the covers and slid inside the cool sheets, careful not to touch him or disturb the bedclothes that were draped over his sleeping form.

'Ah,' came a silky voice from the darkness. 'Mrs Gupta, Meera, wife of mine – for you only this space has been kept, and at last you have arrived to fill it. I have been waiting for a lifetime, my dear; many lifetimes, in fact. Thanks be to Krishna. I shall be forever in his debt.'

That she had returned to him was a miracle, and he held her tight, pledging to never let her go again – not for a second. Meera Gupta had arrived home, and of this fact there was no doubt. None whatsoever.

CHAPTER
TWENTY-SIX

Chandu set the alarm for six-thirty, expecting two deliveries and wanting to get them onto the shelves before opening. Quickly washing, taking care to not wake Babita or Krishna, he made tea, and carried it carefully down the stairs.

About to put the tea on the counter, he saw that it appeared to be almost completely covered with clothes. Definitely ladies, he thought, for here is a sari and petticoat, blouse too, and oh, a jacket on the ground also. Why had Babita been taking her clothes off in the store? Chandu considered himself to be a liberal man. He knew that times had changed, and that women were free to choose their own lives, but no – not this. Why, she could have been seen by any man in the street! No, he thought again. This must stop, and he would tell her so when she woke up.

Attempting to open the door to the storeroom, he

found it stuck, and looking down saw a pair of large platform shoes; red and shiny as a letter box. He rubbed his eyes, then opened them again to study the confusing footwear further. To him, the shoes appeared huge. Why, he thought, they were larger than Babita's head! These were not her shoes, and therefore the clothes did not belong to her either. Glad that she had not disregarded her modesty entirely, there was still a problem. If they were not hers, then whose where they?

Mr Gupta was unable to walk down the stairs, so he could not have put the clothes there himself. Picking up his cup, he took a long, noisy slurp of tea, just as he might have done at a tea-stand on a street corner somewhere in the Punjab.

Then something occurred to him, but he quickly discarded the thought as impossible. Absolutely impossible. No question – never. But men did, he thought, it was the same everywhere. Perhaps Krishna Gupta had found himself able to walk in the night, and had wanted to exercise his back? Now closer to the truth – maybe, he thought, the clothes were Meera's, brought down by him in his night-time walk? But why? He had dressed himself in his wife's clothes in the store at night? Krishna Gupta? Vasuman Krishna Gupta? Surely if this was his way, he would take the trouble to clear up afterwards? Chandu knew he would if this were his behaviour of choice. He would leave no trace of alternative clothing preferences, not even a headscarf!

At this moment, the door to the stairs opened and Babita walked through, her eyes sparkling with excitement. 'She is back, Chandu, she is back!' she cried.

'Who? Who is back?' he asked, confused.

'Meera, of course, who else? What other woman lives at this address? Ah, here they are.' She grabbed the pile of clothes and bent down to pick up the shoes. 'Really, Chandu, whose clothes did you think these were?'

'Well, at first I was thinking that they were yours.'

'You thought I had taken off my clothes in the store in the middle of the night? But you already saw me in my nightdress before we slept!'

'I know.'

'Now I am interested. Please tell me your thinking. You have been watching Columbo on the television, is this not so?'

'Correct! So then I thought who else lives here?'

'Only us, and Krishna. You thought a burglar had left the clothes instead of robbing the store?' She tutted. 'Really, Chandu, the television is hurting your brain.'

'Not burglars, something else.' He looked down for a moment, unable to meet her direct gaze.

Babita's eyes widened, suddenly realising what had been going on in her detective husband's mind.

'You thought Krishna? Mr Gupta? That he had worn these clothes?'

Chandu nodded and smiled. 'Why not? It happens frequently; the newspaper says so.'

'No more night-time television for you, husband. From here on – banned!' She sliced her hand through the air to add final definition to her words, then ran up the stairs, muttering and laughing in turn, leaving Chandu to finish his tea and wonder at the arrival of Meera in the night; removing her clothes in the store, before climbing the stairs to Krishna.

CHAPTER
TWENTY-SEVEN

Meera and Babita spent the rest of the morning talking, the beautiful red shawl spread across the table in front of them. Meera laughed when Babita told her about Chandu's thoughts and conclusion to the pile of clothes that had been left in the store.

'What? He thought that Vasu...? In women's clothes...?' She banged her hand on the table several times and bent over, unable to draw her breath with such an image in her mind.

'Vasu in a sari? And blouse and petticoat?' she shrieked again and covered her face with her hands as though the image was too much to contemplate.

'What is it?' called Krishna from the bedroom. 'Why are you laughing in this way? Is there a plot to kill me? Is this why so much fun is being had?'

'Yes, you have caught us out. Soon you will be killed, and we shall take the money and run away,' replied Babita.

More laughter was heard from the sitting room, and Krishna Gupta sighed. He wanted to get up. He hated being confined in this way, especially with Meera now home. He had an idea to buy her a present, jewellery perhaps, but how was this possible flat on his back like an upturned dung beetle? Maybe Babita could go shopping for him? He would ask her.

At that moment, the lady put her head around the door. 'Meera has gone for a bath. You know the doctor is to come this morning?'

He nodded.

'Good. We shall see what she says, and decide what help is now needed.'

'Thank you, Babita. There is something else... I was wondering if you could find time to buy a gift for Meera? Jewellery maybe? A ring or earrings? The money is in the drawer. Any amount... no limits at all.' He pointed to the chest where the television stood, and Babita nodded.

'This is a very good idea. Of course. I will go out later after the doctor has been, and see what can be found.'

'One more thing. I would like to buy you a gift, as well.'

Babita could hardly believe what she was hearing. A gift? From Vasuman Gupta? Was the man crazy with lying flat for so long and no oxygen getting to his brain?

'Please, I want to buy it to thank you. For Chandu, I will think of something else, but for you – a lady, jewellery, like Meera is to have. Anything you like. Please let me do this or the shame will be too much.'

Babita looked at the man in front of her; barely able to move without strong drugs, totally helpless, crushed, maybe, of the old fire that had blazed within him. And yet, as she had wondered, was the phoenix ready to fly from the ropes that bound him? From the bonds of spite and malice, gifted perhaps by his parents? Meera had told her about Sister Maria Benedicta, and the clever words about the man-boy that was her husband. Would the leopard lose its spots? She hoped so, and yet... and yet... what else might be lost in this process? A man with no spirit was no man at all.

'Thank you. I will accept the offer. What woman does not like to have new jewels? The tide is turning, is that not so? I believe this is the English phrase for change?'

He nodded. 'Yes. I believe it is.'

'Then I have one more to add that was learned yesterday from Stella, the mother of the children I care for.' She paused for a moment to gather her thoughts, and to choose with great care the words that she wished to say. 'To change that which is broken is a good thing; no argument. But care is to be taken in not to throw the baby with the bathwater.'

Now it was his turn to think – to absorb the wisdom of the woman who stood beside his bed; nurse and guru in one – the size of a child, yet with the knowledge of the universe resting upon her shoulders. He felt humbled, and in his low and weakened state tears began to roll down his cheeks, dripping sideways onto the faithful pillow that for so long now had supported his head.

Babita watched this outpouring of emotion from the man who had suffered so greatly over the past few weeks, and longer than that, if the words of Sister Maria Benedicta were to be believed. She took some tissues from the box and began to wipe his face. Yes, she thought, let the tears fall, Krishna Gupta, husband of Meera. Let the tears fall, and this he did, in an outpouring of grief and past hurt – both given and received.

CHAPTER
TWENTY-EIGHT

Later that morning, the doctor introduced herself to Meera, and she and Babita watched as she examined her patient, tapping at his knees with a tiny hammer, and flicking the ends of his fingers and toes to gauge the responses.

'How much pain are you in? Is it any better?' she asked.

'It hurts less as I lie flat, and to turn slightly is also easier, but using the bathroom still has to be done after taking the painkillers.'

'And can you sit up by yourself?'

'Sometimes I can pull myself up a little by reaching like this.' He showed her how he used the headboard to raise himself up slightly when eating or drinking.

'There certainly seems to be some improvement, and your responses are good. Loss of muscle tone is an issue, though, with you lying down so much. I'm going to send someone round to run through a few exercises with you. You'll need to do them every day. A couple of weeks, and I think you'll be much more mobile. We'll soon have you running up and down the stairs again!' She patted his hand.

'I can assist with washing now I am home, so there is no need for a nurse to come anymore,' Meera told the doctor. She had been most uncomfortable when she learned of the visit each morning from a young woman, and had no intention of allowing her to come again. She shuddered at the thought.

'Excellent. Here's another prescription for the next fortnight – just take them when you need them and call the surgery if you're worried about anything. I'll see you in two weeks then, Mr Gupta?' Lucy Shaw, the doctor who looked like a cosmetics representative, waved cheerfully as she left, leaving floral perfume in her wake, to be followed by Babita, also leaving her own trail of French Almond fragrance hanging in the air.

'It's like a perfume shop in here,' complained Krishna, pretending to cough and waving his hand in front of his nose.

Meera grabbed the hand and held it tightly in her own. 'Yes, too many women have been in your bedroom in my absence, is that not so? This is something that as a married woman I will not allow. Shame on you, Mr Gupta,' she teased, before kissing the back of the hand she held, then suddenly dropping it before leaving the room.

Krishna Gupta sighed. Whether or not he was aware of his new name, he had indeed been renewed, as had his marriage. The life of the store had continued to exist in his absence, and the people in it were like the cogs in a clock that constantly turned; interconnected and seamless. Lying in his bed, quiet and alone, he could almost hear the wheels of time, ticking slowly by. He sank a little lower and gave another sigh, but this one of contentment. Never had he felt so cared for, cosseted even, protected from harm and loved.

Perhaps it was the medication? Or that lying in bed for so long had turned his head, and allowed his imagination to run riot away from the confines of his duties – but looking at the remote control now held in his hand, he had a sense of holding the reins to his life. He slid down even further, and pulling the sheets high under his chin, settled to sleep. In his mind's eye, or in a dream, he saw himself in a red and gold chariot, four white horses with red plumes on their heads, almost flying towards a brilliant sunset – all trusting in Krishna to guide them home.

***

'He is asleep,' declared Chandu, the beaker of tea still held in his hand.

'You should have left it. Maybe he will wake and be thirsty. In a moment I shall take it back up,' declared Meera, and Chandu nodded, pleased to be relieved of some of his nursing duties. They had taken the opportunity of a quiet half-hour to discuss the running of the store now that Meera was home. A few minutes earlier she had left the shop, quickly returning with a carrier bag. In it was a bright pink overall, exactly like Babita's, and the two ladies were now a matching pair of shop workers, both giggling when they saw the other.

'I cannot see how you can manage everything,' said Babita. 'The shop needs two people, and there is still nursing to be done. Chandu can deal with deliveries and heavy filling of shelves, and my suggestion is that we will stay for the next week, night-time also, and see how things go. If Vasu can get up and fetch his own tea and take medication, then maybe we can sleep at home from then on. I can still come to the store each day, as long as the taxi will continue to take me to the children.'

'Are you sure? You have done so much already. I worry that you will become very tired with so much to do.' Meera frowned with concern, her eyes worried and anxious.

'I am sure. Actually, I am not tired at all. The taxi is a great help, and Chandu has so enjoyed helping with Mr Gupta. Is that not so, Chandu?'

Realising that he was being toyed with, Chandu moved his head from side to side, deciding to make the most of it. 'Oh yes. It has even made me think that I should leave the hardware store for good, and train to be a nurse. Mr Gupta will tell you himself how skilled I have become. Why, one day I even...' Both ladies burst out laughing, Babita playfully slapping her husband's knee.

'Alright, alright – we know you are the male version of Florence Nightingale. If you are wanting to train, then let me know. I will be happy to support you in this new venture.'

Oh, I am so happy to be home – so happy, thought Meera, and in front of her friends, for the first time in years, she answered Chandu's perfect Indian expression of head movement with one of her own, eyes glinting, and a joyous smile on her face.

'Yes,' she added, 'I too will support those with a vocation. You can work in the store at night, washing the tins and sweeping the floor.'

Chandu held his head in his hands and let out a long groan. 'A new slave-driver has come to the store, India returned. What hope is there for me now?'

At this, all three exploded with laughter, and upstairs Krishna stirred, raised from his deep sleep by the raucous sound.

'So happy,' he mumbled, before falling asleep again.

***

Later that afternoon when Babita had gone to look after Peter and Sasha, Chandu and Meera stayed in the shop, climbing the stairs at intervals to check on Krishna. Unused to working in this way, Meera was impressed by the new-found confidence that Chandu displayed, and how much the customers liked him, often asking his opinion. He had been teased twice that afternoon about 'throwing sunshine,' as the customers called it, and she observed his glowing face, full of pride for both himself, and the store. Leaving him for a moment, she hurried up the stairs and into the bedroom, where her husband was watching the television. He blew her a kiss and held out his hand, which she took, before sitting on the bed.

'Vasu? There is something I need to talk to you about.'

'Of course, what is it? Is there a problem?'

'No, not at all, more that I have made an observation.

167

Chandu – I have been watching him. He works so hard, and the customers love him. I think the time away from you has allowed him to blossom.'

Gupta winced, and seeing this, Meera grabbed his other hand and held both tightly.

'No, you must not take this the wrong way. Sometimes, it is only when the larger force removes itself, that the other light can shine.'

'You want me to leave the store?'

'Of course not, don't be silly, the store is yours and you love it, I know that. No, more I was thinking that it is time to allow Chandu some responsibility of his own. With you lying here for weeks, he has done it all himself with the help of Babita. I know she had done much to assist.'

'I have already given him a raise in salary. Do you think I should give more?' he pulled his hand away and leaned back, pulling himself slowly and somewhat painfully into a more upright position. 'Tell me what is on your mind, my dear, and I might agree or I might not.'

'I was thinking a title should be given,' said Meera, holding her nerve, but unsure of herself with the changed man before her.

'You mean like Prince, or Sir? Yes, I can do that, no problem at all.' He laughed, and as quick as a flash, Meera picked up the remote control of the television and went to stand by the open window.

'Now I have full power over my husband as well as the television. If he disagrees or plays the fool I shall throw the remote to the street, and it will smash to a thousand pieces. What I am wanting is for Chandu to be made assistant manager. That would be his title. 'Assistant Manager of

Mr Gupta's Hardware Store.' She pulled her hand in from the window and carefully studied her husband, trying to gauge his reaction.

'Yes, I have already been thinking about this,' he replied. 'It was to be my gift to him for taking care of everything since my attempt to fly failed so badly.'

'Vasuman Gupta, I have two things to say to you. First – flying must be left to that which has wings. Second – you and Chandu have more in common than was first shown. Oh, and a third. Your wife has decided that she will also work in the store, part-time – no title needed!'

'Very well, then,' he replied, signalling for Meera to toss the remote control back onto the bed. This she did, smiling at him she made for the door, remembering that Chandu was on his own in the store.

'All is in agreement,' said her husband, 'as long as you remember one thing?'

Meera stopped and turned her head. 'Yes? And what might that be?'

'The name of Krishna is preferable. Use it, please.'

'You have heard?' she asked.

'Of course,' he said, blowing her another kiss, this time from the tips of his fingers. 'Even fools have ears, Mrs Gupta, even fools have ears.'

CHAPTER
TWENTY-NINE

The store was still open when Babita got back that afternoon, and she slipped on her overall to take over from Meera on the till. It had been an exceptionally busy day, and each time a customer left and Chandu made for the door, another one came in before he had been able to lock it. Eventually at around six-thirty the shop was clear and quickly turning the sign, Meera called Babita to join her in the storeroom.

'Come, I need to tell you something,' she said, beckoning with her finger as Babita came towards her.

'Am I also to be invited to this gathering,' asked Chandu, 'or is it just for ladies in pink overalls? I can get one… The colour will suit the tone of my skin, is that not so?'

'Women only,' said Meera, slamming the door behind them.

'What is it?' asked Babita. 'Is there a problem with Vasu? Now I am worried. Tell me.'

'No, no problems at all. He is behaving like an angel. I have to remind myself that he is the same man, and not an imposter from the KGB. No, I have great news, but I did not want to ruin the surprise.'

'Surprise? What surprise?'

'Listen and I will tell you. I asked Vasu today to give Chandu the title of Assistant Manager.'

Babita drew in a breath, her pretty mouth falling open for a moment. 'Assistant Manager? Chandu? And what did he say? I cannot believe that you asked this!'

'He said that he had already decided it! We have agreed to keep it a secret until the day before you both leave to go back to your own home, to make a real surprise for Chandu. Perhaps we can have a special dinner to celebrate? What do you think? Are you pleased?'

'Pleased? Pleased? You are insane? I am more pleased than I have words to say. He deserves this so much. For years he has worked like a slave, and for so little.'

'No more,' replied Meera, solemnly. 'Not whilst I am here. I am also to work in the store part-time, so little will happen without my say, you can be sure of it!'

Babita laughed, squeezing her friend's arm tightly. She was sure of it! She would trust Meera with her life, and Chandu's too.

'To stop squeezing would be very wise,' said Meera 'before the flow of blood is stopped and the arm falls off!' Babita hadn't realised she was holding Meera's arm in this way, and let go, embracing her in a hug of pure joy.

'Yes, we can make a special dinner,' cried Babita, her

eyes shining brightly, even in the poorly-lit gloom. 'It will be an evening for him to remember…!'

Meera felt suddenly chilled, and for no reason that she could fathom – ill at ease. The storeroom was dark and cold, although she knew that Chandu would stay in it for the whole day if he could. Despite her happiness about his promotion, she rubbed her goose-bumped arms before reaching for Babita's hand and leading her into the warmth of the shop.

'Ah, the meeting of female minds has come to an end,' said Chandu, slamming the till after removing the large quantity of notes that had accumulated throughout the day. 'The world will be changed from here on, is this not so?' He laughed to himself as he began to climb the stairs, the money wrapped in a cloth bag as an offering to Krishna. 'Watch out, Mr Wilson,' he shouted down, 'your job as Prime Minister is now at risk!'

'Always the clown,' said Babita, and Meera shuddered again, this time noticed by her friend. 'Are you OK?' she asked. 'What is wrong? A ghost has come into the store?'

'I don't know. I feel most strange. Maybe I have a cold coming – honey and lemon for me tonight! Come, we must make dinner before we finally rest. Then we can put our heads together and plan.' She opened the door to the stairs and, one behind the other, the two began the ascent to the flat, Babita making a list in her head of the things she would need to buy. Meera remembered the cowrie shells of her sister-in-law, Suvi, her refusal to give an account of them, and for some unfathomable reason, the face of Sister Maria Benedicta, her silver eyes gleaming, and the deep, rumbling laugh that seemed to have crossed an ocean. She wished she could talk to her now and take both advice and comfort from the woman's undoubtedly wise words.

'I think you are not well,' declared Babita. 'Lie on the bed with Krishna, and I shall cook. Something simple I think, and there is ice-cream in the freezer. Everything is under control.'

If only, thought Meera, making her way to the bedroom and collapsing on her side of the bed, much to the surprise of her husband who had been watching the end of the news.

'If only,' she said aloud, as he started to pull himself up, turning slightly to look at her.

'The saddest words ever said, Meera, and what has happened that you should talk this way?' Returning his gaze, she took in his broad, dark face, large nose, and eyes glinting like black diamonds.

'Cold coming, I think. I shall have lemon and honey after dinner,' she repeated. 'Now let me see what is being shown for our entertainment this evening.' Before he could stop her, she grabbed the remote control from his hand and began to flick through the channels until she found one that she thought might be amusing.

'Babita,' she called. 'Babita… come. The Six Million Dollar Man is on the television. There is much we can learn from the rebuilding of his body to aid Mr Gupta's broken back.' Babita rushed through to the bedroom, onion in one hand, a sharp knife in the other. Chandu followed closely behind, a broad grin already on his face in anticipation of any fun that might be about to start.

'I was already thinking that we should take his recovery into our own hands. Chandu, fetch hot water and towels. This operation might make mess, and you know how proud you have become of the sheets that have been dried by your hands only.' She moved closer to the bed, knife poised… 'Now, no baby behaviour – turn over. Your match has been met one hundred times over and to struggle will be useless.'

Chandu let out a shriek of laughter, slapping his thigh and running to the end of the bed to get a better view. 'Yes – turn, she has a temper, you know this to your cost.'

The sick man held up his hands in surrender, desperately struggling to control the laughter that threatened to cause him so much pain. 'Stop,' he shouted. 'Stop! I give in! I am at your mercy, and if I was able to stand I would throw myself at your feet and beg to be spared, as Krishna is my judge.'

'Krishna? He is always in this house, I have noticed, and to land at people's feet is becoming a habit of yours,' replied Babita.

Chandu let out another howl of delight and banged his fist on the wooden end of the bed. 'Yes, Yes,' he shouted, 'I too wish to land at the feet of those greater than me,' and with that, he threw himself to the floor in front of Babita and grabbed at her ankles.

For the rest of the evening and almost in turn, each of the four would recall the antics from earlier on and laugh and shake in remembrance. Sprawled upon the bed, eating ice-cream, Babita and Meera gave each other knowing looks; the words clear, despite remaining unspoken.

'Yes, we are all home at last! Four Indians together and with Krishna himself to watch over us.'

CHAPTER
THIRTY

The rest of the week went by in a flurry of work and activity. Saturday night was decided upon for Chandu's special dinner, and in the background much planning had taken place. Babita went out to choose the jewellery for Meera whilst she was working in the store, and later that day she had shown it to Mr Gupta, hoping that her choice would meet with his approval.

He was now able to sit up with less discomfort and had made himself tea earlier that day, although the pain dictated that he must lie down again, very soon after. She placed the box on his knees, a dark green velvet embossed with gold around the edges. In Indian culture it was a husband's duty to provide his wife with jewellery, not only for adornment but as a source of revenue, if needed. It was a sentiment much approved of by the traditional Mr Gupta. The gift was very costly, but he insisted, believing that there was much making up to do for time he had lost with his lovely wife. Babita whole heartedly agreed.

He drew in a breath as she opened the lid and let out a low whistle. Nestling in the black interior was a necklace and earring set; the buttery yellow gold standing out like a beacon against its dark background. Each piece had a deep crimson ruby at its centre, and lay inside a nest of sparking diamonds.

'You like it? As soon as I saw it I knew it was for Meera. Can you imagine her face when she sees it? And how it will look when on?' She waited for his response, watching whilst he touched the jewels then held them up for a closer view.

'Beautiful – you have chosen well. I love rubies. My mother had a necklace with rubies this colour all around, each one the size of a pigeon's egg; a bracelet and earrings too. My brother, the eldest, was given it for his wife, but it stays locked away, I imagine.' He snapped the lid shut and Babita placed it in the bag, then pushed it back over to him.

'And for yourself? You have bought something for yourself, as I said?'

She nodded and looked down, unable to meet his eye. She felt shy. It was not every day that she was told to buy herself a piece of jewellery, the amount of money given beyond her wildest dreams. 'Yes, but I feel so awkward…'

'No, stop. I wanted to give you a gift so much. You have been here for weeks, and who else would have come to my aid – even only for Meera's sake.'

'Not only for her sake… Not now that Krishna has come.' They both smiled, and she held out another box, this one square and of the deepest blue, with tiny gold stars on its lid. She hesitated...

'Open it, or are you keeping me in suspense – like a movie?'

She flipped back the lid to reveal a bangle, utterly simple and quite the opposite of the jewellery she had bought for Meera. It consisted of two strands of gold, one yellow, one white, twisted together to make a single rope.

Once again, he drew in a breath, then let out a soft whistle. 'You have excellent taste, my dear, although your taste was never in doubt. Why else did I set you this task?'

'I am very glad you approve. It is without beginning or end, and this is why I chose it. Also, I don't have so much jewellery, and wanted something that I could wear all the time without fear of loss or damage. What I had was sold to pay for fares to England, and the rest is mostly silver.' She held out her fingers for him to see.

'Excellent! You will never need to take it off. What is the point of having jewellery that is never worn?' He paused for a moment, then added, 'like my mother's necklace.'

'You will give Meera her gift later?' she asked.

'Yes, I shall pick the moment with great care,' he replied, and she nodded, wishing she could witness it.

'Almost everything is arranged for tomorrow, and Chandu has no idea at all. His expectations are so small that the potential to disappoint is almost none.' She looked away for a moment before speaking again. 'How lucky we have both been in our marriages, is that not so, although to live with a saint is not so easy...'

'I'm sure he has got used to it by now.'

Babita laughed, lightly tapping Gupta's hand. 'I meant me living with a saint – not him.'

'I knew very well what you meant,' he replied. 'I was teasing – practice is needed, you know, to achieve the standard expected.'

'Ah, yes, practice makes perfect!' She got up. 'You have everything you need? And the exercises... You are doing these regularly?'

'Yes to both, but now is time for a nap. I must make the most of my disabled condition. I fear there will be little time for slacking with Meera and a new assistant manager in the store.'

He slid under the sheets, and Babita went to prepare for her afternoon with Peter and Sasha. Wanting to call in at the boarding house to collect and leave clothes, she left early, asking the taxi driver to drop her there – the walk across the park being a quick and easy one on such a fine day. She hadn't been to her own home for a week, and she opened the windows wide to let in fresh air. It all looked so forlorn, and quite unlike the happy place it had been when she and Chandu were living in it. Despite reminding herself that they would soon be back, it still felt very strange. She wanted to be here alone with Chandu, of course she did, but since the turning of tides and the arrival back of Meera, she felt a solemnness as she looked around her. She would miss them, both Meera and Vasu, that was the truth of it. She would miss them all living in the same house, and the sharing of their lives in such an intimate way. There was much to be said for it.

She also greatly enjoyed working in the store with Chandu and Meera, and hoped that in some way this would continue. With work in mind, she closed the windows again, and within minutes was walking across the park. She had her own key to the house but hated to walk in when Stella was there. 'Hello,' she called, only partially through the door. Some distance away, she heard a voice.

'Come in – we're in the garden,' and she walked towards the kitchen at the rear of the house, and to the garden beyond that.

***

That evening, Babita sat with Meera, planning the dinner for the following night. 'I have two gifts for him, just small things, but I think he will like them. He still has no idea?'

'No,' Meera replied, 'he knows nothing. We must keep him in the store for the whole day, and when he comes up we will be waiting. Vasu wants to be standing, although it won't be for long. He will take his painkillers so he should manage twenty minutes, I think.'

'Will he be able to sit and eat?' asked Babita

'Yes,' came a shout from the bedroom. 'I have been strengthening my muscles all week for the occasion.'

At that moment, Chandu burst through the door. He had gone downstairs to fetch paperwork for his employer, and went through to the bedroom to discuss the details of an order that was placed earlier that day.

'We also have a gift,' whispered Meera. 'A surprise, even from you.'

'Very well. Keeping secrets from your friend? Is this so? Two can play a game like this, Mrs Krishna Gupta. You must be careful!' They both smiled, determined to hold their secrets from the other until the appointed time.

'Things were a little strange with the children today.'

'Really? What do you mean, strange? What happened?' asked Meera, her interest aroused.

'I am not sure, but they are usually so good, and today they were not. Peter cried a lot asking for his mummy, and Sasha drew with ink pen all over the wall. Something has happened, but I do not know what.'

'You tried to ask? I know with my niece, children will often speak their minds.'

'Yes, I tried, but nothing. I think they must miss their father. He is away so much, and she too – Stella. Work is one thing, but he has been gone for many months, from one country to another, it seems, and no mention of a homecoming.'

'Very strange, Babita. Very strange. She is paying you properly?' asked Meera, eyebrow raised.

'Oh yes, no problem there.' She yawned and got up. 'Tell Chandu I am going to bed? No doubt he will be watching television for half the night!'

'No he won't, replied Meera. 'Tomorrow will be a long day, and we all need our rest!'

The two kissed each other warmly, and Babita went to her room. The time has come for us to leave, she thought. Krishna needs to be with his bride, and she with him. I will talk to Chandu, and probably on Sunday we will go home. The thought depressed her, and concern over the children and her job looking after them, added to the insecurity that she felt. 'A transition only,' she said aloud, 'a transition only.'

'You are calling to me?' shouted Meera.

'No. I am talking to myself, which, as everyone knows, is the beginning of madness!'

'Then I am mad already!' Meera laughed. She too felt anxious. She knew that the Kumars should leave, and that time must be spent with Vasu alone. She wanted that… She wanted to get to know her husband again and create an intimacy like that of when they first married, but equally, she did not want to let go of her friend. She wanted to keep her here where she could make sure she was alright, and Chandu, too. The joy that he carried within him had sweetened all their lives, and she wanted it to remain that way.

Chandu had just left the Guptas' bedroom, and came to stand by Meera, who had hastily dropped an envelope onto her knees under the table. 'All is well?' he asked. 'Strange behaviour is everywhere in this household. Am I to be told more?'

'In your imagination!' replied Meera. 'Go to bed and sleep. Saturday is usually busy in the store, especially since sunshine decided to reveal itself.' He grinned and moved his head from side to side, no words needed – it said it all. Meera responded likewise, then raised her hand to gently touch the side of his face.

More alarmed than if he had been slapped, Chandu also raised his hand and placed it over hers. 'I was thinking a smack was long overdue and that this was to be gifted to me!'

'No jokes, Chandu. You are a good man, and I am so glad you are here.'

'Krishna, also?' he asked.

'Krishna, also,' she replied.

He nodded his head, about to say more then deciding against it. He wished the beautiful woman in front of him goodnight, and left the room.

A scene in a play, thought Meera. I have just viewed a scene in a play as if I were watching from outside. What is wrong with me? I must be ill. Quickly tidying up, she switched off the lights and went to her bedroom. The room was in darkness, but the glow from the television sent flickering images around the walls. She watched them for a moment before lying on the bed, still fully clothed.

'What is it, my dear? Something is wrong… Won't you tell me and maybe I can help?' asked her husband, taking her hand and kissing it gently. He smelt the almond perfume that had been on her sleep-sari, and was momentarily taken back to that lonely night, thankful that it was well behind him.

'I don't know how to tell you. Something feels wrong, and I am afraid.'

He sat up, now able to do this with more ease, and putting his arm around her, kissed the top of the glossy hair coiled upon her head. He reached up and pulled away the pins that held it in place, the whole lot then tumbling down – a veritable waterfall of sleek, black silk, heavy and thick like a blanket. In a flash came the words of Shakespeare: *If hairs be wires, black wires grow on her head*. Learned at university, this phrase had stuck with him, and he decided that tomorrow he would take the book from the shelf and read the sonnets again. Too much time had passed…

'Can you say more, so that I can understand what you mean?' he asked.

'Not really. Just that,' she replied. 'That is what I feel.'

'There has been much change, is that not so?'

Meera nodded.

'I think there are more adjustments to be made,' he continued. 'Babita and Chandu will soon go to their own home? This will bring some benefits. You and I can be alone – but there is also loss. Perhaps this is what you feel?'

'Yes, maybe. I will feel much loss when they go, but... I...'

'I am the last one to make any claims to special powers of foresight, but things are often not so bad as is imagined? Is that not so in your experience?'

I barely know this man, she thought. Yet here I am, with my hair loose around his shoulders like a cloak. 'Yes, you are probably right,' she replied. Feeling little comfort she leaned towards him, and without undressing, placed her head on his shoulder to sleep. Television off, he reached out for her hair, now almost invisible in the darkness. He pulled it over him, and with a contented sigh closed his eyes. He thought about tomorrow and the rubies he would give her. Yes, there had been many changes, all good. If only his back would heal quickly, then all would be well. Then he remembered his words to Meera earlier that week. 'If only... the saddest words ever said...'

'Just words, Krishna Gupta,' he thought, 'just words. Tomorrow is another day. Now sleep.'

CHAPTER
THIRTY-ONE

The following morning, after her bath, Meera came back into the bedroom to find the jewellery box upon her pillow. She stood in front of the mirror with her husband behind her. Looking at their reflection she bubbled with happiness; not only at the beautiful necklace draped around her neck, but at both of them stood so closely together – united again.

That Saturday was the busiest day the store had ever had, and Chandu, Meera and Babita hardly stopped. Trapped upstairs, Mr Gupta fretted and worried, wanting to be in his store and in the thick of things, with even the television providing little comfort. Twice now, he had got up to make tea, and stood at the top of the stairs looking down to the shop which he knew was beyond the door. He even went so far as to place a foot on the first step, but his back responded with a sharp pain and he had to lie down again, swearing with frustration.

Be calm, he said to himself – be calm. You are much better, and soon you will be down there and wishing you were here! It had rained a little, and he opened the window wide, glad of the cooler air and the breeze that came with it.

In the store, the three workers were like an oiled machine, frequently laughing and joking, with the customers joining in. At one point whilst Babita was working at the till, tapping in the prices and wrapping the purchases in brown paper, Chandu had been showing a customer the various ranges of paint that they kept, and explaining the differences between them. He picked up a tin and was pointing to its label; the customer nodding and waving his hands in an attempt to describe the colour that he needed.

Seeing that he was being watched by both his wife, and Meera, who was stacking packs of hooks on a shelf nearby, he decided to give them a show. Holding up the tin by its plastic strap he pretended to drop it, and they both gasped, Meera holding her hand up to her chest. Several men had also been watching, possibly in the store with the hope that the small Indian man might repeat the performance they had been told about. They let out a huge cheer, and Chandu gave a bow.

Always the clown, thought Babita, always the clown, and Meera laughed, clapping her hands in glee. Hearing the cheer from his reclined position in the bedroom above, Mr Gupta sighed. If he were to lie here for much longer he would have intercoms fitted. No question! It was like torture to isolate a man in this way!

A few minutes later his wife climbed the stairs,

knowing full well that he would have heard the roar and felt hugely frustrated at not being part of it, or knowing what was happening. She recounted what Chandu had done, still excited and laughing at his daring.

'There were so many people in there, and he knew this. He is like a showman these days. He pretended to drop the tin. They were already watching him with hawk-eyes, and there was a huge cheer. Oh, Vasu, what fun. I wish you had been there to see it.'

'You say he pretended to drop the tin? He might have dropped it, do you think? To explode all over the customer again, like a bomb? The mess, Meera, the mess – you have no idea.'

'With the three of us, the mess would soon have been gone. You are jealous that you were not there? Is that it?'

He laughed. 'Yes! Probably. I miss it so much and want to be with all of you.'

'I know, and soon you will be. I have some small jobs I need you to do for this evening. Remember what the physiotherapist said? A little movement and rest – a little movement and rest. So, here is the list.' She explained what she wanted him to do, and as she was leaving to go back to the store, she turned to add one more thing.

'If he had dropped the paint, I will tell you this. The store would have been filled with hundreds of people all begging for a repeat performance. Yes, Chandu the clown would have had his audience at last.' She left, giggling like a schoolgirl and leaving her husband to plan the chores she had given him, painful back in mind.

***

186

The shop had just closed and Chandu began a quick sweep around before taking the cash from the till. 'Go upstairs ladies in pink overalls. I am half-starved and need my dinner. Half an hour – then I will be with you.'

'He is making it so easy for us,' said Meera, almost at the top of the stairs. They pulled the bolt across on the other side, just in case he should come up before things were ready. All of his tasks completed, Mr Gupta lay on his bed again, having just swallowed two painkillers ready for the evening ahead. Wonderful smells were coming from the kitchen, and bright, shiny balloons had been tied to the backs of the chairs. Pinned to the wall was a long banner with 'CONGRATULATIONS' written on it.

'I told you not to do the banner. Too much stretching,' scolded Meera. 'Are you OK?'

'Of course. No need to worry.' He had only just managed it and was about to give up, but the small amount of pride he had left drove him to complete the task. On the sideboard were two carefully wrapped parcels and a brown envelope, the candles to either side, already lit.

Meera and Babita rushed off to change, and some twenty minutes later they heard Chandu bounding up the stairs, then try to open the door.

'So much energy,' muttered Mr Gupta, and with his hand on the bolt, asked for permission to open it.

'Let me in,' shouted Chandu. 'What is going on?'

'Ready?' asked Gupta, looking at them both in turn.

'Yes!' Babita and Meera answered together. 'Let him in!'

The door swung open and Chandu almost fell into the

room. 'What is happening here? Has everyone gone mad? I am locked away like a prisoner or slave, not allowed into the house? Is that it?'

Feeling a sharp stab of guilt, Krishna Gupta quietly replied. 'Those days are over.'

Chandu looked around him, taking in the banner and balloons, the candles, and the small pile of gifts on the sideboard. 'My birthday has arrived without my knowing? I am being made old before my time?'

Babita walked over to pull him into the room, then gave him a firm kiss. 'Shut up!'

'Ah, now I am happy again. My knowledge of English is limited to words like this,' he replied, and they all laughed.

'Come,' said Meera, taking his hand. 'Tonight we are celebrating a rising of fortune, and a name-giving.'

Chandu looked over to his old adversary, and Mr Gupta winked. 'You mean Krishna?' he asked.

'No, not Krishna! – You!' Babita picked up the smallest package and gave it to him. 'Open it.'

He tore at the wrapping with shaking fingers, eventually pulling out a long white badge, a sturdy safety pin stuck on its back. He turned it over to read what was written on the front.

Mr Chandu Kumar
ASSISTANT MANAGER

Chandu looked at each of them in turn. 'This is a joke?' he asked.

'No!' they all shouted.

'Not everyone jokes all day long, like you,' said Babita. 'You have been made assistant manager of the hardware store. Are you pleased?'

'Pleased? Are you insane?'

Meera remembered Babita saying the same thing and laughed. 'So, do we have a new assistant manager amongst us?' she asked

'Long overdue,' he replied, 'but I accept the position with great thanks and gratitude.'

'Hooray for Chandu. Newly appointed assistant manager of Mr Gupta's Hardware Store!' shouted Babita, overjoyed that at last her husband was being taken seriously and his value acknowledged.

A few hours later they had eaten an enormous meal, and leaning back in their chairs, Mr Gupta walked slowly behind them to collect the envelope and the parcel that was yet to be opened. He had gone to lie down for an hour, and had also taken more tablets in order to see the evening through. Giving the parcel to Babita, he held the envelope in his hand and waited.

Babita pushed it across to her husband. 'Just a small thing,' she said, 'for your new status.'

He picked it up and began to feel it all over. 'I can guess what this is. A pink overall, to match the other workers.' It was indeed an overall, although not pink but dark green, with various pockets to hold bits and pieces from the store. Chandu thought of the nails he had collected over the years, and the symbolism that was placed on their sharp points; each one a marker for the pain and suffering he had endured. Babita clearly thought the same and their eyes met, both acknowledging the

189

past and hoping that the worst was over for good.

Meera saw the look, and although not aware of its content, understood that something of significance had passed between them. 'One more,' she said, as Mr Gupta handed the envelope to Chandu. They all watched as he tore it open, pulling out a piece of white paper.

'What is it?' asked Babita. 'Read and tell me. You have been given another grocery shopping list?' Krishna stood up, his back now screaming with pain. Seeing this, she grabbed the paper from her husband's hand and began to read it herself.

'Receipt for one large television set to include delivery and connection. Chandu? You have read it? You know what you have been given?'

Looking stunned, he nodded.

'Your tongue has fallen out? Now you can watch yourself on "This Is Your Life," throwing paint on a customer's head.'

Mr Gupta laughed, although leaning heavily on the table and clearly in considerable discomfort. 'You like it?' he asked. 'Are you happy?'

Babita was unsure if Chandu would answer at all, but a few moments later he smiled, head moving to either side. It said it all, no words needed.

'At last,' she said. 'I was thinking that your new position would be taken from you now you have been struck dumb.'

'Thank you,' he finally said, 'thank you. Now we both have television, begin to prepare yourselves for my appearance. Two-three months only, then I shall be in front of you.'

'I shall look forward to it,' said Mr Gupta. 'I was going

to give you a watch to make sure you would not be late for work.'

Chandu laughed. 'Never,' he said. 'No deduction in salary needed.' In saying little, much had been conveyed – the subtleties of language having never been used so appropriately, nor for better purpose.

'Now,' said Mr Gupta, 'I must leave you, but not before a toast in the English tradition.' He raised his glass, the others following suit. 'Good health and prosperity to us all.'

'And long live Mr Gupta's Hardware Store,' added Chandu, and the glasses were raised again.

Reaching the bedroom door, Gupta turned to take one more look at the colourful scene before him, fixing it in his mind for posterity. He would use the image to remember how close he had come to the total destruction of all that he valued the most. Such moments were the essence of joy, and of far more worth than cash accumulating in a till. Having decided this, he finally lay down to rest his aching back.

***

In bed later that night, Meera handed her husband a small wooden box; a carved figure of Krishna on its top. Inside, sat in black velvet, were two gold wedding rings – one larger than the other – each set with a small ruby at its centre.

'I thought a fresh start for us both? English style?' she said, hesitantly, suddenly unsure of herself. A Hindu marriage did not dictate an exchange of rings, although he had given her one before they came to England for the purposes of correctness, and to save any awkward questions that might be asked.

He smiled, taking the smallest from the box and placing it on her finger. She took the other one, repeating the gesture. 'An English wife is no longer needed, Mrs Gupta, but I shall wear the ring until the day I die.'

'And in the life after that?' she asked.

'Yes,' he replied. 'We shall recognise each other by the rings, and all will be well.'

The Guptas' lives had come full circle. The love they once shared had returned. Perhaps through Dharma and the learning that had taken place, or, as in the dream of Krishna with the reins held firmly in his hands, they had taken control of their own destiny – by deeds, words, and the love of others…

CHAPTER
THIRTY-TWO

After everything was cleared away from the previous night, Babita packed their things, and a taxi arrived to take them home. Chandu would be back in the store at eight the following morning, and it was agreed that she would still come to work for three mornings and all-day Saturday, at least until Mr Gupta was back on his feet. This was a huge relief all round; Meera concerned about the amount of work she would have to do, and both happy that they would see each other so often. A salary was negotiated and, although sad, the parting had not been so bad as they thought.

Babita left two small packages on the bed of the spare room, one for each of them. She had been too shy to give them before, a little fearful, perhaps, because of their lack of monetary value, considering the gifts that she and Chandu had received.

She had bought Mr Gupta a beautifully embossed hardback copy of Shakespeare's sonnets. One evening, a few weeks ago, she was looking through the book shelves at the Guptas' home, and found a tattered copy dating from his university days. She remembered this, and thought he might appreciate a new one. For Meera, she bought a pair of antique silver hair-combs, studded with moonstones and found in the local market.

Standing in front of their old home, they watched as the taxi drove off, almost reluctant to go inside. 'It feels like such a long time,' said Chandu, 'and yet only a few weeks in total.'

'Nearly six,' replied Babita, shocked at how much time had passed.

'That long? Come, we must go inside or we shall be arrested for street loitering.' He picked up their bags and unlocked the front door. He felt like an intruder, but it smelt the same – boiled cabbage and gravy. He wrinkled his nose.

'Yes, I know,' agreed Babita. 'Hot spicy curry tonight, and the smell will be covered over.' Meera had packed a bag full of food, and inside their room with the windows flung wide open, she began to put things away. It was ridiculous, she thought. She had lived here for years but felt lost, like a child that had just left its parents. Yet she had been the parent, certainly for much of her time at the hardware store. Then it struck her…Was her feeling of loss for that reason entirely? She was no longer the parent, nor was she ever likely to be one again – neither to a fully-grown man like Mr Gupta, or a child.

'Out!' said Chandu. 'We should go for a walk to settle ourselves, and things will feel better when we get back.'

***

Within minutes they were walking through the park. The late summer flowers gave off a heady scent, and the dry, almost yellow grass released a fragrance of freshly baled hay.

'It smells like India,' he said, 'in a village away from town.'

'Yes – very dry and dusty, and with heat in the earth. Do you miss it?' she asked, realising that this was a subject rarely brought up between them.

'Sometimes. Not really the heat, though. The rain I miss the most – proper rain, not like here.' He told her about the floor washing at the store, and the smell given off; evocative even to his employer and spoken about between them some time ago. 'Here, all is mild; in India, there are extremes – both good and bad, but they give a feeling of being very alive, pulled from one side to the other.'

Babita was surprised by the eloquence of this statement from her husband, although there was no reason why this should be so. He had depth, she knew that, so often hidden by the fooling around. None of this was new to her except the words themselves and the impact they had... That was new. Perhaps they had both changed? Certainly she had felt some shift take place inside her, but that was one of uncertainty and discomfort, not romance and poetic reverie.

'Your words surprise me,' she said. 'Maybe there is also a poet hidden in your skinny body, waiting to burst free?'

He laughed. 'Yes, a poet. Shakespeare and Keats, Milton and Byron; I remember them all from school.'

'Then,' she said 'I shall buy you a book also. No more Attila the Hun, but poetry for you like Krishna Gupta.'

She told him about the book she had left on the bed, and the combs that were bought for Meera. 'He has much romance within him,' she added. 'Like you, kept hidden from view.'

'But Babi, is this not what we all do? Hide that which affects us the most? You also are guilty of this behaviour. Tell me honestly that this is not so!'

He is right, she thought, and anyway, try as one might, attempts to hide things from others were so often futile. In her own experience she knew that this was true.

'Enough, you are beginning to sound like a sage, and soon I shall lose you to a monastery in Nepal!' Before he could reply, she grabbed his hand and pulled him onto another path – the one that would lead them towards 52 Park View. 'Come, I want to show you Stella's house.'

'We are going in?' he asked. 'I am not dressed for visiting royalty, and the homes of the rich and famous.'

'No, of course not! I will show you the outside only. They are not royalty but are rich, I suppose, and she dresses the famous. Remember? I told you.'

'Ah, yes. Then we should go inside, for as you know, I am soon to be on "This Is Your Life," and correct clothing will be needed.' Back to the clown, she thought, and thumped him lightly on the arm.

'Ow, Ow,' he yelled! 'Now you have become my abuser, with Krishna moved into the body vacated by Attila the Hun.'

She laughed, then raised her hand to thump him again. This time, he ran off down the path – Babita following closely behind, shouting, 'Come back, come back! You are my slave, and escape is not an option.'

'Escape?' he thought as he ran. 'From you? Clearly you are hiding from the truth; no doubt at all.' He dived behind a bush, springing out as she ran past and making her jump.

They continued to walk until she suddenly stopped, pointing to a large house across the street. 'Look, over there, the red door. We can walk by, and look at the same time.'

'Ah, yes, like spies. As you have already witnessed, I have special skills of deduction that surpass even the best secret agent.' He was referring to the clothes left on the counter in the store by Meera, after her late-night return.

'Stop,' said Babita, 'no more joking, we are here. Look, the door is open.' Holding his hand, she pulled him back into the shadows under the trees, and they leaned against the park wall to watch. Two men appeared to be removing furniture from the house and were loading it into a van. Along its side was written 'Moretti & Sons, International Removals.' There was no sign of Stella or the children, and Babita and Chandu observed in silence as the house was slowly emptied.

'Shall we go?' asked Chandu, gently pulling her back towards the park.

'Do you think she is leaving?' she asked. 'Why did she not say? What about Peter and Sasha?'

'I don't think she will be leaving them behind, Babi. Maybe she isn't leaving? Just changing the furniture?' He didn't think that this was the case. They were leaving, there could be little doubt about it. 'She said nothing at all?'

'No. The children were upset, and behaved badly the last time I was there. That is all. What shall I do?'

'You still have the key?' he asked.

'Yes, of course.'

'Then on Monday afternoon you go to the house as usual and let yourself in. All will become clear at that time. If they are gone, then you will know. Finished.'

'I suppose so. Dr Greene did say that she was hoping to go back to Italy.'

'They are very rude people if they do not even leave you a note. Do not upset yourself. You have the job at the store, and I have had a raise. You can look for another small job if you wish, but I think it will be a while before Krishna can work full-time again, or if he will even wish to.'

She nodded. 'Yes, I also thought this.'

'Good. We are in agreement. Quick march home… we have strong curry to make to fill the house with a good smell. No more cabbages and gravy!'

***

That evening after dinner Chandu walked up and down the room, tape measure in hand, trying to work out the best position for his television set, and the siting of the aerial point. Babita lay on the bed staring at the ceiling. She felt like she was sliding backwards after feeling so positive in recent times. Later that night and unable to sleep, she crept silently to the armchair, pulling the blanket over her. She stared into the darkness, her head blank of thoughts; feeling nothing except confusion. When Chandu left in the morning, she crawled into the bed and slept, waking just in time to quickly dress and walk across the park to Stella's house, and confront what might await her there.

She turned her key in the lock, and as usual put her

head around the door and called. 'Hello? I am here.' She waited... but heard nothing. Slowly, she pushed the door wider and went inside. Walking from room to room, she saw that most of the furniture had gone, leaving bits of newspaper and discarded items on the floor. Upstairs was the same. Chandu was right. They were gone, and not even a note left for her. Feeling exhausted, she carefully locked the house and quickly walked back home.

When Chandu arrived that evening, he found Babita in bed asleep – her face resting on a list of job vacancies. Still fully dressed, her sari was crumpled and twisted, and with the sheet screwed up around her tiny body, he was reminded of the beggar children sleeping on the streets in Delhi; their clothes in rags and newspapers under their heads.

Quietly making a simple meal, he sat in the armchair and worried. He worried that she would sink into a hole so deep that he would be unable to reach her. He recalled the night in the hospital when his greatest fear was that she would disappear, and despite his searching, would remain unfound. It had brought a panic into his chest, so great that he could barely breathe, and now he felt the same panic – gripping like a hand around his throat.

***

In the flat above the hardware store, Meera lay on the bed with her husband, who was reading aloud from the book Babita had given him.

'It's not so bad on our own?' he asked.

'No,' she said, smiling. 'Not so bad at all. She will be here tomorrow, and a new routine can be made.'

'Exactly, don't worry, all will be fine. I want to try the stairs at the end of the week. If I lie here much longer, I will go crazy.'

'We shall see. No more flying, Mr Gupta. Maybe coming down on your bottom will be better?' She laughed at this thought, and he snapped the book closed.

'You mock me? A disabled man? Shame on you, Meera Gupta. For this you must make tea – milk only and not too weak.'

She got up from the bed and went through to the kitchen. Waiting for the kettle to boil, her thoughts drifted back to Babita. How was she? Had there been any further developments with the childcare job? Chandu seemed to be his usual self at work today, and she felt reluctant to keep asking him about his wife. Kettle boiled, she filled the pot. Anyway, she would see her tomorrow and could find out for herself.

'Where are you?' came a shout from the bedroom. 'Am I to die of thirst here, Mrs Gupta?'

'Coming,' she shouted back, quickly pouring the tea; milk only and not too weak, for her disabled husband dying of thirst in the flat above the hardware store.

CHAPTER
THIRTY-THREE

Babita woke at six the following morning and took a bath whilst everyone in the house was still asleep. Chandu usually got up at seven, and she crept around the flat, tidying and making their lunch. She felt guilty for her behaviour yesterday, and for sleeping away the afternoon and evening. She hadn't even prepared a meal for her husband, which she felt was the least she could do if she was at home. She felt low and very disappointed that Stella would just walk away without saying anything. Where were those poor children now?

Wanting to cheer herself up, she put on the flowery salwar kameez bought by Meera, although just the thought of being in the store had, to some extent, done that. Chandu had been watching her as she moved about, looking for signs that might tell him how she was. Having gleaned nothing apart from the fact that she looked like a flower meadow, he let out a groan and then slid out of bed, landing with a thump on the floor.

Babita jumped. 'What are you doing? Time to get up, not slide around like a snake.'

'How are you? I was worried last night.'

'I know – sorry. I went to Stella's house and it was empty. They are gone, and not even a note. Nothing.'

'Very rude. No manners at all. I would like to tell this woman how to behave!'

'I felt no anger when I was there – just disappointment, and concern for Peter and Sasha.'

'Well I feel anger at such ignorance. Today will be better, Babi. You shall see your husband for the first time in his new overall and name badge with no nails in the pockets. And you will see Meera…'

'I know. Hurry up. Your breakfast is on the table, and I have made double rations for your lunch.'

'And for your lunch?' he asked.

'Single only. I am not a horse!'

Chandu got himself ready for work, still watching his wife from the corner of his eye. If there was another day like yesterday he would talk to Meera – finished. He gave a loud clap as though to cement his decision, making Babita jump again.

Chandu had only just raised the key to unlock the rear door of the shop, when it was flung open to reveal Meera, overall on, and the beautiful moonstone combs that Babita had bought glowing against her black hair.

'At last,' she said. 'I have been waiting for ages.'

'We are early,' replied Chandu. 'Babita has also been waiting since six o'clock this morning to come here.'

202

Ignoring him, Meera grabbed her friend's hand, pulling her through the storeroom and out into the shop. 'How are you?' she asked. 'Have you settled back in the flat? The children? Any more news? You look tired...'

'Wait,' replied Babita, 'only one question at a time, please. First, I am OK. Second, it was very strange to be back home. I felt unsettled and lost. Third, the children are gone. On Sunday Chandu and I watched whilst the house was emptied. Then yesterday I went as usual and they were gone. Everything gone.'

'Not even a letter for you?' asked Meera, still holding Babita's hand.

'Nothing left, just rubbish on the floor. To them, I was this rubbish.'

Ah, thought Chandu, who had been listening to this exchange. The truth was now coming out. He remembered seeing her lying on the bed last night, looking like a beggar-child sleeping in rags. She felt that she was rubbish only, and this was how she had looked. 'No,' he said aloud, still in the storeroom. 'Not rubbish! Never.'

'Rubbish?' said Meera. 'You? If I see this woman I shall show her that it is she who is rubbish! I shall give her this...' She raised her hand and made a sharp swipe through the air as though to slap Stella's face. 'Wham!' she said, 'this way.' She repeated the gesture in the opposite direction. 'And again, on the other side. Wham! How dare she?'

'Don't upset yourself,' said Babita. 'It is finished with. Your final statement about looking tired? Well, my sleep has been bad these past two nights, but now it will be alright. There is no need to worry. Come, let us organise ourselves and the work to do.'

Meera followed her, leaving Chandu to sort out the change for the till. She was still fuming with outrage at the treatment Babita had received. Breathe deeply she told herself, or your blood pressure will rise. Her thoughts drifted to the day the brick had come through the window, and her accusation to Mr Gupta that he was blind to the reality of their life in England. She would discuss it with him again later. Life in England was not all bad, she knew that. Most likely equal parts, good and bad, like so many things. Some equilibrium restored, the two ladies in their pink overalls split the work to be done, and the door of the hardware store was unlocked, ready for another day of business.

***

At lunch time, Babita went upstairs to see Vasu, or Krishna, as she would now always think of him. Fully dressed, he was lying on top of a beautifully embroidered blanket; a book held out in front of him.

'You are accepting visitors?' she asked, and without waiting for a reply sat on the edge of the bed, curious to see what he was reading.

'Babita, my dear. Yes, of course.' He held the book out to her. 'Look – the book you gave me. It was such a co-incidence I cannot tell you, for only a few nights before, a quote had come to mind, and I was to read my old copy again. Thank you.'

'Coincidence?' She shook her head. 'One of the things I find so difficult here in England is the desire to have practical understanding of everything.'

Krishna pulled himself higher up the bed, wanting to

engage in a subject that interested him very much, and always had. 'Say more?' he asked, intrigued.

'Forgive me if I don't explain this well, but here there seems to be always a desire to break things up – to separate. How can it be that I am buying you this book when you had already thought to read it? The two must have connection. How else?'

'Please say more?' he repeated.

'It is the same as the job I had looking after the children. I went to the doctor about my health, and he knew of the job. A coincidence? Or already connected and my destiny?'

'Destiny. Ah, now there is a subject to discuss. You have kept your Hindu beliefs despite your many years here. I fear I may have lost some of mine, but with all that has happened lately perhaps it is time to reconsider. You say "had," with your children's job. Has this finished?'

Babita told him what had happened. 'I don't understand why she said nothing, but I suppose for her there was a reason.'

'You are upset?' he asked.

'I was, but not now. Enough talking about me. How are you? Is your back recovering?'

'Definitely, although slow – slower than I hoped, but a little better each day. I am wanting to be down in the store so much.' He let out a long sigh.

'Not long now, and you will be there.'

***

It was Friday, and Gupta could bear it no longer. He had to get downstairs, even if he might only make it back up

205

again on his hands and knees, like he had done before. The three musketeers, as he had taken to calling them, were all there, and he was going to join them. His mind was made up! He stood at the top of the flight, looking towards the closed door at the bottom. A handrail had been fitted that week, and he held onto it tightly as he took the first step, bringing the other foot down so that both were together before going to the next one – like a child might do.

The movement pulled at his back, but not unbearably so, and he continued this slow progress to the bottom, and his very own Nirvana. He paused on the final step for a moment, then turned the handle and swung open the door. Hearing his footsteps, and lined up together, were Meera, Chandu and Babita; all quietly waiting for the master to descend.

He walked through the door, closing it firmly behind him. At last he thought, his spirits soaring. At last I am here! He walked slowly around the store making a few adjustments, checking for dust, and generally taking it all in. Chandu went into the storeroom, emerging with the bucket of water and mop to begin his daily floor-cleaning duties.

'Ah, the wet floor. How I love this smell… like India after the rain.' He turned to see his wife and Babita watching him, both still saying nothing.

'Mr Gupta has returned to his hardware store,' said Chandu, beginning to swish his mop back and forth.

Slowly walking behind the counter and to the bottom of the stairs, Mr Gupta opened the door ready for his ascent.

'You will be crawling on your hands and knees like a baby?' Chandu asked, head shifting from side to side – so very Indian; so very him.

'No,' answered his employer, 'no more crawling needed.' Or kneeling, he thought, and began to climb the stairs. On the first step, he stopped – carefully turning around. 'Carry on,' he said. 'Clearly the assistant manager has everything under control. I chose well.' He looked at Chandu, mop still in motion, a proud smile now on his face, which said it all.

No words needed.

CHAPTER
THIRTY-FOUR

1975

As Mr Gupta predicted, adjustments were made over the following year, and a new routine had established itself. His back continued to heal, and as the weeks and months passed, he spent increasing amounts of time in his beloved store. Business continued to improve, and the growing trend of DIY brought many more people through the door, which increased sales further. Meera and Babita worked three mornings each week and all day Saturday, and he and Chandu covered the rest, with both ladies helping out further if necessary.

It was suggested that they work different days to spread out the staff ratio, but Meera refused, wanting to be with her friend as much as was possible. Each Saturday evening once the store had closed, all four climbed the stairs to eat together, talk and play card games. It was hot, and they sat at the table with windows flung open in the hope of catching any breeze that might blow through. Even the door of the shop was wedged open, the jangling bells now in silent repose.

On one of her weekdays off, Babita shopped and cooked, took a walk in the familiar park, and fed the swans that were so often there. Each time she saw them, she recalled when she had sat on the same bench after the loss of her baby; engaged in trying to make sense of what had happened. It no longer hurt in the same raw way, but neither was it forgotten, and she supposed that her understanding from that time had been correct. That which had once lived would always continue to do so, and this gave her great comfort.

There had been another family of cygnets since then, and she took many photos of them with the small camera that Chandu bought for her birthday. Some were stuck to the walls of their room with dates written underneath; a marker of times past like Chandu's nails, although these were no longer being collected.

Her other day off was spent with Meera, and she continued to prepare her friend a traditional Indian meal, even though this food was no longer banned in the Gupta household. It had become a ritual, even down to the handwashing in a plastic bowl with petals floating on its surface, these varying depending on the time of year. At the end of each visit, Meera would return home with a dish of whatever Babita had prepared, saved for her husband's evening meal. He also looked forward to this regular event, and the surprise dinner that would await him when he climbed the stairs from the store at the end of the day.

Sunday was spent with Chandu, sometimes watching television; sometimes walking around the area in which they lived. The heat had intensified as the summer went on, each day dawning with another bright blue sky. She revelled in it, wearing light cotton clothes, washed each day and dried in hours in the garden at the back of the house.

They had discussed moving several times and even visited a few flats closer to the Guptas', but the rents were high and would take up almost all of their increased income. The idea hadn't been ruled out, but for now at least, they decided to stay put. On a few occasions, Babita had looked through the papers for other jobs she might like to do on her free afternoons. Finding nothing that interested her, and with the increasing business at the store, the idea was pushed to one side and forgotten.

***

One morning in mid-August, Chandu opened the door of the stairs and shouted up to Meera. 'Mail arrived from India.'

She quickly went down to collect it, guessing correctly that it was from her brother, Manju. They wrote regularly, and occasionally spoke on the telephone, but Meera loved the letters and looked forward to getting them. He wrote beautifully, often describing images and scenes in such a way that she felt she was there, and she tried to do the same for him. He was hoping to come over next year, bringing Delilah with him, perhaps leaving her there to spend the rest of the summer with her aunt and uncle.

Each time she received a letter from him – even before she opened it – she would recall the night spent outside listening to the jackal choir, and her prayers to keep her husband and Babita safe. She marvelled at this instant transportation across time as she tore open the envelope, pulling out the thin blue airmail paper covered with her brothers handwriting. Lying comfortably on the bed she began to read, Manju starting as always with a rundown of their health and the weather. In recent letters he spoke of the increasing frailty of their father, and Meera scanned the pages looking for this news first. Their father, he said, was now refusing all food, only drinking beakers of buttermilk liberally sprinkled with nutmeg three times a day and nothing else, not even water. He continued to lie on the verandah for most of the time, stood up only to use the bathroom, and said nothing at all. The doctor had visited and, according to Manju, shrugged his shoulders, saying there was nothing he could do. He might last a few weeks or another year. It was impossible to say...

At the end of the letter he told her not to worry. He was of the opinion that their father would not die for several months yet, and if this changed he would let her know. There was always the telephone, after all. She was relieved to hear this because she didn't want to leave Vasu on his own again so soon, not only for his sake, but her own. She would miss him, and hoped that her father would indeed continue to survive on the buttermilk given to him at regular intervals. She was due at Babita's later that morning, and putting the letter in her bag began to get ready.

The store was busy when she came down half an hour later, and she waved to both her husband and Chandu as she left, not wanting to disturb them. It was hot, and she crossed the road at intervals trying to stay in the shade as much as possible. At the boarding house, she rang the bell, using her own key to let herself into the cool tiled hall just as Babita was coming down the stairs.

'So hot,' she gasped, 'almost like India,' and she fanned her face with her hand to try to cool herself.

'Come, I have ice-cubes in the cooler and will make you a drink,' replied Babita pulling out a chair for her friend. 'I think I have forgotten how hot it was in India, but most certainly hotter than this. I like it – the windows open all the time, and laundry dry in a few hours.'

Sitting opposite each other at the table, Meera thought how well Babita looked, and said so.

'Yes,' Babita replied. 'I am well. I was thinking the other day that I have not been to the doctor for nearly a year! I was going to go about Stella to see if he knew anything, but then I thought, no. What happened was not his fault, and best to leave it alone.'

'Yes, agreed. You are so happy with your store job, and a little time to yourself. Everything has turned out well, just like Vasu said.'

Babita got up. 'Time for food. Something a little different today because of the weather.' She brought the bowl for Meera to wash her hands. She had dropped honeysuckle and jasmine flowers into it, and stood watching until Meera had finished. 'I have an extra cooling treat for you.' She went to the fridge and took out a tinfoil parcel, opening it to reveal a soft, muslin cloth which had been soaked in rosewater for her friend's hot face.

She thinks of everything, thought Meera, humbled, as she so often was in Babita's presence. As she allowed the cool cloth to do its magic, she watched as Babita took chicken kebabs with a mint and yoghurt dip from the fridge, as well as various side dishes to go with it.

'Eat,' Babita said. 'There is plenty made, enough for Chandu and Vasu later.'

This was one of Meera's favourites, and she filled her plate. 'You are not hungry?' she asked, noticing that Babita's plate had very little on it.

'A little indigestion,' she replied, patting her stomach.

'Indigestion? The spicy food does not agree with you?'

'Most things, really. If I eat smaller amounts, then it is better. I was thinking it might be my age,' she laughed, 'but I am feeling very fat these days!'

'Yes! I am having to be careful too. Mr Gupta, he prefers more shape,' she giggled shyly, 'but I am happier to be slim. Mint tea – I shall buy some on the way home, and you can drink it in the store tomorrow. Vasu has this for indigestion and says it helps him.'

An hour later, dishes washed and everything tidy, they decided on a gentle stroll given their discussion on excess weight. With their figures in mind they headed toward the park, once again staying under the trees as much as possible. Throwing a few crusts of bread to the swans, Babita explained how she had come to terms with her loss the previous year, and how the swans had helped with this process.

'I was so worried at that time,' said Meera, 'it almost sent me crazy. But here we are. Much has happened, has it not, and yet we are still all together and stronger than before.'

'Yes, stronger, but different. I am not the same as I was then. Come, shall we lie under the trees? Who knows when we shall see weather like this again?' Babita led her friend to a large cedar tree, perhaps several hundred years old, and they lay on the dry prickly grass, arms under their heads, gazing up at the fragments of blue sky visible through the dense foliage.

'I love the smell,' said Babita. 'The heat makes it stronger.' She drew in a deep breath to inhale the pungent, aromatic fragrance.

'It reminds me of my father,' replied Meera. 'He used a cologne that smelt like this, and I have never forgotten it. Sometimes, when he was out, Manju and I would go to his room and put a little on ourselves. It would linger for the whole day.' She gave a huge sigh. 'Today I received a letter from him – Manju, I mean, not my father.' She told her friend about its contents and what had been said about her father's health.

'I brought it for you to read, but I left my bag in your flat. He lies there all day long and eats nothing at all. The doctor came but said there was little he could do. I fear that I shall be called to India very soon, and of course, I shall go.'

'But you would rather stay here with Vasu?' asked Babita, astute as always to the emotions of others.

Meera laughed. 'Yes, this is true. When I remember how things were… I think that you were responsible for much of this change. I shall be forever in your debt.'

Babita pondered on this statement for a moment. It was true that she played a part in the changes that had taken place in Meera's marriage, but overall, felt she had received far more than she had given, from both Vasu and her dear friend. 'There can be no debt between friends,' she replied. 'Is this not the truth? Let us never use that word again. If one needs, the other gives and so forth. Nothing must ever be owed between us, or we shall become bound by the act itself.'

Once again she has moved beyond me, thought Meera. They remained silent for a while, the warmth from the hard ground seeping into their bodies and the fragrance from the trees, permeating their minds. Feeling like she was melting into the earth, Meera closed her eyes and drifted into a deep and dreamless sleep. She was woken by a gentle shaking on her shoulder, and opened her eyes to see Babita's smiling face.

'You have been asleep for half an hour,' she said. 'I was thinking that I would have to leave you here and fetch Vasu to carry you home!' She stood up and held out her hand. 'Come, we need tea.' She hauled her friend up from the ground, and arm in arm they strolled slowly back through the park, their bodies languid from the hot sun.

A group of young people walked past them carrying a large cassette player. The beat of the music combined with their laughter and happy faces raised their spirits further. It was a perfect summer's day, and one which Meera knew she would never forget. Later, she took a cab back to the store, and that evening sat with Vasu, watching whilst he ate the kebabs and various accompaniments that had been wrapped and carefully placed in her straw shopping bag.

'Very tasty,' he said. 'Babita is a good cook.' She read him the letter that Manju had written, wanting to talk about the possibility of her returning to India in the not too distant future.

'Don't worry. If you have to go, I will manage here. Babita can come more often if she wishes. I will lose weight like last time, and you will return to a new, slim husband.'

'As long as it is not one who is flat on his back!' she replied. 'When I go, I will only stay for the minimum time.'

'Yes, Mrs Gupta will miss her husband too much to stay longer. Is that not so?' he teased.

'Do not let your head swell too much, Mr Gupta,' she replied. 'Perhaps I might change my mind and stay for a year!'

'Never! I would come and fetch you, and there would be an end to it!'

Yes, she thought. He would come and fetch her; he would claim his wife as his own and, whether old-fashioned or not, this pleased her very much.

CHAPTER
THIRTY-FIVE

When Babita and Chandu arrived the following day, Meera was, as usual, waiting for them. As promised, a packet of mint tea had been bought and a cup was already on the side, waiting for the kettle to boil.

'Try this,' she said to Babita. 'I will have one also. I like the taste.'

'And me?' asked Chandu. 'I too have a fat stomach that needs to shrink.'

'Your stomach is as flat as a board! Ordinary tea for you,' replied Meera.

There were several large deliveries that morning, and both men were in the storeroom for much of the day. It was busy, with many people on holiday and undertaking work to their homes. Babita particularly enjoyed helping people choose paint colours, and quite a few customers now asked for her by name if they needed assistance. She stayed later than her usual half day, and it was nearly three when she eventually left. The store had become hotter as the afternoon went on, and with so little air coming in she had developed a headache. Meera fetched painkillers for her and made iced water for them all. The walk home felt particularly long taking her more than half an hour. When she got back, she drank another large glass of water and fell onto the bed; a cold cloth pressed to her forehead. Later that afternoon she was sick, and when Chandu came home, she was sick again.

'You have a stomach bug, I think?' he asked later that evening, hating to see her suffer in any way.

'Yes, I think so. Don't worry. I no longer feel sick, and the headache is almost gone.'

'If you are not better tomorrow then you must go to the doctor. I shall telephone from the store at lunchtime and we shall see.'

'Alright, Chandu, there is no need to worry. Being sick and a headache is a very common thing. Tomorrow I am sure I will be fine, and you will have upset yourself for nothing. Let me sleep now.'

As she had assured Chandu, the next morning she did feel a lot better. She was still a little queasy, but the headache was completely gone, and if she rested today she was sure that a full recovery would be made.

***

At the end of August the hot weather finally broke. It was a Saturday, and the heat had become unbearable – even for Babita. All four of them were in the store serving and

218

clearing up at the end of the day. There was a long, low rumble and the lights in the shop flickered.

'Here we go,' said one of the customers who was standing at the till paying for his goods whilst Babita carefully wrapped them. 'I thought it would break today, and a good job too!'

There were a few more rumbles of thunder accompanied by bright flashes of lightening, and when the shop was finally empty, Chandu quickly locked the door and turned the sign. Rain began to fall, huge drops quickly soaking the dusty pavements and parched earth. A few moments later it became a torrential downpour, accompanied by the frequent flashes that lit the dark, grey sky with streaks of yellow. Babita stood by the door watching the rain run down the street in a mini torrent, with Chandu standing behind her. As he had said, he loved storms of any kind and felt exhilarated by them.

'You will have to stay here tonight,' said Meera, 'or take a taxi. You will be soaked right through to your skin in ten seconds if you go outside.'

'Shall we see how long it lasts? We usually stay until ten, and can decide a little later,' replied Chandu, desperate to get outside and feel the full force of the elements.

After their meal and the usual card games, Meera opened the window to see if the rain had eased off. 'It is less, but still raining. You would like to sleep here?' she asked, hoping that they would say yes.

'I know what I would like,' said Chandu. 'A large umbrella, and we can walk. I would enjoy this very much.' He looked at Babita to see how she felt about his suggestion, and she nodded.

Ten minutes later Babita was wearing a raincoat of Meera's that almost reached the floor. Huddled together under a giant striped umbrella, they walked home in the fresh, clean air – dry, but with the rain still falling around them.

'This was a good idea. After so much heat it is good to breathe cool air again,' said Chandu, inhaling deeply. 'It gives me energy!'

Babita was enjoying it too, but struggled to keep up with Chandu as he bounded along, excited and happy.

'Slow down,' she said. 'My legs are shorter than yours.' She felt a little breathless, but with the slower pace this reduced, and they were soon home.

'I'm glad we came back,' she said. 'We can watch a little television in bed, but if you would rather not...' This was a tease, because it was Chandu's favourite pastime and would never be refused. Several hours later she was soundly asleep, but he was still leaning against his pillows watching the flickering screen; completely absorbed in a world that was altogether so different from his own.

Babita got up early the following morning to take her bath, slipping quietly back into the room, not wanting to wake her husband. Like many Indian women, she had never got used to stripping off in front of him, usually managing to keep an item of clothing on, thus maintaining some level of personal modesty. Chandu had his back to her as she pulled off her bathrobe, first drying her back and shoulders, then raising her arms to rub her wet hair with the same towel.

Unbeknown to her, he had woken up and turned to see what she was doing. From behind, she looked like she always had, although slightly thinner. Almost too thin, he thought, deciding to ensure that she ate more. She had always been slim, but not like this. She then turned a little so that he was almost seeing a side view. Her head was bent over, and she was vigorously rubbing her hair with the towel, still unaware that he was watching her.

What is this, he thought, as he looked? She had definitely lost weight, but her stomach was quite the opposite. It protruded considerably, and he couldn't help but be shocked by its appearance. Without doubt, there must be something wrong with her! For a brief moment he wondered if she was pregnant, but this thought was dismissed almost as quickly as it had come. The shape was wrong entirely and spread too far across her front. Realising that she was about to complete her hair drying, he quickly turned his back so that she wouldn't realise he had been watching. She would be very angry if she knew he was doing this, which saddened him greatly, even though he had got used to it.

As he lay there, waiting until he knew she would be dressed, he thought about what to do. She was stubborn, and had never responded well to demands. He would have to play this carefully, but one thing was for certain; she needed to see a doctor, and he would do all he could to make sure that she did... and soon. If she refused, he would talk to Meera. The two were very close, and he was sure that Babita would listen to her friend's advice. Hopefully, with pressure from them both she would see that she was overpowered and would do as she was told.

***

Chandu always cooked breakfast on Sunday mornings, usually scrambled eggs on toast, and they would sit at the table together instead of Babita hovering around, serving him in the Indian style. He put the plates on the table and sat down, wanting to make sure that she ate something – deciding that if she didn't eat enough, he would raise the issue that was now worrying him so much. 'What shall we do today?' he asked. 'The rain is on and off which will affect our choice.' He watched as she ate, considering their options for the day ahead.

'You can choose. I don't mind,' she replied, picking up her toast and taking a small bite from the corner.

'You are going to eat that toast instead of nibbling like a mouse?' he asked, unable to contain his concern any longer.

'I am not feeling very hungry this morning. I think I ate too much last night and am still full – you have it.' She pushed the plate across to him, and he pushed it back.

'No, you must eat, Babi. You are becoming thin, and this is not good.'

'Thin? You are wrong, I am fat! My stomach is like that of a pregnant woman,' she replied, her voice becoming raised. 'But I am not pregnant,' she added quickly, not wanting him even for a second to think that she was, nor raise any hopes that should have died a long time ago.

'You feel full? You ate little last night, also. I noticed this and so did Meera. You feel sick again?' he asked, remembering the vomiting from earlier in the week.

'Only a little. I am fine. Stop making a fuss.' She got up, wanting an end to the discussion that was now making her feel uncomfortable.

'No Babi, not this time. You must go to the doctor. If he says it is nothing, then fine. You will make an appointment tomorrow? For my peace of mind only, if not for your own?'

She thought for a moment. She didn't want to go to the doctor after not having seen him for so long. She didn't want to be asked any questions about Stella after having successfully laid the issue to rest. She didn't want to be poked and prodded, thinking she had gone through enough of this when she lost the baby two years ago. She looked at her husband, taking in the distressed and worried face; his hands held in front of him, almost in a position of prayer.

'Very well – I agree, but no more questions now, you promise?'

'I promise!' Chandu let out a sigh of relief. He had expected to fight a harder battle, and would most certainly check if she had made the appointment tomorrow. 'So, how shall we spend our day? There are several films at the cinema, one, a horror movie which I know you love, and The Pink Panther, although I already agreed with Krishna that we might go to see this together. Perhaps we could all four go next week?'

'You know I hate horror movies, so you can go on your own if that is your wish!' she replied. 'It may be a good idea to see the other movie together, though. I know it is your favourite, and also Vasu's. To watch you laugh is great amusement in itself. Ask them tomorrow when you go to work. We need to buy food from the store, but unless you can think of anything else, I am happy to stay here and sew my quilt.'

For the whole year, Babita had been slowly stitching together a patchwork quilt. It had grown considerably, and the brightly coloured squares of varying patterns now covered her knees and draped onto the floor as she stitched – stopping every now and then to admire her work.

'Very well. To the store first, then I shall read and watch TV. We can go for a walk later if the rain stops,' replied Chandu, their day now decided.

CHAPTER
THIRTY-SIX

Chandu was gone by seven-thirty the following morning, and Babita had the day to herself. Keeping her promise, she called the surgery and was offered an appointment that afternoon, as a cancellation had just been made. Although still reluctant, she accepted it, knowing that it would please Chandu and stop him worrying, which would be good for them both. Arriving at the surgery a few hours later, she had only just sat down when her name was called. As she thought, Dr Greene quickly raised the issue of Stella.

'I wanted to talk to you about it, but you haven't been in for such a long time. I hope you weren't too upset?'

'I was upset... Not that the job had ended so soon, more that she would leave without so much as a note to explain herself. But it was a long time ago now, and is behind me. Don't worry, it was not your fault. Let us leave it in the past where it belongs.'

Very wise, he thought. He had no answers anyway, since Stella left no messages for anyone, not even his wife who considered herself to be a friend. Someone said that Stella's husband was involved in shady dealings of some sort, possibly drugs, and had been arrested, but no one knew for sure.

'You're right, and sensible as always, Mrs Kumar. Now, tell me why you're here.'

'My husband made me come – he worries all the time. I think it is probably nothing, but I have felt a little sick on occasions and my stomach is bloated. I feel full even before I have eaten and have an upset tummy occasionally. That is all. My friend also has bloating and her husband does not make this fuss.' She shrugged her shoulders as though to dismiss Chandu's worrying entirely.

'And have you actually been sick?' he asked.

'A few times. Three in total.' She hadn't told Chandu about the other times, not wanting to upset him further or give him more worry.

'Have you lost weight? Any pain? Wind? Indigestion?' He continued to ask questions. From past experience he knew that she disliked being examined, especially near any intimate areas. The nurse was brought in last time and it had been fine, but he didn't want to distress her without need. 'From what you've told me, it's quite possible that you have something called IBS. Irritable bowel syndrome.' He explained, and Babita listened carefully, knowing full well that Chandu would expect a full run down later on.

'I can give you some tablets that might help, but I would like to ask you to keep a food diary over the next two weeks, making a note of anything that gives you worsening symptoms. Some people find fatty, spicy food an irritant, others too much fibre – others not enough. If you keep the diary, you should be able to work out what might be causing the problem.'

'Of course. I will do this,' replied Babita.

'Good. I need you to make an appointment in a fortnight. If there are no improvements, I shall need to examine you. You have had cysts in the past and needed surgery to remove them, so we shall certainly have to check out that side of things and run a few tests.'

Babita took in the slightly raised eyebrows, and realised that the last statement was in fact a question. 'Very well, Doctor. I shall do all you say, and if it doesn't get better then I will agree to an examination.' On the way home she bought a small notebook for her food diary, and later that evening told Chandu what was said and the instructions she had been given.

'You will do as he says and take the tablets?' he asked. 'And have made the appointment for two weeks?'

'Of course. Please stop worrying.'

He said no more, but remained unconvinced by the doctor's diagnosis. His mother had died from cancer of the stomach and became greatly distended as she progressed with the disease. Two weeks only, he said to himself. Then, if tests were still not done, he would involve Meera, and go to the doctor himself and demand more investigations. If the doctor resisted then he would meet his match!

***

At the same time as Babita was telling Chandu about her appointment with the doctor, he was in his surgery having just seen his last patient of the day. He had been unable to get Babita and her symptoms from his mind, and wished that he had insisted on an examination and basic blood tests there and then, whether she liked it or not. Under normal circumstances he wouldn't be quite so concerned, but it was her past medical history that bothered him, and resulted in the anxiety he was now feeling. If it was more serious, then two weeks would probably make little difference, he knew that, but even so…

On his way out, he checked that Babita had made another appointment. Finding that she had, and in twelve days' time, not fourteen, because of the times available, he let out a sigh of relief. He would already have ruled out the simplest and most obvious cause and he could take it from there, wasting no time at all in sending her for tests if he needed to. Slightly more at ease, he went home to his family and a large gin and tonic – usually reserved for Saturday evening. Being a conscientious doctor was undoubtedly stressful, and although the alcohol went some way to helping him relax, the niggle at the back of his mind refused to shift entirely. It's just twelve days, he said to himself – just twelve days…

***

The week flew by, and on Friday, instead of the usual meal at the boarding house, the two ladies decided to go into the city. Meera wanted to go to Harrods because of a particular perfume that could only be bought there, also declaring that she would be treating them both to lunch.

When Chandu arrived at the store that morning, instead of getting straight to his duties, he asked Mr Gupta if Meera was awake, since he wanted to speak with her.

'Go upstairs,' he answered. 'Go up, she is dressed and eating breakfast. Is everything OK?'

'Not really,' he replied. 'Babita is unwell and will not be able to go shopping.' He ran up the stairs, and Meera beckoned him over to sit at the table with her.

'Sit down. What is it? Babita?' she asked, the toast now back on its plate uneaten.

'Sick all night,' he replied. 'She is better this morning and has drank milk, but she is not well enough to go shopping. She says to go on your own, and she will see you tomorrow in the store.' As Chandu knew would be the case, Meera looked shocked and stood up.

'Go on my own? When she is in bed, unwell and sick? She is crazy? What fun would there be for me in this situation?'

He held up his hands as though to surrender. 'I told her this would be your reaction, but she insisted I tell you to go.'

'Humph. I would rather be without new perfume for the rest of my life than do this.' She banged her cup down on the table, spilling tea on the white cloth. 'I shall buy chicken soup and go there now,' she added. 'I have the key, and if there are any problems, I will call you.'

'Thank you. Now I can stay here and not worry?' he asked, as though trying to reassure himself that this action was the correct one.

'Go, go - I will attend to things.' She waited for a moment, but Chandu still didn't move. He continued to sit at the table, playing with a few grains of sugar that had been spilled and pressing them between his fingers.

Realising he was still worried, she spoke again, gently patting his back at the same time. 'Don't worry, I shall call the doctor if there is need, and will let you know. Relax and enjoy your work.'

He nodded, and ran back down the stairs, the door banging loudly behind him.

Collecting everything she thought she might need, and throwing it into her large bag, she grabbed an umbrella from the stand and hurried down the stairs. Within minutes she was in the small grocery store nearby buying soup. Then, as quickly as her platform shoes would allow, she hurried to the boarding house and the sick Babita – her best friend and ally, sister, mother and daughter rolled into one.

***

Babita was lying in bed, although had got up, washed, and made herself tea before Meera arrived. She was expecting her, knowing full well that her friend would never countenance going shopping if she knew Babita was unwell.

'I knew you would come. You should have gone shopping – the sickness has stopped now. Nothing to worry about. I told Chandu to not make a fuss, but you know how he is?'

'There was no fuss. He told me how things were, and I came. You are very naughty!'

Babita laughed. 'Naughty, me? You are the naughty one! Come, sit down – I was to sew my quilt today. Look, see how it has grown.' She pushed it across to Meera, who stood back up; shaking it out to see the progress that had been made. It was almost big enough to cover the double bed and was a riot of colour and texture.

'Beautiful,' said Meera. 'I would never have the patience to do this. You have enough squares to sew, or shall I buy you more?'

'I have plenty, thank you.'

'I am worried. You are looking thin in your face. You see the doctor next Friday?'

'Yes. I am keeping the food diary as he asked, but so far I am unable to see that it is any particular thing that makes me unwell.'

'You would like me to come with you when you go?'

'No,' said Babita firmly. 'There is no need. I like him very much, and trust what he says. I shall rest for today and will be at work tomorrow. If you want to look after me, then make tea. I shall sew, and you can tell me more stories from when you were in India.'

Meera stayed for the rest of the day, making sure that Babita ate the soup without being sick, which she did. She told her about the jackals' choir, her niece Delilah, and about her father when he shouted out 'silence' after having not spoken for months. She left about an hour before Chandu was due home, far more worried than when she arrived.

That evening she told Vasu about her day, and her fears for Babita's health. 'There is something wrong, Vasu, I know it. The doctor does nothing but ask for lists of food. What use it this? He is a fool!'

What Meera did not know, was that when Chandu got home that evening, there was an envelope on the mat behind the front door addressed to Babita. It was from Dr Greene, asking her to attend an appointment at the surgery on Monday morning. He had felt distracted all week, unable to clear his head from the concern he felt for his patient. He would rather look a fool, he thought, than be negligent. To anyone that knew him, this was ridiculous; he was an excellent doctor – one of the best. He was kind, caring, thoughtful and professional. However, he had no fear of the opinions held by others. He needed no praise to boost his ego – not at all. Dr Greene's greatest motivator was the respect he had for himself. If he lost that, then he lost everything.

CHAPTER
THIRTY-SEVEN

As she had said, Babita arrived at work with Chandu the following morning. She had eaten a little breakfast, but still feeling breathless found that she needed to walk more slowly. Meera was waiting, the kettle boiled ready to pour, and with a list of less arduous jobs for Babita to do, although she knew this might give rise to some argument. They were still going to the cinema that evening, eating before they went, and Meera had already decided that she would insist on them taking a taxi home.

At lunchtime, the two women went upstairs because Meera had some clothes she wanted to show her friend. She had also spread several large pieces of fabric over the spare bed. Brought back from India, she wondered if they might be suitable for Babita's patchwork quilt.

'One moment,' she said. 'I have another piece,' and she dashed into the bedroom to find it. Although she would never admit it, Babita felt exhausted. She sat down, and then raised her legs onto the bed to stop them aching. When Meera came back in, she found her fast asleep. Deeply concerned, she covered her with a blanket before going back down to the store. As usual it was very busy, and Chandu didn't notice that his wife was missing until mid-afternoon.

'Where is Babita?' he asked Meera.

'Having a rest. Leave her there – we can manage here.' Seeing the panic in his eyes she tried to reassure him. 'Try not to worry. I think she is weak from her recent illness. Resting will help.'

'Not worry?' he replied. 'Tell me you are not worried, and then I will not worry also.'

She let out a long sigh. 'Yes, alright. I am worried, but what can we do? She sees the doctor on Monday, and from there we will become involved. No more messing about, and if she fights us, then a fight is what she will receive. Two against one.' She banged a fist into the palm of her other hand to show she meant business.

Chandu felt better for hearing Meera in fight mode. It made him feel less helpless knowing that he could count on her support in this way, and he got on with his work. A few hours later Babita slipped back into the store, unnoticed until Meera saw her talking to a customer. He was clearly enchanted by the pretty little lady in front of him, and paint chart in hand, she helped him to choose what he wanted. Meera sadly shook her head. How would this all end, she wondered? Standing at the till a few minutes later she could hear the telephone ringing above her, but having neither the time nor inclination to run up to the flat, she ignored it – and it was soon forgotten.

Babita seemed to pick up as the afternoon went on, and the four went to the cinema as arranged. Great fans of 'The Pink Panther,' Chandu and Vasu laughed all the way through, wiping their eyes at intervals before the next bout of laughter rendered them helpless again. This amused their wives far more than the film did, and when they left all were relaxed and happy – a cab taking them home, stopping at the hardware store first.

They had just got into bed when the telephone rang. Mr Gupta got up to answer it, quickly coming back into the bedroom.

'Not Babita?' she asked, her eyes wide with fear.

'No. It's Manju. He said he tried to call earlier, but I explained we were in the store. Hurry, he wants to talk to you about your father.' Meera quickly got up and went to the phone, her husband following her.

'He is worse, I think,' said Manju. 'and I thought you should know. The doctor came again and said the same as before. He might last for many weeks like this but was unable to give any accurate timing. He might also die tomorrow. It takes Suvi an hour to get him to drink his buttermilk, and today he hit it from her hands to smash on the floor.'

'At least he has some strength left,' she replied.

'Maybe, although he now struggles with his cigarettes. One fell on the blanket and caught fire. Delilah threw water on him to put it out.' Meera remembered the plume of grey smoke rising as her father lay on the verandah, used as a guide to him still being alive.

'Suvi says she can manage, and not to worry. It's such a long way when the timing is not known, but the choice is yours. I keep thinking about how he used to be...'

Meera heard a quiet choking sound, assuming correctly that her brother was struggling to control his emotions. She felt torn. She wanted to be with her father in his last days, of course she did, but she wanted to stay here too. Not just because she didn't want to leave her husband, but because of Babita. Who knew how things would go if she was not there to assist, and Chandu would need help if her friend refused to take care of herself properly. Hearing another stifled sob, she made up her mind. She had to go to India – this was her father, after all.

'I will come,' she said. 'On Monday, I will give you the times.' Back in bed, she told her husband about her fears of going to India and leaving the Kumars without support.

'Try not to worry. I will do all I can. Maybe Babita will get well quickly and everything will go back to normal.' Secretly, he too felt concerned. He had observed her today and, although smiling and happy, her thin face looked a little sallow. He knew that many Indians had this colour when living in colder countries, but even so, it was a change that he had not noticed before.

'I will do everything I can to take your place. I promise you this – everything. And even if there are health problems, surely it can be dealt with?' he added. 'From what Manju says, I think your father will not last many more weeks – two-three at the most. Without food or water, he cannot survive. No one can.'

Meera knew that Vasu meant what he said. He would help if needed, but Babita would most likely refuse any help from him. She might even refuse to see him at all if she became increasingly unwell. Even Chandu might find it difficult to ask his employer for assistance. She would speak to him before she went, as well as to Babita. She would be very strict with them and make a plan for emergencies. Sleep did not come for several hours, as images played through her mind of her father lying on his death bed, disappearing in front of her. She saw herself in the park with Babita – the swans, and the warm earth beneath them as they lay on sun-soaked ground. She saw the quilt that Babita was making; the bright, vivid colours flashing in front of her like lights.

'Stop,' she said to herself, 'enough now,' and she turned towards her husband, putting an arm around his waist. As she fell asleep she smelt cedar – strong and pungent like her father's aftershave or the trees in the park on that hot afternoon...

CHAPTER
THIRTY-EIGHT

Babita sat opposite Dr Greene as he explained why he had made her an earlier appointment.

'I thought it best not to wait any longer, Mrs Kumar, given your past medical history. I hope I didn't alarm you?' he asked.

'Not really. I thought it might be something like that,' she replied. 'I kept the diary you asked for but was unable to see that any particular foods caused me to feel sick or unwell. My appetite is small, but I have been eating.' She pushed the notebook across to him so that he could see the lists of what had been consumed and when.

He studied it carefully. 'And the tablets? Did they help at all?'

'Not really – sorry,' she replied.

'No need to be sorry – it was worth a try. Have you had any other symptoms at all? Any pain or breathlessness? Tiredness? Anything else?'

'I have felt breathless a few times when walking back from work. My husband goes so fast, and lately I have been unable to keep up. I was sick a few times the other day. No pain really, maybe a little here…' She pointed to the small of her back bringing her hand across to the right.

'Just in your back and on the right side?' His heart sank. He didn't like the sound of this at all. He had been right to bring her back in, and picked up the telephone to ask for a nurse to act as chaperone whilst he examined his patient.

'I shall have to examine you, Mrs Kumar. I'll be as quick as possible, but without it I won't know how to progress. The nurse will be here. Are you alright with that?'

Babita was not alright with it. She hated to be looked at in this way. However, sitting opposite the doctor she could see his concern, and knew that he wouldn't do anything that wasn't necessary. 'Very well, then,' she said. The nurse came through the door and helped her onto the couch, exposing the areas which needed to be examined.

'Let me know if anywhere is particularly uncomfortable,' he instructed. Babita closed her eyes, and at one point during the examination the doctor and nurse looked at each other, both quickly looking away again. Ten minutes later Babita was back in the chair opposite Dr Greene, watching as he struggled to find the words that would alarm her the least, yet make her understand that further action must be taken.

'Mrs Kumar, as you are already aware, your stomach is quite swollen with fluid.'

'It is not fat, then?' asked Babita, feeling relieved.

'No, not fat. It would be better if it were. The fluid might mean that there is something else going on, and you are definitely tender on that right side, both front and back, as well as around your stomach. The breathlessness might suggest that there is fluid around your lungs as well. I need to take blood tests, the nurse can do that today, and you will need x-rays and scans, but that will have to be done at the hospital.' He paused for a moment to tick off a few things on a list he had made. 'I'll arrange for those straight away, and hopefully can give you the times before you leave, but I want to refer you to a specialist. Do you remember Mr Ellis who operated on you some years ago?'

Babita nodded. She remembered him very well. 'Yes, of course.'

'Good. Well, I shall refer you to him. In fact, I'll try to get hold of him, or his secretary, whilst you're having the blood tests. It's a lot to take in, I know. Is there anything you want to ask?'

'Babita thought for a moment. 'Yes,' she said quietly. 'There is one thing.'

'Of course. What is it?'

'Am I going to die?'

Dr Greene felt like he had hit a wall. She had asked the question completely without emotion, like asking for a glass of water, or for the time of the next bus. He wanted to be honest, but was unsure if that was appropriate. Her liver was enlarged; he had felt that, and there were other masses in her abdomen that he couldn't identify. Her lungs were congested, and she appeared to be slightly jaundiced. It didn't look good, and he was definitely very concerned.

'Mrs Kumar, it might be best if your husband was here to support you?'

'No. I asked you a question, and trust that what you say will be truthful. Chandu panics easily and will make it harder for me.'

'Very well. The truth is that I can't answer that question without some test results and specialist opinions. There do appear to be some problems, but if we get the tests done as soon as possible, and you see the consultant, we should be a lot clearer about what is actually wrong and what can be done. I promise I won't hold anything back from you when I have answers, and neither will Mr Ellis.'

There was a knock on the door, and the nurse reappeared. 'I can do the blood tests now, Mrs Kumar.'

Babita got up and went to follow her.

'I'll just make a few phone calls,' he continued. 'Please don't leave without seeing me first.' With the door closed, Dr Greene sat down in the chair, rubbing his hands rhythmically through his hair. He knew he was right in not giving an opinion without more information. Without wasting any more time he picked up the phone, and began to make the appointments that his patient so urgently needed.

***

When Chandu came home that evening, he demanded a full replay of Babita's visit to the doctor. He had wanted to go with her, but she refused, saying she wouldn't go at all if he insisted on coming.

'He gave me blood tests, and tomorrow afternoon I must have x-rays and a scan. There is no point in asking to come. You will not be allowed into the x-ray room, and

and no results will be given to me anyway. On Thursday afternoon I see Mr Ellis who did the surgery many years ago. After this, I may know more, or he may want more tests.' She sighed. 'All these tests – it takes my time away, and I want to be in the store with Meera.'

Meera had told him today that her father was dying, and she must return to India. She asked that he not tell Babita. She would tell her tomorrow, she said, because there were other things they needed to discuss. Chandu had no idea how they would manage with Meera away if Babita became more unwell, or needed to have surgery from Mr Ellis, like last time. He would want to be with her, but this might mean that Mr Gupta would be alone, and that was almost impossible these days with the store so busy.

Babita served his dinner as usual in the Indian style, but when he had finished, she didn't sit down to eat her own like she usually did. 'I had eggs earlier which makes me less sick,' she explained, when he asked. 'Please Chandu, no fuss. I will eat when I can.'

He felt helpless and out of control. She excluded him from almost everything and he could do nothing. He began to feel the panic rise in his chest, and went to stand by the window to take deep breaths of air. It was raining but still warm, and Babita insisted on it being open saying she couldn't breathe properly otherwise. After she left the room to have a bath, he leaned his head against the cool glass. Who could he turn to when Meera left? Who would help him?

***

Babita lay in the deep bath, the water almost up to her chin. Her stomach was not entirely covered, and she prodded it with her finger. She knew Chandu was upset, but didn't know what to do for the best. If she told him about Dr Greene's frightened face and the worried look between him and the nurse, then he would panic, and she would be unable to pacify him, except through anger. Her eyes were not fully closed whilst she was being examined, and that one single glance had told her everything that she needed to know.

She felt nothing then, and felt nothing now. Tonight she would sew her quilt, and tomorrow they would go to the store. She would see Meera and Krishna. This name still made her smile, especially when she remembered how it first came about. Chandu would be happy in the dark storeroom, safe from harm, and she could sell paint.

In bed an hour later, she spread the quilt over her as she attached more pieces. She had cut squares from the fabric Meera gave her, and they blended perfectly. Two more rows all around and it would be big enough. She would stitch on the backing, and then it would be finished. 'Just in time for when I shall need it,' she said aloud.

Chandu was watching television, and looked over to see her admiring her handiwork. 'Very beautiful,' he said. 'It will keep us warm in the winter.'

Babita said nothing and continued to sew.

CHAPTER
THIRTY-NINE

As usual, Meera was waiting for them the following morning, and she held Babita's hand as she led her up the stairs to the flat. 'I need to talk to you – come.' Five minutes later they sat at the table, tea in front of them.

'I have to go to India,' said Meera. 'Manju called me. Father now refuses his buttermilk and can surely not last much longer.'

Babita looked away. 'When will you go?' she asked.

'Thursday,' replied Meera, missing nothing of her friend's distress at the idea of her leaving.

'So soon? I hoped... I wanted to be with you.'

'I know, I know. You are unwell, and I wish to stay here, but he is my father...' Meera's voice began to rise and she wrung her hands, her eyes pleading with Babita to not make the separation even more difficult than it already was. Babita still looked away, and Meera continued to try to reassure her, as well as herself.

'Please, I will be back soon in just a few weeks. With no food or drink, how can he last longer?' She felt even more torn, not realising that Babita would react in this way. A piece of her was wanted from both sides, and to do one meant to hurt the other. 'What can I do?' she asked, beginning to cry.

Babita reached out to hold her friend's hand. 'No, no, please don't cry. He is your father and you must go to him. I shall work in the store and help Vasu and Chandu until you come back.'

'But you are sick. How can you work?' asked Meera, looking at her friend's thin face. 'You are not even eating properly, and without me who will feed you?'

Babita smiled and reached up to wipe away a tear glistening on Meera's cheek. 'I will feed myself! Have I not done so for many years now?'

'You must promise me that you will – Chandu and Vasu will also be instructed. If I am told you will not eat then I shall come back, and my father will die without his daughter!'

'Ah, now you resort to blackmail. Is this so? Meera, I am shocked! I never thought to hear this from you!' They both smiled at each other, amused by their own words as well as each other's.

'I have not even had tests yet,' she confirmed, 'so there is nothing to worry about. If I am tired, Krishna can pay for a taxi. If too tired even for this, then I shall stay in bed and they can manage together. I have television and radio, and my quilt to sew.'

***

Downstairs, Mr Gupta took Chandu to one side. It was early, and the store was empty. 'You know Meera has to go to India?' he asked.

'Yes,' replied Chandu.

'Good. We shall be on our own for a few weeks at least, but she is worried about Babita, and how you will cope if she becomes more unwell.'

'I also am worried. She will not listen to me and tells me nothing. She refuses food and will starve.' He became upset as he spoke, and Gupta gently placed a hand on the small man's shoulder.

'You will not be alone with this, do you hear me? I have made a promise that I will support you in any way that is needed. If you have hospital to attend with Babita then you can take a taxi – I will pay. I can manage here alone for a few hours. She can work with us for as long as she wishes. It may be best this way, and we can watch her. She can rest upstairs if necessary. I think that Meera will not be gone very long – one month at most. If you need anything then you must not be afraid to ask.'

Chandu nodded. 'Thank you. I agree to keep her with us is a good idea, even if she is unwell. Next week we should know more, and can make plans, but... I...?' He faltered, struggling to finish what he was saying.

'What is it? What were you going to say?' encouraged Mr Gupta, his hand still on Chandu's shoulder.

'I don't know what I will do if she dies. My life will become empty, and I am very afraid of this.'

As he was speaking, Gupta felt Chandu's body relax under his hand, the result perhaps of expressing the things that he feared the most. 'It is good, I think, to share what you feel. I know you would rather say these things to Meera, but I will listen when she is not here. Try to not move too far ahead... as yet you know nothing. When all is known, then a plan will be made. It may not be as bad as you fear.'

Listening to this, Chandu felt very grateful for the support that he was being offered. In truth it was all he had, and he would need it, or he would break and be of no use to Babita at all. She was sick, very sick, he knew that without any tests to confirm it, and he was sure that Mr Gupta did too. At this point Babita came through the flat door and began her usual morning duties of tidying and dusting the shelves.

When Meera followed a few minutes later, it was clear that she had been crying. Letting out a huge sigh, her husband was about to go over to her when the door opened and two customers came in, both tradesmen with long lists in their hands. The working day had begun. Maybe this was for the best to give them all some respite from the difficulties that undoubtedly lay ahead...

Later that day, Babita went to the hospital for the tests that had been arranged for her. As she already knew would be the case, she was told nothing except that the results would be with Mr Ellis on Thursday. At home that evening, Chandu told her that he would be coming with her to see the consultant, and that it was already arranged with Mr Gupta, including the taxi that would fetch them and bring them back.

'No need. I shall go alone,' she quickly replied.

'You are misunderstanding me,' said Chandu, standing up from his chair at the dining table, where he had been watching her pushing food around her plate. 'I did not ask for your permission to attend. I advised you that I would attend. There is a difference.'

'And I told you that I did not require it,' she responded, 'I will go alone.'

'I am coming, and if you refuse me entry then the doctor will see your behaviour and demand that I come in as a husband who cares for his wife.' There, he thought, I have done it. This response had been practised with Meera whilst Babita was at the hospital, who believed that if dealt with firmly, Babita would back down.

'You have been talking to Meera?' she asked.

'Yes, I have.'

'What about the store? How will Vasu manage on his own all afternoon?'

'It will not be all afternoon. Two hours at most, with a taxi both ways. The decision has been made.' He went to the sink to wash the dishes, his back now turned to her.

'Very well. You may come. It will save me having to repeat everything, I suppose.' Babita felt deeply ashamed of herself. She was being unfair to Chandu, even with the response she had just given. Meera told her this at lunchtime today, and she knew it was true, but struggled to stop herself. Many wives might share more with their husbands, but what was the point? How would it help if they both cried together each night, making promises that would be impossible to keep about love and eternity, and the next life about which they knew nothing?

She might try to have this conversation for Chandu's sake if not her own, but what she craved most was detachment from emotional drama. If she was to cope with what she knew the future held, then this is what she would need. She loved Chandu very much. Perhaps more like a mother, a sister, or a playmate, than a wife, but maybe this was because it was all she would allow herself to be? Meera had said something that shocked them both, coming quite out of the blue and perhaps riding on some of the hidden anger she felt, or despair at a situation that was beyond her control.

'You are treating him badly so that he will hate you! Is this it? Then you will feel free of the bondage that this type of love brings? I am no Guru, Babita, nor do I have the intelligence of you and Vasu, but I do have eyes and a heart. If you believe in reincarnation and are seeking to not return, then your behaviours and actions must be pure in order to transcend. Surely you know this?'

Babita had stormed from the room, appearing a minute later in the shop before leaving for her hospital tests.

She got up and went over to Chandu, his back still turned. Putting her arms around his waist, she held him tightly; he eventually turning around to face her and kiss the top of her head.

'I am sorry,' she said, 'forgive me.'

'Nothing to forgive,' he replied, kissing her again.

***

In the flat above the store, Meera recounted to Vasu the conversation that was had that afternoon, as well as Babita's response. 'I feel so helpless pulled this way and that, and soon to be thousands of miles away. She is a saint

249

and I love her very much, too much... but at times she is so stubborn, which makes her blind.'

He considered this for a moment. 'All true, but I think she is also afraid. She would not be human if this were not so. My dear, I hate to see you upset like this. You will need your strength for India and your father. I will see to things here as best I can, and will telephone with any news, I promise.'

Trusting that he would do as he said, Meera went to get out her suitcases ready to pack tomorrow, hoping that like last time, Babita would be there to help her.

CHAPTER
FORTY

Babita sat on Meera's bed, folding the clothes that were handed to her, and placing them in the suitcase by her side. 'It seems like no time has passed since we were last doing this,' she said. 'You have spoken to your brother again about your father?'

'Yes, last night. There is no difference. A few sips each day of buttermilk through a straw but nothing else. I am looking forward to seeing Delilah. She will have grown, the boys also.' Changing the subject entirely she asked about Babita's hospital appointment on the following day. 'I shall be flying when you have your appointment, but Vasu will call me the next day. If you tell him, he can pass a message to me. You will do this, please?'

'Yes. I will tell him all I know, but there may be more tests to have,' she replied.

'You have eaten today?' asked Meera.

'A little. I feel so full all the time, it is hard.'

Meera sighed. 'I shall be back as soon as possible. There is no holiday this time. If necessary, you will move here, and I will feed you by hand until you become fat!' They both giggled at the thought of this. It was rare that they argued, and when Babita arrived that morning she had kissed her friend and apologised, both now feeling far more relaxed than they had for some time.

'There,' said Meera, closing the large case. 'I think this is enough. I thought two cases, but there are no gifts this time.'

'What time do you leave? I shall be here?' asked Babita.

'No. I leave at six, before you arrive. Vasu is coming with me and should be back by eight, but you and Chandu can open the store if he is delayed.' They heard shouting from the stairs.

'Come, Babita. It is time to go home. A cab is waiting,' shouted Chandu.

Meera opened her arms to hug her friend. 'Remember, tell Vasu everything, and eat! Even milk is good, and do what the doctor says.'

'Of course. I hope things go well. Send me postcards? I will pin them to the wall.'

'Every day,' promised Meera. 'Every single day, I will send one.'

***

At the airport the following morning, they stood before the metal gate – so symbolic the last time they were here of the barrier that had been between them. Today there were no barriers and Meera held her husband close, not caring what anyone thought.

'I will miss you so much,' she said. 'Don't forget to telephone tomorrow about Babita. Oh Vasu, I am so worried about everything.'

He held her face in his hands and kissed each of her cheeks in turn, much as she had done to him before. 'Please try not to worry, my dear. Try to relax and make the most of the time you have with your father, and your brother and Delilah. You are so fond of them, and they you. At least there will be no plans made to kill me on this trip!'

She laughed. 'You must behave then. No more falling down the stairs or young ladies in your bedroom. I am a traditional woman, Mr Gupta, and some things I will not tolerate.' They embraced again, and Meera walked through the metal gates to where he could not follow, quickly turning to blow him a kiss and he responding likewise.

On the plane she was disappointed to find that the seat beside her was empty. On several occasions she had fantasized that Sister Maria Benedicta might be there to offer her wise words and advice, and she felt very alone. It was almost as though she was being forced into a position of solitude in order to contemplate and come to terms with her difficulties herself. She slept a little, but for most of the journey gazed out of the window seeing nothing but clouds and sky; unsure of what was to come, either in the place she was going to, or the one she had left behind.

***

Manju came to meet her alone, and feeling less disorientated she soon spotted him in the crowd, waving his arms and shouting her name. He gave her a big hug seeming reluctant to let her go, and she gently pulled away to look at him. He appeared to have aged, but she supposed she might look this way to him, even though only a year had passed. He took her bag and they walked toward the exit. Meera suddenly stopped, remembering something. 'Wait... I need to buy postcards. Many postcards.'

'Why? You can buy a few later in the week. I will take you to get some.'

'No, I want them now. I will explain in the car.'

He followed her to a small shop by the exit selling books and newspapers, with several stands of postcards over to one side.

'All different, please,' she said, and he helped her to select as many varieties as he could, intrigued as to why she was buying so many. She had one of every type and thought she was finished when her eye caught one more, tucked behind the others and almost obscured from view. It was of a pair of swans drifting on a calm lake toward a coral sunset. She took two and Manju paid for them, insisting on doing this despite her objecting.

'I can't even buy you a few postcards?' he asked, shaking his head.

'Not a few. There are at least thirty!'

He shrugged his shoulders. He was a wealthy man. It meant nothing except in the giving of a gift, which made him happy. They came out of the shop and walked towards the exit. 'It's pouring with rain. The season has been much worse than when you were last here. The car is right outside. Jump straight in and I shall put your bag in the boot.'

He wasn't exaggerating, it was indeed pouring. Proper rain, as she knew Chandu would call it, not just dribs and drabs like in England. She smiled when she thought of him and hoped he would be alright with her away. Manju interrupted her thoughts.

'Now, tell me about the many people who are to receive postcards from India. I'm intrigued!'

Meera smiled. 'There is no great mystery. I fear you will be disappointed with my answer. Do you remember me telling you about my friend, Babita?'

'Of course! She is the one with spirit and fire and a temper to match. I love feisty women and so she has remained in my mind. I even dreamed about her once. Tell me...'

Meera began the tale of what was happening in England, and the fears that she had for her dear friend's health. 'She looks so thin and yellow.' She reached out for her brother's hand and held it tight, tears slipping down her face. 'Manju, I fear that I shall lose her. For some time now, I have felt...well...'

'Yes? Tell me. You can tell me anything...'

'I have felt strange, Manju, like something awful was to happen that would change my life for ever. Not father dying, not that, something else...'

'You mean your friend? She is this sick?'

'Maybe,' replied Meera. 'She has had tests and expects the results today.'

'You have always been a little this way, Meera; even as a child. Delilah is the same. I'm not sure about my beliefs in such things, especially fortune-telling cowrie shells and matching horoscopes before marriages are made, but sometimes people do have special gifts. Yes, I think this is so, and maybe you are one of those people? Do you think you are?'

'No,' said Meera. 'Definitely not! No – not special gifts, more I think that I feel things very deeply. If I love, I love deeply, and the opposite also!' She laughed. 'I am temperamental, but just sometimes I get strange thoughts and feelings.'

He gently squeezed her hand. 'And when will you know how she is?'

'Vasu will telephone tomorrow. If she dies, Manju... if she dies, what shall I do? I am here, and she is there. How will I be able to care for her?'

'Slow down, Sister. You must not run away with things in this way. When you know, then you can plan.'

Meera nodded and let out a deep sigh, held perhaps for weeks. Her shoulders dropped, and she felt exhausted. 'Yes, you are right. But she means so much to me... If anything happens to her, then such a hole will be left that can never be filled. Never...'

She put her head against his broad shoulder, and little was said for the rest of the journey. The rain continued to pour down, and arriving at the house she ran to take shelter under the verandah, Manju following closely behind. He had come without umbrellas and they were both soaked, rivulets of water running down their hair and faces.

'You look like you have just been swimming,' she said.

'So do you,' he replied, laughing as she wrung the water from the long plait she had just taken down from its pins. 'Let's go inside to get dry before we catch colds. You know how easy it is in the rainy season; warm and wet with bugs everywhere.'

Suvi was waiting in the hallway with towels, having seen through the window how wet they were. 'Why did you not have an umbrella, Manju?' she scolded.

'Actually, I really enjoyed it,' said Meera. 'I have not been so wet in decades. It was like a spiritual cleansing,' she laughed.

'Yes, we are both cleansed of past bad deeds. Is that not so? What a very refreshing thought,' replied Manju.

Meera leaned over to kiss her sister-in-law, who was beginning to look annoyed. Being careful not to drip on her, she took the proffered towel and began to rub her hair, still feeling exhilarated. Taking in the disapproval and discord between her brother and his wife, she thought it a great shame that they were so unhappy. Although she and Mr Gupta had had their differences, for the most part these were now resolved. Whilst not there to witness it, she knew that Babita had played a considerable part in turning things around, with her frank talking and care of Vasu when he was at his most vulnerable.

'Go and get changed,' said Suvi. 'I will bring your case. Delilah is in bed but was very excited about seeing you.'

A little later she sat with her brother in front of a small wood stove in the kitchen. It was the same one that was there when they were children, and they had always loved it. Suvi tried to get rid of it, but Manju refused, saying if she ever did then she could go back to her parents for good. Although this happened many years ago, Meera had never forgotten it. The wood crackled in the small grate, which gave both of them comfort after their earlier soaking.

'Would you like to see father before you go to bed?' he asked.

'Yes, please, I would like that,' she said, realising that she hadn't asked about him at all, but had spoken about Babita instead. They walked through the dark corridors and into their father's room; two small nightlights flickering on either side of the bed. He lay absolutely still, his face drawn and thin and his eyes tightly closed. There was no bidi between his lips, and no smoke was rising to tell them he was alive. For a moment Meera wondered if he was already dead, and Manju and Suvi had not noticed.

She reached out to gently hold his thin hand, and finding it slightly warm to the touch she felt relieved. Continuing to hold it she spoke to him, her voice lowered to a whisper, as if she were in a temple or church. 'Daddyji? Daddy? It is me, Meera. I have come from England to be with you and shall stay for as long as you wish it.' There was no reply, but feeling a weak pressure on her hand she looked down, Manju following her eyes at the same time. There was no doubt about it... Her father had squeezed her hand and her heart leapt. He knew she was there and wanted her to know that he was glad! He seemed to have fallen asleep again, or had drifted off in his mind to another place – one where his children could not go. Quietly, they left the room.

'Manju? I think I would like to sleep with him if this is possible? Not tonight, but tomorrow. If a cot could be brought in I will stay in his room. This is why I have come, after all.'

'Yes, Sister. You are right, of course. Two cots shall be brought in, one on either side. I shall stay with you whenever I can, and him of course, until he goes... I'm so very glad that you are here,' he said. 'I wish you had never left...'

CHAPTER
FORTY-ONE

When she woke the next day, Meera opened her eyes
to see Delilah staring at her, gently stroking her
aunt's hair with her forefinger.

'Delilah, there you are. I missed you last night, but it
was late. You are at school today?'

'Yes,' she replied, sounding like she was sulking. 'I
want to stay with you, but mummy says no.'

'Then mummy is right. School is important, or
how will you get to the university in England and study
archaeology?' She paused for a moment. 'Or have you
changed your mind?'

'No!' Delilah almost shouted. 'Never – nothing has
changed.'

Meera laughed. 'Stand back so that I can see you
properly.' She sat up in bed to take a good look at the niece
that she hadn't seen for so long.

'How you have grown!'

'Of course,' Delilah replied. 'It is what children do, Auntie. They grow, like I imagine you and daddy did.'

'You have become cheeky too,' said Meera, laughing again. 'We shall have to see about that, if you are to stay with me and Uncle Vasu next summer. Your English has greatly improved, and your hair... so long...'

'I want to have it cut,' said Delilah, 'but mummy will not allow it.'

'Soon you will be able to choose for yourself,' replied Meera.

'Have you never wanted to cut yours, Auntie? It is almost the longest hair I have ever seen!'

Meera thought for a moment before answering. 'No Delilah, I have never wanted to cut it – not even when I was young. I know that to you it might seem old fashioned, but even now I think that long hair is beautiful – I know uncle Vasu also thinks this. But the decision will be yours to make soon enough.'

'Delilah, where are you?' called a voice from the hallway.

'It's Mummy. She told me not to disturb you, but I couldn't help it.'

'Then go,' said Meera, 'hurry now, and I shall see you later.' Delilah slipped through the door, and Meera got out of bed and went to the bathroom. She wanted to arrange things so that she could be with her father, and from what she saw last night, there was little time to lose.

Later that morning, Suvi went to visit her mother.

'She goes every day,' said Manju. 'I don't mind, it gives me some freedom, and anyway, I'm often at work. I have taken two weeks off whilst you are here, so she can be with her mother all day if she chooses.'

'Things are not going well between you?'

'No they are not! We have even discussed divorce, but her mother keeps interfering. I think when Delilah goes to university then it cannot be avoided any longer. She is aware of how things are, and so are the boys. Nothing can be hidden from children, is that not so?'

'That was certainly the case with us,' Meera replied. 'I am sorry that it has come to this. Perhaps next summer if you are to bring Delilah over, you should stay for a few weeks yourself? A break might be good for you.'

'I shall give it some thought,' he replied. 'Maybe it's not such a bad idea.'

***

The rest of the morning was busy with cots being moved into their father's room. Later that afternoon, Meera sat at her father's old teak desk to write her first card to Babita, keen to catch the last post of the day. She told her about her lonely flight and the rain, how her father held her hand, and how much this meant to her. She told her about sitting in front of the stove with her brother, and that he sent his best wishes. Lastly, she told her that she loved her, and would speak to Vasu later to get news of her visit to the consultant. I will send another card tomorrow, she wrote. Until then I send a million kisses…

At intervals throughout the day, she pushed a straw into her father's mouth for him to take small sips of buttermilk. He drank a little each time, but pushed the straw out with his tongue when he had drunk enough. She tried him with water, but he rejected this entirely. She asked the servant for a small sponge, and every hour or so, moistened his lips to stop them becoming dry, speaking to him gently, telling him about the hardware store and her life in England.

He had visited several times, and once or twice she was sure that his fingers squeezed her hand. He loved to travel, and if he would squeeze her fingers for anything, it would be this. Looking for a towel, she opened his drawers, pulling out a few things and carefully rearranging them. Then she came across a cut-glass bottle, its top made of beautifully carved amber. Instantly recognising it, she pulled off the stopper to smell the liquid that was still inside. It hadn't changed at all, and she moved to the side of the bed to gently place two dabs – one on each of her father's wrists, to allow the wonderful fragrance of cedar to fill the room.

'Daddy, can you smell it?' she asked. 'It is exactly the same!' He made no sound, nor squeezed her hand, but when Manju came in a few moments later he recognised it immediately.

'You have found it? Can I see?'

She handed him the bottle and he opened it, dabbing himself on the wrists like she had done to her father. Two tears slid down his face, one from each eye as the years fell away and they were children again; their father tall and strong, his mind as sharp as a knife and with a tongue to match. Meera knew exactly what he was thinking, and they sat together to watch the shadow that was their father, quietly slipping away…

CHAPTER
FORTY-TWO

Babita and Chandu were sat in a cab, en route to drop him back at the store. It was raining again, and stuck at traffic lights, Babita watched as the people scurried past, trying to keep dry under umbrellas and coats. Chandu was on the other side of the seat as far from her as was possible. He stared straight ahead to the back of the driver's head; his eyes fixed and unblinking and his body totally still. He looked as though he was in a trance, and Babita quickly glanced at him before looking away again, letting out a huge sigh as she did so.

The appointment with Mr Ellis had not gone well. He examined her again and, some ten minutes later, sitting behind a large desk, gave his opinion on her condition. He spoke quietly and carefully, but for the most part Babita looked away, barely acknowledging what he was saying. Much was left for Chandu to absorb and consider; not just the mass of information given, but also to formulate pertinent questions about treatment and the future, or even if there would be a future to contemplate at all.

'Mrs Kumar, Mr Kumar... I've got the x-ray and scan results here, and most of the blood tests are back. I need another scan, but I'll talk to you about that in a moment.' He sat forward and adjusted his glasses as though preparing himself. 'There appear to be several large masses in your abdomen, Mrs Kumar, and others on your stomach and liver. The liver is almost totally obscured, which might explain the yellow tinge to your skin and the whites of your eyes. You might have noticed this?'

Chandu nodded. 'Yes,' he said, 'I have noticed.' He looked at Babita, her head turned to one side.

'Mrs Kumar, are you listening? Would you like a glass of water?' In his time as a consultant he had seen many reactions to bad news, silence being one of them, and he spoke again as gently as he could. 'Mrs Kumar? Would you like to write things down as I speak? Some patients find that helpful.'

She turned her head to look directly at him. 'I am listening,' she said, her voice brittle and monotone. 'I want no water, nor do I require a pen. Please continue.'

'Very well. One of the masses covers your right ovary and is particularly dense in that area, so it might be the primary tumour. Your lungs also seem to be affected. I need you to have another scan. It's a type of x-ray, but much more sophisticated and will give greater detail and from different angles.'

'Please speak plainly, Mr Ellis, are you saying that I have cancer?'

Chandu visibly winced, horrified at what he was hearing from the doctor, as well as Babita's rudeness. Seeing this, Mr Ellis raised his hand, not wanting any friction between husband and wife, especially in a case as serious as this.

'Very well, Mrs Kumar. In my opinion, I would say that you very likely have multiple cancerous masses surrounding your internal organs.' He looked as he spoke, trying to gauge how she was receiving the information he was giving. His patient gave nothing away, still not even facing his direction, so he decided to continue.

'From what I have been told, it would seem that the growth of the tumours has been very fast. That is less good in treatment terms, since fast growing tumours are usually the most aggressive and difficult to deal with.'

'But Doctor, surely you can operate like last time?' asked Chandu, his voice almost pleading for reassurance that something could be done.

'Now you are being ridiculous,' said Babita. 'This is nothing like last time, you do not understand at all. Tell him, Mr Ellis. Tell him I shall soon be dead, and then we can go home.'

'Please, Mrs Kumar... let me finish before we engage in a discussion about death. With the greatest of respect, your husband is very worried, and it might help him if I can explain fully?'

She turned her head away again, and sighed as though she were bored. 'Very well, carry on.'

'If the scan confirms what I believe, then we have a few options. The usual next step would be to remove as many of the tumours as possible. We can test for various things at the same time and would at least know what we were dealing with. It would be major surgery, I can't pretend otherwise, but has sometimes prolonged life considerably. However, we have recently started using a new drug, and in some cases the results have been very promising.'

'No surgery. You know as well as I that it would be useless, let us not pretend otherwise.'

'Babita, please, please, we must try,' cried Chandu, desperately, grasping her arm.

'There is no "we" Chandu. This is me and my body. The drugs I will try, but no surgery, big or small.'

'Very well, Mrs Kumar. Look, this is what I suggest. I will arrange for the scan tomorrow morning, and I want you to see the oncologist after that. He will be the person who will look after you during the treatment. You can take the drug in tablet form, and depending on how things go you might be given radiotherapy afterwards, but that can be discussed in the future. I believe I am right in saying that you get on very well with Dr Greene, and have known him for many years?'

This statement seemed to have a beneficial impact on Babita, and she answered in a much more normal voice, her body seeming to relax a little. 'Yes, I like him very much. I would be happier to be treated by him if possible, Mr Ellis, and at home.'

Noticing the change in his patient, Mr Ellis began to understand a little about the lady in front of him, and her reluctance to be interfered with in any way, especially by those unknown to her. 'Good, good, then I'm sure he will help in any way he can. I shall liaise with the oncologist and Dr Greene, and between us we will do the very best we can for you, Mrs Kumar – the very best.'

Babita thanked him and left, closing the door quietly behind her and leaving Chandu still in his seat. She had done this deliberately so that he could ask what he wished without her there to interfere or make him feel awkward. Realising this, Mr Ellis went to sit next to him, pulling the chair closer and leaning forward.

'People react very differently to these things, Mr Kumar. Your wife has taken a very direct and matter of fact approach, but don't be fooled. She will need support and understanding – things are often not what they seem. Do you understand?'

'Yes, Babita makes me very angry with this behaviour, but she is my wife and I know she has much feeling, often buried deep inside.'

'Good man. Now I think you have questions for me? Ask away...'

CHAPTER
FORTY-THREE

Chandu stood on the pavement and watched as the cab pulled away to take Babita back home. He felt confused. Not in the sense that he hadn't understood what the doctor had said. He fully understood it at the time, but now it seemed like a jumbled mess in his head and this scared him. He looked through the window of the store to see Mr Gupta behind the counter, several customers standing in a line waiting to pay for their goods. In a flash, he remembered the brick smashing through the glass to land at Babita's feet. He could even hear the noise that it made, and he wanted to run – run and never come back. Then he felt a hand on his shoulder, and turned to see Mr Jackson, the ever-present cigarette dangling from his lips, and a concerned look on his face.

'You alright, mate? You look like you've seen a ghost!'

At that moment Mr Gupta appeared at the door, and

between them, they led him inside. 'Just one moment, please,' he said to his customers, leading Chandu up the stairs and pulling out a chair for him to sit down. He put an arm around his shoulders and leaned over, almost whispering into his ear.

'Stay here. You will be safe, and I will come as soon as the shop is empty.' Chandu nodded, and Gupta disappeared into the dark stairwell, closing the door behind him. Two hours later, with tea in front of them, Chandu seemed less bewildered and slowly began to recount the events of the afternoon.

'She was very rude to him,' he said.

'Hmmm, that doesn't surprise me. You know how she is...'

Surprisingly, Chandu gave a proud smile. 'Yes, this is Babita,' and he went on to tell Mr Gupta what had been said, and the treatment that she was to receive.

'When she left and you spoke to the doctor alone – what did he say?'

Chandu shook his head. 'He said that the scan would give more details, and the new drugs may extend her life.'

'He gave an amount of time?'

'Not really. He said much would depend on the scans and how she might respond to the treatment, but that it was very serious. He... I asked...'

'Take your time, I can wait. He said more?'

Chandu picked up the almost cold tea and drank it all in large noisy gulps. Then, looking straight into Mr Gupta's dark eyes, he spoke again. 'He said... that she would be unlikely to survive the disease indefinitely.'

'And Babita? How was she when you left?'

'Nothing. It was like nothing had happened and she was angry with me for making a fuss. A fuss! Can you believe this?' Chandu's voice began to rise as his distress grew. 'I am making a fuss because most likely my wife will die? She is insane as well as sick?' He reached across the table and grabbed Gupta's arms tightly, one held in each hand.

'What shall I do? What shall I do? Krishna, help me. What shall I do?' He threw back his head as though he might burst into song, but instead let out a howl like that of a wild animal, its leg caught in a trap and broken, doomed to die in agony. If Meera's jackals howled in their choirs with an untitled song of sadness, then Chandu's howl was one of solitary torture, with no escape or release. He dropped his head down onto the table, cradled it in his arms and sobbed. 'Help me, help me, Krishna,' he pleaded, in a strangled voice, 'help me – help me.'

Half an hour later, Mr Gupta went with Chandu in a taxi to take him home. As soon as he got back, he picked up the telephone to call Meera. He waited a long time for the call to be put through, and eventually, after a series of clicks, he heard her voice.

'You are late. It is midnight here.'

'Yes, sorry. I had to take Chandu home and the lines were busy.' He told her what had happened at the hospital, and Chandu's distress. If he expected her to break down, then he was wrong. She was calm, as though in knowing the truth, her fear of what might be had been released. As with Babita, he doubted that this would continue, but for tonight he was glad of it, since he was struggling to control his own emotions and felt exhausted.

'I need to cut myself in half, Vasu,' she said. 'I need to cut myself in half.'

***

That night he lay in bed, his mind shifting backwards and forwards over the past few years. He too remembered the brick through the window, and his own petty, spiteful behaviour which left him wracked with guilt and shame. He remembered the exploding paint tin; the care he had received from Babita when he injured his back, the rejuvenation of his marriage and how much love and laughter had been shared in this very room. It felt like yesterday. And what of tomorrow? He wanted Meera to come back, but knew that this would not happen until her father died. He wanted to reverse time. He would gladly lie on his back in pain for another year in order to correct the massive fracture that had now taken place between the people he cared for the most. In this turmoil of memory and regret he finally fell asleep, just as dawn announced the arrival of another day.

***

In India, Meera lay on the cot beside her father's bed. The rain still fell outside – the sound providing a backdrop to the flickering candles as their reflections danced around the walls. Unable to sleep she got up to sit beside him, and holding his hand began to tell him about her friend, Babita. She told him about their weekly meetings for lunch, her caring for Vasu when Meera was last here, and their afternoon in the park. She told him about Babita's illness, and her own fear of a loss that might be too great to survive. As she spoke, her father gave her hand small squeezes, acknowledged gratefully by his daughter as signs of support and affection.

'Thank you, Daddyji,' she said. 'I knew you would understand.'

***

Chandu arrived home to find Babita in bed; her unfinished quilt spread over her and fast asleep. As he had done so many times over the years, he went to sit in the armchair, pulling the blanket over him. His earlier outpouring of emotion had left him calm, and in this much quieter frame of mind he too reflected on the day, and began to order his thoughts with the information he had received. This done, he closed his eyes, sitting further back in the chair to watch a series of images slowly being played out like a slideshow.

The first was of the day Babita had been introduced to him as a potential marriage match, in her now-dead aunt's house. She had pulled her dupatta-scarf low over her face so that he couldn't see her properly, and he smiled, thinking how little she had changed. The second was when he swung her round after hearing about her new job with Stella's children, and then another of them running through the park as though they were still children themselves. The fourth was of Babita sat up in bed, stitching her ever-growing multicoloured quilt. The final image was of her rushing into Mr Gupta's bedroom;

onion in one hand, knife in the other, called to perform surgery by Meera after watching 'The Six Million Dollar Man' on television. He remembered her comments about Krishna, her wit as sharp as the knife she held, and he, Chandu, throwing himself at her feet.

And there I shall stay, he thought, and slept.

CHAPTER
FORTY-FOUR

When Chandu went to work the following day, Babita stayed in bed for a while, dozing at times, and at others, thinking. She had an appointment for a scan that morning, and another an hour later with the oncologist. A cab was already arranged to pick her up, with an agreement that she would call when she needed collecting. She fully intended to go into the store if there was still time, wanting to occupy herself, and keep some routine to her day with a job that she enjoyed very much.

She was fully aware that her behaviour caused Chandu distress, and was sorry about it, intending to apologise later. Apologies, she thought... my life is to become one of constant apologies for bad behaviour. Then she felt indignant. This is my life – I have entitlement to choose, but Chandu? He would see this differently, as most likely would everyone else.

She got up, made tea, and began to get ready to go out, her thoughts now turning to Meera. Had she been told? She thought it most likely that she had, by telephone last night. Without doubt she would stay in India until her father died, which might be for weeks or even longer. Babita was unsure how she felt about this. If Meera were here there would be another drama to deal with, probably on a daily basis along with constant cajoling of do this, do that, eat this, drink that, and so on. But she would help to support Chandu far better than Mr Gupta might do, which would definitely be a good thing.

As she reached out to open the door, the brass knob felt very cold in her warm hand. It gave her a jolt as though she had received an electric shock, and maybe she had, but in that moment she felt her own flesh as never before. 'I am alive...' she said aloud, the words reverberating through her head as though a bell had just been struck. 'And soon I shall be dead.' Her tongue felt dry in her mouth, and she raised her hand to feel the wetness as she licked it. Overcome with dizziness and the beginnings of another headache, she quickly went to sit on the edge of the bed until it passed.

Outside, the taxi waited, its driver inhaling deeply on his cigarette, then blowing a great plume of smoke out of the window and into the damp air. Within a few minutes Babita stepped out of the front door, and once she was sat inside he set the meter; its ticking sound marking the total sum that would need to be paid, and the amount of time that would forever be lost.

Almost three hours later she was back in a cab again, and on her way to the store. The scan had been simple enough, after which she had waited for nearly an hour to see the oncologist.

'Mrs Kumar, I've looked through all the x-ray results and the blood tests, and yesterday I spoke with Mr Ellis. We won't get today's scan results until tomorrow at the earliest, but I agree with him that we should proceed straight away with the drug treatment.' He paused for a moment and looked around. 'Is there no one with you?'

'No. I am fine on my own, my husband is working.' Chandu had wanted to come with her, but she refused, saying he wouldn't be allowed in the scanning room anyway, which was true.

'Very well, if you're sure.'

Babita nodded.

He went on to explain the treatment, which was to be by tablet and would be given in stages. 'It might make you feel quite unwell. People vary, but the specialist nurse will explain everything to you in a minute. You will be able to contact her if you need to, and I'm told that Dr Greene is going to monitor things?'

'Yes, I would prefer that.'

'Of course. You will need another scan in four weeks, and then we can work out the further treatments from the results.' There was a knock on the door, and the nurse came in.

'Before you go, is there anything you want to ask me, Mrs Kumar? I know you only saw Mr Ellis yesterday, but you might have thought of more questions?'

'No, nothing thank you, Doctor,' she replied, getting up to follow the nurse from the room, quietly closing the door behind her. The oncologist went to stand by the window and watched whilst two pigeons fought over a

277

scrap of bread on the wall outside. Mrs Kumar's coolness was unusual. Normally he was faced with a barrage of questions, often tears or quite understandably, fear. Walking back to his desk, he called for the next patient. Time would tell, he thought, time would tell.

Babita arrived at the store – both men busy as usual, and she slipped through to the back to pull on her pink overall. The headache had increased, and she quickly swallowed more aspirin before starting her first task. Mr Gupta thought she looked very unwell, and as soon as he could went to talk to her as she dusted the shelves; tidying and rearranging as she did so.

'My dear, are you alright? Later you can tell me about the hospital, but you look pale. You have eaten? There is food upstairs… please help yourself.'

He sounded so much like Meera that she laughed. 'Just a slight headache. I will eat later. There is little to say about the hospital, so I will tell you now. No results from the scan yet, and I have medication to start from tomorrow. It might make me feel unwell, but the nurse said each person reacts differently.'

'You must rest. Would you prefer to come and live here whilst you are taking this medication? Then we can care for you if you need it.'

Babita thought how things had changed that he would speak to her with such kindness. The nails that Chandu collected were now little more than memorials to the past, and were no longer being added to. Time had pushed them with its bony fingers to the back of the cupboard, where the dust and cobwebs grew in collusion to hide the hurt from sight.

'Thank you, but I prefer to stay at home for now. Let us see how I am feeling after I begin the treatment,' she replied. 'I will still cook for you twice a week, as before.'

'No, Babita, there is no need. It is I that should cook for you. Please...'

Babita laughed. 'You are wishing to poison us all and hasten my end, and also that of Chandu? Now we are hearing the truth, Vasu, and husband of my best friend! What would she think?' She laughed again.

'It is true my skills in cooking are not advanced... I have an idea. Would you like to speak to Meera this evening after we close the store? I was to call her. Six here is ten-thirty there. It would be a great surprise for her, and good for you as well?'

'Yes! Yes, I would like that very much,' and who knew when she might be able to do it again, she wondered. 'Yes,' she repeated. 'May I be the one to speak first?'

'Of course,' he replied, and feeling a little happier, went back to his work.

***

Meera spent the whole day with her father, Manju coming in and out at intervals with snacks and drinks. She saw Suvi a lot less than when she was here last, although she was always around at mealtimes, and in the evening when the children were home. The eldest, Devi, would soon be leaving for University in Oxford, and often sat with his aunt in the evenings to discuss the city that she had visited several times. She saw little of her younger nephews, who preferred to spend time with their friends, or stay in their rooms. Delilah usually came to find her straight after school, delighting her aunt with tales from the classroom.

Her father continued to take sips of buttermilk, and she read to him for a while, pulling books from the shelves and reading a few passages from each. She had written another card to Babita, telling her about finding her father's perfume bottle with a small amount of the precious fluid still inside, and asking for a long letter by return. As the evening wore on she sat talking to her brother as she held her father's hand. He had drunk a little more today, his eyelids fluttering slightly as she read, although now appeared to be deeply asleep.

'Go to your proper bed,' she encouraged. 'I can call if there are any problems.'

As he got up to leave, they both heard the telephone ring, and Manju went out into the passage to answer it.

'It will be Vasu, come on.'

'Vasu, is that you?' Meera asked, letting out a cry of delight when she heard Babita's voice, staying on the phone for twenty minutes with just two of those spent talking to her husband.

'That will have cost a fortune,' teased Manju, as he kissed his sister goodnight. 'Still, I'm sure he can afford it!'

Lying on her string cot some ten minutes later, Meera ran through what Babita had said. She didn't doubt that the whole conversation had been watered down to prevent her from worrying, but at least she was starting the medication tomorrow and that was something. Turning on her side, she saw that her father's hand had slipped from the bed and was now dangling in mid-air. She got up to place it back on the covers, stroking it for a while in case he had become distressed and was trying to reach out for her. She gave it one final squeeze, and he gripped it back, clearly not wanting to let her go.

When she was sure he was asleep again, she pulled on her robe and went outside to the verandah at the back of the house. The rain had stopped, and the sky was full of stars; a crescent moon hanging low over the vast empty plains. She could smell woodsmoke, probably from one of the servant's houses at the bottom of the garden, and sitting on the swing seat she rocked herself back and forth. She could hear the jackals, although not in their choir like the last time she was here, but with sharp yelps and shrieks coming randomly from the blackness. She wondered if she was hearing the young practising their voices before being allowed to join their parents in collaborative song? Whether true or not, she liked the idea of it, finding the natural and ordered progression of nature soothing at such a difficult time.

**

Returning to the bedroom, she saw that one of the nightlights had gone out, and quickly took another from the drawer and lit it. She had come to see the candles as signifiers of life, rather like the bidis had been, wanting to reject any potential symbolism that was being enacted in her father's room. 'Goodnight, Daddyji,' she said, bending over to kiss his forehead. As she did this, she saw that her own narrow cot was now occupied by a sleeping Delilah, the black mantle of hair so like her aunt's, draping over the edge of the pillow to settle like a pool on the tiled floor.

As one light goes out a new one replaces it, thought Meera, rather like the young jackals outside engaged in tuning their voices to eventually replace their parents. Quietly climbing into the cot that Manju set up for himself, she acknowledged the greater force that surrounded all living things and began to recite her prayers – the whispered words floating around the room before disappearing altogether.

CHAPTER
FORTY-FIVE

Babita had now completed the first course of medication, and suffered greatly. The drug made her very sick, her mouth became sore and she itched all over, almost to the point of distraction. Dr Greene was called out twice to administer anti-sickness injections, and prescribed more tablets for the itching. The headaches had grown in intensity, and failing to get any relief from standard painkillers, she was given something much stronger. It made her woozy and sleepy, but this was preferable to the pain and so she took them. It was nearly three weeks since she had seen Mr Ellis, and she was beginning to feel better, with most of the side effects from the first course of treatment now gone.

The pain, however, had increased in her stomach, abdomen and back, and Chandu called the surgery to ask for another visit before going to work. Mr Gupta had tried to insist that they move in with him, but Babita refused. She wanted to be in her own home, she said, but the main reason was that she didn't want to be watched over all the time, nor harassed as she saw it, with constant questions about how she was feeling. Neither did she want the pity which she knew would be present in increasing amounts as time went on. That would be the worst and most inevitable outcome of her progressive illness, and she feared it would be the one thing that might break her own resolve, and the barrier that enabled her to live with the pretence needed to spare the feelings of others.

As it was, she lay quietly in bed watching television or listening to the radio, the window wide open and her quilt spread on her lap; now almost complete. April called in from time to time, and had even attached the pink satin backing using her sewing machine, leaving Babita to fix tiny sparkling beads around the quilt's edges. She could make tea, go the bathroom and prepare a simple meal for Chandu when he came home, although this was becoming more difficult since the food smells made her feel nauseous.

So far she had received seven postcards from Meera, and each was pinned to the wall where they were frequently taken down and re-read. She had only written to Meera once, describing the treatment and how sick it made her feel, but keeping the descriptions to a bare minimum; focussing instead on other things like the stories April told her about the children in her class, or the weather, or Chandu's constant fussing which made her irritable and then guilty in turn.

Dr Greene was given a key to the front door to make entry easier for both him and Babita, and had just pulled up outside. As Chandu had once done he stood for moment, looking up at the old house covered in creeper. Now late September, it was a brilliant, flaming red, and the small front garden was still full of fragrant roses and other flowers, untamed and thriving. Putting down his bag, the thoughtful doctor quickly gathered a small bunch for his patient, thinking she might appreciate the sentiment and enjoy them throughout the day. With these in his hand, he opened the door and let himself in.

Expecting him, Babita had carefully bathed and tidied the flat. She was dressed in her flowery salwar kameez, now too big but still pretty, and easier to wear than a sari which she found uncomfortable with the folds of fabric tucked around her swollen tummy. She looked at herself in the mirror, and seeing more changes to the face that peered back at her, quickly turned away. Hearing a tap on the door she let Dr Greene in, and he handed her the flowers.

'They were in the front garden, and I thought you might as well enjoy them before frosts kill them off.' As she took them, he was struck by the irony of his words and swallowed, telling himself not to be stupid or become over-emotional.

'Thank you – I shall put them right here.' She indicated a small table by the side of the bed which held a tray full of medicine bottles, as well as a small bowl of shiny beads and a sewing kit.

'Your husband called the surgery to say you were in pain all last night? Any other symptoms? How is the nausea?' he asked.

He pulled out a chair and sat down, placing his bag on the floor, with Babita sat opposite him. When he first started to visit her at home she would offer tea and biscuits, but these were always refused, and now she had stopped asking.

'Yes, we are sorry to bother you again. The pain was bad, and the tablets did not work very well. I do still feel sick at times, especially with food smells, but not like when I was taking the treatment.'

'How is your appetite?'

Babita looked down at the table. 'I try to eat, but it is hard. It feels like there is no space for it to go. If I force myself then I am sick.'

He stood up. 'Let's have a look at you. Stay where you are for minute, and I'll listen to your chest. Then, if you don't mind, lie on the edge of the bed and I'll have a feel of your tummy. No need to remove any clothes. What you have on is very thin and should be fine.'

He washed his hands at the sink, and as he examined her, the words that he said as he gave her the flowers came back to him. He swallowed again – not to quell nausea as Babita might have done, but in an unconscious attempt hold down the fear that he felt for his patient's future. 'You have another scan in a week, and that will tell us how well you have responded to the drug treatment. I want to run more blood tests and will send the nurse around to do that, probably this afternoon, if that's ok.'

Babita nodded. 'Yes, I shall be here. The masses inside me, they have not shrunk as was hoped. I have felt them myself when in the bath. What is your opinion, Doctor?'

'I can feel them too, but it isn't that simple. The scan might show areas of shrinkage that can't be felt with a hand, so we need to wait and see. Without doubt you will be given further courses of drugs, so prepare yourself for that.'

Babita nodded again.

'You need nutrition,' he continued, 'so I'm going to write a prescription for a food replacement which I want you to have at least three times a day, more if you can. I'm going to up the strength of the pain medication as well. This will be in liquid form, and I'll get the nurse to bring it round later with the supplements and show you how to take it. Oh, I nearly forgot, I've left a few surgical masks on the table to help with the food smells!'

'Thank you. You are always very kind,' she replied, walking with him to the door.

'Are you sure you're alright here on your own?' he asked. 'Wouldn't you prefer to go and stay with your friend who owns the store where your husband works?'

'Please don't worry,' Babita replied. 'I much prefer it here. I can do as I wish and am happier this way.'

When Dr Greene had gone, she arranged the flowers he had given her in a small glass vase, placing them on the bedside table next to the tablets and sewing kit. Together she thought they portrayed a simple pastiche of her life, and she lay down on her side to study them further. Leaning forward to smell a pretty pink rose placed in the centre of the bunch, she suddenly jumped back, as a large black beetle crawled out from its heart; pincers waving in warning. Feeling nauseous, she pulled out the bowl that was so recently offered to Meera, then full of warm water and petals to wash her hands in before eating. To Babita the beetle looked like a tiny devil – a harbinger of the doom that she knew was in front of her, and she retched.

It was the twin of the blackness that lay within her, and she retched again, feeling disgusted that something so vile was now slowly eating her away.

***

When Chandu came home that evening there was no supper waiting. Babita was curled up on the bed, hidden under the multicoloured quilt, with not even her face showing.

'Babi? You are sleeping?' He gently tried to peel the quilt back, and she grabbed at it from inside, trying to prevent him from revealing her.

'Babi! Stop this! Why are you hiding in this way? Sit up and we can talk. Tell me what is wrong and I will help you.'

'You cannot help. No one can help me,' came a muffled reply.

As though he were lifting a child from its cradle, he slid his arms under her body and lifted her onto his lap, the quilt partially falling away to reveal her tear-stained face, which she then covered with her hands.

'You must not look at me – please Chandu, you must not look,' she pleaded, turning to hide herself against his chest.

'What is it? Tell me, Babi. You are in pain?' He began to feel panic rise up into his throat and took a deep breath, slowly letting it out again as Dr Greene had advised him to do. Babita now started to sob, struggling to release herself from Chandu's grasp.

'I am finished, Chandu, I am finished,' she shouted. 'The devil is within me and I am finished. Do something, Chandu, do something!' Her voice became louder with each word, and finally grabbing the quilt she fell back onto the bed, tightly covering herself up again.

Hearing the shouting from below, April hurried downstairs and gently knocked on the door, then opened it and stepped inside.

'What is it?' she asked. 'Can I help? Do you think you should get the doctor? Go and call him, and I'll sit here until you get back.'

***

Half an hour later, with Dr Greene kneeling by the bedside, Babita lay still on the bed – the shouting now stopped, and the quilt covering just the lower part of her body. He had given her a sedative to calm her down, and as he talked Chandu stood to one side and watched, as usual feeling helpless.

He spoke about her illness, explaining in simple terms the way the disease might progress. He used carefully chosen words to counteract the fear that his patient clearly felt, wanting to remove any stigma that she had apportioned herself, dug up perhaps from old wives' tales heard many years ago. After each bit of information, he asked the same question, 'do you understand?' and she would nod her head, or quietly ask something which he would respond to.

'Thank you, Doctor. You are right, I became frightened and panicked. The explanations have helped. I should have asked for them before.'

'It doesn't matter, please don't worry. I'm going to give you a little more sedative so that you get a good night's sleep, and will pop in tomorrow on my rounds. We can talk again then, and I'll rearrange for the nurse to come in the afternoon with the supplements and pain relief.'

'Thank you. I was too upset to go downstairs. Please apologise to her,' replied Babita slowly, as she drifted into a deep, drug induced sleep.

CHAPTER
FORTY-SIX

The week that followed was much calmer, and Babita settled into a routine that included the new medication and food supplements. She disliked these intensely, the thick creamy texture making her retch as she swallowed. One evening, Chandu made a large pot of vegetable soup, and finding she could tolerate this well, it became the only thing she would eat. She had gone for the second scan, and two days later she and Chandu went to see the oncologist for the results.

Mr Ellis was also in the room, and together they told her that there had been no shrinkage of the tumours at all, and some had grown. She was given another course of drugs, and was offered daily visits from specialist cancer nurses, which she refused.

'I am not being difficult this time, Chandu,' she said. 'I just feel no need for it. I will feel ill, and I know this. I do not need nurses to witness it nor talk about it, and if I want this in the future I will tell Dr Greene and he will arrange it.'

He called in to see her when she was halfway through the course, and once again offered specialist support at home, but received the same reply as Chandu. The pain, however was much more under control, and arranging to see her in a few days' time, he left, feeling upset and almost as helpless a bystander as Chandu.

Mr Gupta was desperate to see Babita, but she repeatedly put him off. She had been unable to get to the store at all, and he knew that Chandu did everything in the house, including cooking and laundry. He sent him home an hour early most evenings, and even offered to find temporary staff so that he could stay home all the time. However, Babita said she didn't want it, and that was that.

Chandu had fallen apart at work on several occasions, and it broke Gupta's heart to see him this way, crying and upset one minute, then getting on with his work the next. It was like Chandu inhabited two different worlds, and in truth he supposed he did. Being in the store kept him going, and gave some normality to a situation that was becoming worse as each week passed.

Meera's father was still alive, and he missed his wife terribly. After talking to her on the phone, he made a decision that in the week following Babita's second drug treatment, he was going home with Chandu to see her, whether she liked it or not. If she died, which he feared was becoming increasingly likely, he would never forgive himself if he had not visited and spoken to her.

***

Three days after the second batch of treatment had finished, Mr Gupta agreed with Chandu that this evening was as good as any for his visit, and he went out to buy flowers and a small basket of fruit that he thought she might like. He also bought a jigsaw puzzle that Chandu said she enjoyed now that her quilt was finished, and he cut a board to go under it so that she could do it whilst in bed. He also bought some women's magazines that he knew Meera liked, piling it all into the taxi after they closed the store. He felt nervous, and so did Chandu. Neither had any idea how Babita would react, although from past experience he might end up with the flowers thrown in his face. He smiled as he thought this, and shared the idea with Chandu who laughed.

'To have the flowers thrown in your face would be a pleasant thing. But a smack, then you would know you had angered her – then you would know. Of course, you have experienced this. I forgot. Yesterday she threw yoghurt, and such a mess you would not believe.'

Like before, he spoke as though he were proud of these actions, and would clap his hands to applaud the fight that his wife still had left. Chandu the clown had made very few appearances of late, and Mr Gupta missed them.

'I would be honoured to receive a smack,' he replied, 'even two. I may just offer my face and see what happens.'

'You should prepare yourself,' Chandu said, his voice now sounding more serious. 'She is very thin, and her hair is less thick. Her colour is also not good. April from upstairs bought her new nighties as the others were all too big to wear. She is a good friend to us.'

'You have bought a gift to thank her?' Mr Gupta asked. Meera told him before she left to ensure that these things were taken care of, thinking that Chandu might be too upset to remember.

'Yes, Babita told me what to buy.'

Chandu's hand shook slightly as he pushed his key in the lock, and before letting Mr Gupta into the flat, he popped his head around the door to check that Babita was not in any situation that might compromise her modesty. Then, opening it fully, they both walked in.

'Ah,' she said, pushing a book from her knees and holding out both hands. 'I was wondering when Krishna himself would be making a call. If he left it much longer, it might have been too late.'

'No, please don't talk like this, you will become well again,' Gupta replied. Walking over to her he held the tiny, almost fleshless, hands in his own large ones, and bent to kiss her cheeks.

'I wondered if you might be angry with me for arriving like this, but you have refused me so far. If there is a slap that you would like to give, please go ahead. It will be my honour to receive it.' He proffered his face, and she reached up and pulled him closer, returning his kisses likewise.

'I have gifts. Look, flowers, and a puzzle of London bridge. I made a board to fit with edges so you can put it on your knees if you are resting in bed. These magazines are Meera's favourites – and grapes. You will eat them?'

'Yes, a few at a time,' she replied. 'Thank you. You are very generous.' An image of the nails in the cupboard so close by suddenly came to mind, and she pondered on this for a moment...

'Babita… Babita, you would like tea, or you are ready for soup?' asked Chandu.

'Tea, please. Sorry Vasu,' she said, 'the medication makes my thoughts drift a little. Tell me about Meera. You see the cards she has sent me?' There were more than twenty pinned to the wall, all much thumbed around the edges. 'She said she would send one each day, but the post is not always reliable. She has been gone six weeks now.'

Gupta stayed for almost an hour until Babita became so tired that she slid down the bed, struggling to keep her eyes open.

'I should go, I have exhausted you,' he said, standing up. She struggled to get up with him, and he reached out to hold each of her hands in his own.

'No, no, stay there. You must rest, and then you will become well.' He remembered her saying something similar to him after his accident, and once again desperately wished he could turn back time, or bargain with someone using himself as collateral to save her from this illness. He bent over to kiss the back of her hand, and placing it gently down, noticed the twist of yellow and white gold slip out from under her sleeve.

'You still wear it all the time – the bangle without beginning or end?' he asked.

'Of course,' she replied. 'I have never taken it off.'

CHAPTER
FORTY-SEVEN

The condition of Meera's father worsened, and he was now barely able to drink at all. The hand squeezing had stopped altogether, and the doctor was called once again.

'He cannot go on for much longer. His heart is weak, and I think you must accept his passing very soon. To be honest, I am amazed that he has lasted this long.' Manju showed him to the door, and beckoned Meera to follow him outside.

It was hot, and although the monsoon season was almost over, the garden still lush from the rain. Meera thought how beautiful it looked, yet how different it was from England.

'I wanted to talk about father's funeral. It's hard to know if he can hear or not, so I thought it best if we came out here,' said Manju, sitting down on a long teak bench set against the side of the house.

'Yes of course. He left instructions?'

'Detailed and precise – in writing too. There is a small crematorium on the Yamuna river not far from here. It's very quiet and private. He arranged it all some years ago.'

Meera nodded. 'Yes, he would have done this. And the ashes?'

'In the river. He has said no fuss. No one other than family, and no wailing or weeping women – no ceremony.'

In India, women were often excluded from Hindu funerals, but Meera knew that this was not what her father meant. A strong believer in emancipation, he would want her there, but would find any drama abhorrent. The family had certainly never been strict as far as religion was concerned, but she was glad he chose to follow tradition after his death.

'I am finding it hard to let go,' she said. 'He was always so strong, and if there was a problem, he could solve it – anything at all.' Tears started to trickle down her cheeks, soon outpacing her attempt to wipe them away.

'I know. All last night I was thinking these same things. My religious beliefs are dubious to say the least, and to be honest, I struggle to make sense of any of it.' He wiped away a few tears of his own, and reached for Meera's hand to hold it tightly. As though reading her thoughts, he asked about Babita.

Meera shook her head. 'Vasu says he visited her, and she was resting in bed. They spoke for some time, but he cried on the phone, Manju, he cried! For him to do this? I am almost out of my mind with worry.'

'You must leave as soon as the ashes are in the river. Father said this must be done at sunrise the next day with no days of mourning, and he is right. I would also want this. Would you like to see the letter he wrote?' asked Manju.

'No need,' replied his sister.

'You shall see the will, of course. Everything is left jointly to you and me; all fair and square.'

'Just like Daddyji,' said Meera.

'Yes, just like him.'

***

The following evening, Meera opened the windows of her father's room. The air smelt stale and it was warm outside, with a gentle breeze blowing. She lit a small incense cone and quietly moved around, dusting and tidying, the light fading as the sun began to set. Suddenly, a gust of wind flew in, sending the light curtains billowing into the room, and instantly snuffing out the candles.

Despite the warmth, Meera shivered, once again fearful of the symbolism being played out in front of her. As before, she quickly relit them with shaking hands, desperate to hold together the tangible fracture of time that she had just witnessed. Overwhelmed with grief she began to cry, not just for her father's imminent death, but for her own fragmented self. Images of her long-dead mother came to mind, and then, out of nowhere, came the smiling face of Babita, leaning over her in the park under the cedar tree – trying to wake her up.

Unaware of what had just taken place, Manju came into the room and sat beside the bed, carefully straightening the sheets and pushing back a few stray silver hairs that had blown across his father's forehead. Looking up, he saw

Meera's tear-stained face, and reached out a hand towards her. 'Come, Sister, and sit beside me for a while. It will soon be time, I think.'

Their father died two hours later, his eyes firmly closed; no smoke rising, no movement to be seen. His children were beside him, his hands held tightly in theirs, each wanting to never let go, yet knowing that they had no choice. The bidi smoke had been a signifier of life, and its absence, death. He had played his part with all the ingenuity and brilliance that he had and, if only for a brief moment, the family stage was empty – its curtains drawn back, yet denying entry to any interlopers until every last floating fragment of breath had gone. Then, after a few moments silence, the performance was over.

***

The following evening, Manju and Meera stood on the steps that overlooked the river, their father's pyre in front of them, waiting to be lit. There were fires on the other side of the shore where more cremations were taking place, and the red sun hung over them all as it made its slow journey downwards, until it could be seen no more.

How very fitting, thought Meera, as Manju stepped forward with a flaming torch in his hand, to release their father's spirit from the body that it no longer required. Suvi and the children stood further back, all four of them far taller than their mother. This reminded Meera of her thoughts about the jackals and the way of all living things, in replacing that which had preceded them.

Dressed in white, she realised that a shift had now

taken place amongst them, all one step further down the road to their own death. Manju came back to stand beside his sister, the pyre now well ablaze – the smell of incense floating heavily on the air.

The following morning, just as the sun was coming up, they went back to the Yamuna alone. Sitting on the steps with the glowing sun reflecting on the dark water, they scattered their father's ashes into the river that would carry him on his final journey, and to the next life that awaited him. They stayed until the sun was fully risen, then standing up Manju held out his hand.

'Come, Sister,' he said. 'You now have a different journey to make.'

***

At the house, her father's room had already been thoroughly cleaned, and the mattress and cots removed.

'As though they are trying to erase him,' she said aloud, although knew that this was a ritual that took place after death, stemming from a need to remove any disease that might remain. Going to the desk, she took out the perfume bottle to put in her case to take home, then went to bathe and change her clothes.

Manju booked her flight for two days' time, and the following afternoon he took her shopping. They were both subdued, but she wanted to buy things for Babita, and this would be her last chance to do so. After dinner, they sat outside and talked.

'I have decided to definitely stay in England for the summer next year with Delilah – six weeks in total. I am owed the time from work, and a change of scenery will be a good thing.'

'I shall look forward to it. We can show Delilah the city, and can visit Devi in Oxford if he stays there for the summer. I shall discuss things with Vasu, and will let you know.'

She wanted to spend her last evening sleeping outside, and just two charpoys were set up, her nephews and Suvi preferring to sleep in the house. Upset by her grandfather's death, Delilah had gone to stay with a friend, and two hours later just Meera and Manju lay under the stars, side by side.

'I think I will not be back for a while, Brother, so it is good that you will come next year. I keep wanting to look behind me, expecting to see father with his bidi – smoke rising upwards.'

'I know. I do this all the time,' he replied. 'I think it will be my last memory of him and the one that will stay with me.'

Disappointingly, the jackals were silent, and Meera lay awake thinking about what she would find in England on her return. She had not spoken to Mr Gupta for a couple of days, and had tried to call him earlier, waiting for a long time only to be cut off without warning. From here on, she decided, her job would be to look after Babita, and she would go to visit her the morning after she was back to see what was needed. She fell asleep to the sound of her brother's gentle snoring, but woke with a jolt a few hours later. Disorientated for a moment, she sat up and looked around her, seeing nothing unusual.

'What is it?' asked Manju, also sitting up quickly, then

lying back down again. 'Ah, your choir has returned to serenade your departure, is that not so?'

He was right. It was a fitting finale to her stay in India, and also of her father's life, and she settled back on her pillow, tears streaming down her face unchecked.

CHAPTER
FORTY-EIGHT

Babita continued to deteriorate, and now struggled to walk for any distance, even around the flat, without becoming breathless. On Monday, Chandu went with her for the scan, three weeks after the completion of the last drug treatment. Feeling unable to repeat the journey two days later to see the oncologist, Dr Greene agreed to visit her that afternoon with the results and any plans for further treatment. She hadn't told her husband this, saying that the date had been moved to the end of the week, and he would be able to accompany her to the hospital then. She was lying on the bed when the doctor arrived, and called out for him to enter when she heard him come up the stairs.

He looked around the room for Chandu, who he expected to be there. 'Your husband isn't here?' he asked. 'I would much rather he was. You shouldn't have to discuss these issues without him, and to be honest, I'm not happy about it.'

'Dr Greene, I prefer to do this on my own. I know what you are going to say, and Chandu will be very upset. You do not seem to understand, none of you do, that this places extra burden upon me to make sure he is alright. I am tired – I no longer have the strength for it.'

He sat on the chair by the side of the bed, and let out a sigh. He understood what she was saying, but he too felt a huge burden, and greatly appreciated the quiet presence of her husband. Though lacking confidence, he thought Chandu had much to offer, and believed him capable of far more than she so often gave him credit for. 'I do understand,' he replied, 'but I think you are wrong. I will discuss the scan results with you, I have no choice, but I shall come again after surgery on Friday to have a further discussion with you both. He'll be back from work by then, and we can make a plan together. Agreed?'

She smiled. 'You are becoming quite a negotiator, Doctor. Very well, then. Agreed!' Now devoid of her rings because they were too big, she held out her tiny hand which he shook gently, fully aware of her frailty.

'How are you managing the pain?' he asked. 'I think the nurse brought more morphine yesterday?'

'Yes, I have plenty. I do what she says and take regular amounts. At night sometimes it is worse, and I take a little more.'

'Good, that's fine. The scan results showed no reduction in the size of the tumours. I'm sorry.' He hung his head as though it were his fault, and Babita reached out to pat his knee.

'I already knew. Please, you must not blame yourself. I knew at the very beginning – you also.'

He nodded. 'It might be best if you were to move to a hospice where your care could be managed constantly.' He had mentioned this before, as well as specialist nurses throughout the day, but she refused everything. 'Or Chandu needs to stay home. Surely his employer would allow him the time off in the circumstances?'

'Of course he would. May I discuss these options with him, and on Friday we can tell you our decision?'

This was quite a turnaround, and Dr Greene was surprised but greatly relieved to hear her response. He got up. 'Can I get you anything before I go? Would you like some tea?'

'Only if you have some with me,' she replied.

***

When the doctor had gone, Babita slowly got up and washed the tea cups. She was in pain, but ignoring this she went to the drawer, pulling out the ochre silk sari with the green velvet border that Meera had bought for her. She pulled off her nightie and dressed herself carefully, winding the sari in the correct way to make the folds at the front. It was extremely difficult. She felt weak, and her upper arms shook as she tried to hold the fabric in the right place before tucking it over her distended stomach.

Now totally exhausted, she sat on the edge of the bed and brought her head down so that she could brush her hair without the effort of raising her arms. Opening the small wooden box that held her jewellery, she put the rings on first, keeping her fingers slightly curled so that they wouldn't fall off. She then carefully picked up the earrings that Meera had given her for her birthday. Slowly fixing them to her lobes, she shook her head slightly so that they swung against the sides of her face, and enjoying the fluttering of the cool metal on her cheeks, she repeated this gesture several times. Feeling like she was moving in slow motion she stood up again, and suddenly overcome with dizziness, clung onto the side-table until it passed. She picked up two bottles from her medicine tray, and making sure the window was open as wide as it would go, leaned out for a moment to look at the autumn colours of the leaves, glowing in the bright sun.

Slowly lowering herself into the armchair, she sat back and let out a sigh of relief. The time had come, and she was glad. She had suffered enough, and the thought of continuing to inflict pain on those most dear to her could no longer be borne. Chandu now wore the look of a hunted animal, and she wanted to ensure that his torture was brought to an end. Meera would soon be back, perhaps in a few days, and she too would be devastated by what lay waiting for her; a person not dead, not alive, but halfway – a position for which there was not even a name. Krishna would care for them both, she knew that. His strength surpassed all of theirs put together. He was like a fortress at the top of a mountain, and would provide safe shelter for as long as it was needed.

Taking the top from both bottles, she carefully drank the bitter fluid until every drop was gone. Closing her eyes her head fell back, and her body relaxed into the chair and beyond it; floating like a bird in the sky on a warm summer evening. Now soaring, then diving low and rising up again, she saw other birds to either side of her – beautiful white swans formed in an arrow and flying away for the winter. Feeling the strength in her wings and the wind in her feathers, her heart soared as she flew and, aiming towards the sun, Babita knew that she was going home.

***

When Chandu arrived back that evening, shopping bags in his hands, he immediately saw his wife in the chair on the other side of the room. Assuming she was asleep, he quietly set about making himself a meal, and attended to the other duties that were now his responsibility, including making another batch of soup. A few hours later and wanting to go to bed, he crept over to where she sat, reclining comfortably on the chair with her head to one side.

He reached out to gently shake her. 'Babi, wake up, it is time for a little soup, and then bed.' Her arm felt cold and stiff, and worried that she had become chilled, he quickly moved to the other side of the chair to see her face. Her eyes were open and unblinking, and her mouth seemed to be smiling, yet still she made no response. Now scared, he shook her again, this time more roughly and with both hands. 'Babi,' he shouted. 'Babita, wake up! Stop playing games.'

Suddenly feeling weak he dropped to his knees, and at the same time saw two empty bottles lying on the floor. He looked at her again, now noticing the best sari and jewellery. Then something in his brain clicked. He heard the noise of it quite clearly. It sounded like a door closing, and feeling momentarily confused he stood up and looked around him. All was as it should be, familiar and safe, and as though he suddenly understood, he picked up the blanket from the arm of the chair and gently draped it over his wife, tucking the sides in carefully.

'Sleep here, then,' he said. 'You need rest, and tomorrow you can eat soup all day long and build up your strength.' Still fully clothed he climbed onto the bed, pulling the patchwork quilt over him and closing his eyes, shivering slightly despite the thick cover. Barely moving at all, he remained awake for the entire night, his mind devoid of any thoughts of Babita, or the hardware store, or anything that he might have to face the following day.

Sensing the stillness that had descended upon the room, a small spider came out from its hiding space in the cupboard under the stairs. Oblivious to the events of the evening it began a nocturnal forage for food, returning just before dawn to a web of its own making behind the tins of dusty nails. Although no longer marking time or suffering at the hands of Mr Gupta, they were, perhaps, still symbolic of the torment that was to come for the small Indian man hiding like a child under the quilt made by his dear dead wife.

Time may have stopped for Babita, but for Chandu it would continue, this now manifest by the rising of the sun which shone through the window and onto the bed; slowly warming the multicoloured quilt, and the broken man beneath it.

CHAPTER
FORTY-NINE

The following morning, and for the first time ever, Chandu was ten minutes late for work. Mr Gupta thought he looked dishevelled. His clothes were creased, his hair was in disarray, and immediately he felt concerned. 'Are you alright?' he asked. 'Would you like to use the bathroom? Please make yourself breakfast if you have not had time to eat. I know you have a lot to do at home.'

Chandu said nothing, but went upstairs, coming back down fifteen minutes later looking more like his old, dapper self.

'Do you not think it would be a good thing to go home at lunchtimes? I know Babita has resisted, but you might feel better if you did. Take a taxi. I will pay.'

Chandu agreed. 'Yes, this is a good idea. I can then make sure that she eats, and if she objects I will tell her the order has come from Krishna!'

'Yes,' Gupta replied. 'Tell her that, and please, there is no need to rush. I can manage alone for a few hours. Also tell her that I shall be visiting again this weekend, and to place an order for anything she requires to keep her amused. Meera should be home within a week, but until then these duties belong to me.'

A little happier, although not entirely, he watched Chandu carefully throughout the day. As agreed, he left at twelve to go home, refusing a taxi, saying he would walk quickly as the exercise would do him good. As though in a trance, he went to a small park around the corner and sat there for an hour – seeing and hearing nothing. Then, guided by instinct, he got up and walked back to the store.

'That was quick!' said Mr Gupta. 'Is everything alright?'

'Yes, all fine. She was sleeping, and there is soup made last night, so I came back.'

Although very busy, Chandu was sent home early with instructions to eat a good meal and rest. Throughout the day he had behaved like an automaton – swishing the mop across the floor, unpacking boxes and taking money at the till, these tasks established through years of repetition. His care of Babita had now been added to this list, and staring straight ahead he walked home and let himself into the flat. The window was still wide open and a few leaves had blown in, landing on the floor by the sink. He picked these up, and looking across to Babita still covered in the blanket exactly as he left her last night, his brain gave another click. As though in rewind, he remembered that she needed to eat, and heated soup made the previous evening.

Picking up the small table that held her medicines, he now put this beside her chair. The flowers he had bought her were dead, and he threw these away before rearranging the bottles and jars carefully. Then he placed a large mug of hot soup next to her, and spoke. There was no voice as in normal speech, not that anyone would hear. The voice was in his head only, but to him it sounded as it always had. 'You must eat the soup, Babi. It is hot, so you can rest a little longer and then it will be ready.' He nodded his head as though she had replied, and like the previous night he crept fully dressed under the multicoloured quilt and slept. A few hours later there was a light tapping on the door, and Chandu stirred, hearing April calling his name.

'Chandu? Are you there? Babita?' She knocked again, this time a little louder, but there was no response. She tried the handle but the door was locked, which was unusual. She often called in to see Babita when she got home from work, but there had been meetings, both last night and tonight after school, and this had prevented her from doing so. She looked at her watch – not even eight, but maybe they had decided on an early night, or just wanted to be alone? Not entirely reassured she began to climb the stairs to her own flat, deciding she would try again tomorrow. If she still couldn't get in, then she would call Mr Gupta at the store.

***

Although on time the following morning, Chandu looked even more dishevelled than the previous day and once again, Mr Gupta sent him upstairs to wash and eat some breakfast. The store was very busy, but he still insisted that Chandu go home to check on Babita and have a break. He had called Meera the previous evening, but unable to get through he intended to try again later. If he wasn't happy after his visit on Sunday then he would call the doctor, and extra care would need to be arranged. With this plan made he relaxed a little and, that evening, after the shop had closed, he climbed the stairs to the flat feeling easier in mind.

***

Chandu arrived home early, and emptied Babita's still-full mug into the sink. He boiled a kettle to make tea, and using her favourite china cup and saucer placed it on the side table and stood in front of her, his mind speaking the silent words that no one else could hear. 'I am back. You are very naughty, Babi, to not drink the soup. I shall tell the doctor and you will be given supplements.' He screwed up his face as though it were he that disliked the taste so much, then carefully retucked the blanket around her before climbing into bed. He was woken about an hour later by loud knocking on the door, and pulled the quilt further over his head to shut out the noise.

'Babita? Chandu? Are you in there? It's April, please let me in.' She had tried to visit Babita earlier, but finding the door still locked and with no response to her calling out, she went back upstairs, leaving her own door open so that she could hear Chandu when he arrived home. Hearing footsteps an hour later, she crept to the top of the stairs to see him going into their room, quietly closing the door behind him. Feeling relieved, she waited for another half an hour then went down to try again. 'Chandu? Babita? It's April.' She paused for moment to listen, and hearing no sound at all, knocked louder, then tried the handle to see if she could get in. Like the previous evening it was locked. She was now feeling very concerned, and banged again, this time with her fist. 'Chandu? I know you're in there!' she shouted. 'Open the door! It's April, and I'm worried about you both.' Hearing a noise behind her, she turned to see Dr Greene hurrying up the stairs, leather bag in hand. He had heard her shouting as he let himself in, and standing beside her he too banged the door with his fist, making it rattle in its frame.

'You're sure they're in there?' he asked.

'I saw Chandu go in about half an hour ago, although I was beginning to wonder if Babita had been taken to hospital?'

'Not that I know of, and I'm sure I would have been told as I'm listed as her main medical support. Something's wrong. Stand back, I'm going to try to force the lock – it looks quite loose already. I'd rather not take any chances...'

April moved away as he rammed his shoulder against the door – repeating this until it flew open and hit the wall behind it, then swung back and forth a few times until it stopped. Part of the frame had splintered, but the lock was still intact and he rushed in, April following closely behind. Babita was in the chair at the far end of the room; a blanket tucked neatly around her. Almost running across the room he gently touched her neck, quickly realising that she was dead, and most likely had been for a while.

'She's dead?' asked April, her heart pounding in her chest.

'I'm afraid so – perhaps for a day or two.' At that moment they both heard a scrabbling behind them as Chandu flung off the quilt and flew out of the room; fully clothed, but with bare feet and a look of terror on his face.

'Chandu,' called Dr Greene. 'Chandu, come back, it's alright – come back!' He ran after him, but already outside Chandu slammed the front door and was gone. April began to cry, and the doctor put his arm around her, thinking for a moment. 'I'd better call the police and an ambulance.'

'But surely…'

Knowing what she was going to say, he answered quickly. 'There will need to be an autopsy, so she'll have to go to hospital. The police need to find Chandu, and fast. The poor man will need help. It's probably best if you go back to your own flat, and I'll tell the police where they can find you. They'll probably want a statement.'

'Yes, of course,' replied April, deeply shaken, despite her outward calm.

Gently taking his arm from her shoulder, he followed her back into the hall. 'Will you be OK? Is there anyone who could come and sit with you for a while?' he asked.

April thought for a moment. 'Yes, I have a friend who lives not far from here. I'll phone her when you've finished.'

'Good,' he replied. 'It might help to have someone there when the police arrive.' After she left, he went downstairs to use the telephone. Miss Grant was stood beside her door, and he reassured her as best he could. 'An ambulance will be here soon, so it would probably be best if you go back into your flat.' As soon as her door was closed he made the calls and then went to wait outside. Far more distressed than his professional front allowed him to show, he took a deep breath and let it out slowly, like he had taught Chandu to do. As he waited, he wondered what he could have done differently – anything at all that might have changed the terrible events that had unfolded over the past few days. He could think of nothing. Each person had played their part, he included, all trapped within the confines of law, duty and the complexities of love.

He had asked for no sirens, and the police pulled up quietly outside the gate, then followed him into the house. April had just put the phone down after calling her friend, and stopped him for a moment.

'I think I should call Mr Gupta. He's Chandu's employer and a close friend, you see. He might know where to look for him. It'll be dark soon, and I can't bear to think of him outside, cold and frightened, and not even shoes on his feet.'

'I agree,' replied Dr Greene. 'Hang on...' He ran up the stairs, and a few minutes later, called back down. 'Go ahead. The police are going to put a search call out, but the sooner he's found the better!'

CHAPTER
FIFTY

Mr Gupta had just tried to call Meera, and once again was unable to get through. This was not unusual since calling India was notoriously difficult, but he wanted to talk to her about Chandu, and ask when she was coming home. Feeling deeply frustrated, he went into the kitchen to make himself tea, and had just filled the kettle when he heard noises coming from downstairs. The kitchen was directly over the storeroom, and he stood still for a moment, kettle in hand, to listen.

At first he heard nothing, then... there it was again, scraping and banging sounds as though furniture was being dragged around. Thinking someone had broken in through the back door, he quickly went to the phone and called the police. Then bolting the door up to the flat, he went to stand by the window and wait for them to arrive.

Some ten minutes later he heard a siren, and watched

as they pulled up outside. Leaning out of the window, he shouted down to the street. 'At the back! They have entered through the rear door.' Deciding that it would now be safe, he crept down the stairs, switching on the shop lights when he reached the bottom. He could hear the police shouting, and encouraged by their presence, put his hand inside the door to the storeroom then switched on the light.

'Over here, sir. We've got him – he isn't armed,' called one of the officers.

Mr Gupta hurried to where they were stood and looked down to see a small bedraggled figure huddled in the corner, head covered with his hands, and no shoes on his dirty feet.

'C'mon, up you get.' Grabbing the intruder by his shirt, the policemen hauled him into a standing position.

Mr Gupta gasped with shock as he recognised the man in front of him. 'Officers, I am so sorry, there has been a mistake. This is my employee and friend.' He reached across to gently push back the hair from Chandu's face in order to look at him properly.

'Chandu, what is going on? Why are you here... and looking like this?'

A two-way radio then burst into life, and a minute later one of the policemen replied. 'It's OK, he's here. We've got him – he's at the hardware store.'

Chandu began to shake, and thinking he might collapse Mr Gupta put an arm around his waist and almost carried him up the stairs, the police following closely behind. He sat him down then placed a thick blanket over his shoulders just as the phone rang. Thinking it might be Meera, he went to answer it.

'Excuse me, officers, this is important,' he said. It wasn't Meera, but April, and he listened in silence, interrupting only once to tell her that Chandu was safe. 'Thank you, April, thank you. Please also thank the doctor.'

Making tea for them all, an exhausted Mr Gupta sat down. Chandu had stopped shaking, and sipping the hot drink he looked around him, his eyes constantly returning to Gupta, as though fearing he might be left at the mercy of the uniformed men sat at the other side of the table. 'Chandu,' he said. 'You are safe. No one will harm you whilst I am here. Soon you can have a bath and go to bed, but first, please tell us what has happened. The officers are only here to help.' Mr Gupta felt like he was talking to a child, and continuing to coax and encourage, Chandu's story was told.

***

Two hours later Chandu had taken a bath, and wearing pyjamas that were four sizes too big, was soon fast asleep in the spare room.

Mr Gupta was also in bed, reflecting on the evening that had just passed. Babita was dead. These were the words that kept coming to him. Babita was dead, and the poor soul that was her husband had continued to make her food and tea – sleeping in the bed they shared, and coming to work the next morning. He tried to grasp an image of her from his memory, but just as the face came into focus, it slipped away again into the darkest and most unreachable recesses of his mind.

'Unjust!' he said, angrily. It was unjust that someone

like Babita should have suffered in this way, with Chandu being driven to the very brink of insanity. But since when had justice played any part in the lives of so many people around the world? They were just two more to face the backlash of an unknown degenerate force that lashed out when least expected. Much to the confusion of the police officers, throughout the interview Chandu had repeatedly referred to him as Krishna, and feeling totally alone he now called upon his namesake to help him, and give him strength in the days ahead.

'Help me, Krishna,' he whispered. 'Help me...'

CHAPTER
FIFTY-ONE

A few hours from landing, Meera had spent much of the flight asleep. The plane was full, and once again she was forced into a position of silence; the man to her side keeping his head hidden behind a book, making it very clear that he didn't want to talk. Now desperate to be back, she began to plan the days ahead. Like last time, Mr Gupta had no idea that she was arriving. She had tried to call but was told that all the lines were busy, eventually deciding that she would phone from the airport, and take a taxi from there.

When she thought of Babita she found it hard to breathe, placing a hand on her chest to monitor the racing heartbeats and try to slow them down. Soon, she said to herself. Soon you will be there, and can feed her and give her strength to fight the illness. Her mind flitting from one thing to another, she thought about Manju and

Delilah coming for the following summer. Where would they sleep? There was only one spare room, and to sleep on the sofa for six weeks was too much for any of them.

Before she left, she agreed with her brother to sell a piece of land for development on the other side of town. This would bring a sizable amount of money for each of them. She would need to talk to Vasu again about moving. It was a conversation that had been raised many times, both knowing it was a good idea, but neither having the impetus to make it happen. Now it would happen, she thought. A nice house near to the store, and Babita and Chandu could have the flat. She would give it to them for nothing but knew they would object, deciding to suggest the smallest amount that she knew they would accept. Her thoughts went to Babita – so pale and thin, and she closed her eyes, overcome with fear.

Noticing the heavy breathing and heaving bosom, the man behind the book congratulated himself on not starting any conversation with the Indian lady by his side. Checking his watch, he turned the page – relieved that there was just one more hour to go.

***

After landing Meera collected her case, then searched for a payphone to call her husband. Each one she came across had a long queue of people waiting, and swearing under her breath she gave up and went outside.

She gave the cab driver the address, and making herself comfortable recalled the last time she had made the same journey. The flight had been later that time, and it was dark outside... In an instant, Meera decided she would go straight to Babita's. It would only be about nine-thirty when she got there – not too late, and they would probably be watching television. She could call Mr Gupta from the payphone in the hall, and go home an hour later. Leaning forward, she knocked against the dividing glass and spoke to the driver. 'I have changed my mind and now want a different address!'

Raising his eyes, he listened politely to the beautiful Indian lady sitting behind him. 'No problem, love,' he replied. 'No problem at all.'

Happy with this decision, she settled back in the seat and dozed in her taxi cocoon – the city slipping by in a constant stream of bright lights and people. Forty minutes later she found herself standing on the pavement, her suitcase beside her and a large bunch of keys in her hand. It was dark, and finally finding the right one she let herself into the house. The case was heavy as she dragged it behind her, bumping it up each step, eventually arriving outside Babita and Chandu's door. Unused to visiting in the evening the whole house seemed very quiet, and she knocked gently before calling out.

'Chandu? Babita? It is me, Meera.' Hearing a noise, she turned to see April coming down the stairs towards her. She looked as though she had been crying, and suddenly feeling anxious her heart began to pound. 'What is it? What is wrong?' she asked. 'April?' Without waiting for an answer, she began to fumble with the keys again, trying to find the right one for the flat door.

'No, wait!' April reached out to hold Meera's hand. 'I need to talk to you. Please... just for a moment, come upstairs. I'll take the case.'

Meera followed her in silence. She felt close to fainting... Something was wrong, she knew that – very wrong. 'What is it, please tell me. Is it Babita? Chandu? April, tell me!'

Sitting down beside her and holding her hand tightly, April began to describe in detail what had happened, starting with her concern from the previous day through to the events of that evening – Dr Greene's forced entry and finding Babita, then Chandu's fleeing. At first, Meera didn't respond. Realising she was in shock, April continued to hold her hand and patiently waited, knowing that she would speak when ready to do so. Tears began to slide down Meera's cheeks, and April got up to fetch tissues, gently wiping her face with shaking hands. Eventually, her voice broken with suppressed emotion, Meera spoke.

'Chandu? Where is he? He is safe?' she asked.

'Yes,' replied April. 'He's with your husband at the store. The police found him there. They believe that Babita deliberately took an overdose of her medication...'

'Yes, she would do this to prevent more suffering for him. This is how she was. Also, she hated to be touched and viewed by strangers. Traditional Indian ladies are often like this, but she... even in front of me she was unhappy to remove clothes.'

'She was a lovely person. I shall miss her.'

'Lovely?' Meera thought for a moment. 'Yes, she was this word, but more – far, far more.' She stood up. 'Thank you, April. You have been very kind. I must go now.'

'Shall I call you a cab?'

'No. I am going downstairs to the flat. Thank you again, but please – do not disturb me there or call my husband. I need to be alone.'

'Yes, of course, I understand. Will you be alright?'

Outside the Kumar's door, and with the hallway fully lit, she could now see the damaged frame. Despite being loose, the key still fit, and she let herself into the dark room. When everyone had left earlier that evening, the always-open window was firmly closed, and Meera went to open it again. Babita's body was shut in a frozen box in a hospital, and until she was cremated this was how the window must stay, in case any part of her had remained, perhaps waiting for her friend to come.

No longer crying, Meera switched on the light and looked around her. The bed was unmade, and in the corner was the chair that Babita had died in. Walking towards it, she saw that the blanket was now placed over the back; the soft cushion still showing where her dearest friend had so recently sat. How strange, she thought, that even when we are gone, our body still leaves its imprint behind for others to see.

She wanted to light incense, and got down on her knees to open the cupboard where she knew it was kept. Taking out the small box, she was about to close the door when something caught her eye. Tucked into the corner was the toiletry set she had given to Babita some years before, telling her to use straight away and not keep it for any special occasion. That Babita had gone without hurt Meera greatly, and more tears began to stream down her face.

'Oh, Babita,' she cried. 'Babita, come back... come back... I am still here, and you have left me behind... come back...' Sobbing as though her heart would break, she crawled to the bed and pulled off the patchwork quilt that Babita had sewn. Curling up under the open window, with the quilt wrapped tightly around her, she continued to call for her friend; the words now turned into a ceaseless chant of lament that filled the room with sorrow.

***

Unable to sleep, Mr Gupta telephoned India again, and was told by Manju that Meera left yesterday. 'I think she may have gone straight to her friend, Babita. She was so worried.'

Quickly explaining what had happened the previous evening, and realising what Meera would discover when she got to the boarding house, Gupta agreed. 'You might be right. I shall leave now to look for her and will call you later.'

Hearing someone come up the stairs and stop outside the Kumars' door, April hurried down and told Mr Gupta about Meera's arrival last night, and her request to be left alone. Asking her to wait, he used Chandu's keys to open the door to the flat and went inside. At first, he couldn't see her, and looking around the room again, his eyes were drawn to the open window. Then he saw the huddled figure beneath it, almost entirely covered with Babita's patchwork quilt.

'Meera, I was so worried.' Helping her up from the floor, she flung her arms around his neck and clung to him.

'Vasu, she is dead. Babita is dead,' she cried.

'Come, let us go home and we can talk – the taxi is waiting. Look, here is April, she will take you down.'

Hearing her name, April stepped into the room. 'Can I help?' she asked.

'April, please can you take Meera to the taxi and I will be down in few minutes.' Putting her case and bag in the hall, he quickly tidied the room, stopping for a moment to study the rows of postcards pinned to the wall – sent by Meera every day, just as she promised. The final one was of two swans floating on a lake towards a beautiful sunset, and shaking his head, he sighed – his eyes filling with tears.

Closing the window and securing it firmly, he took one last look around the room, before locking the door and going downstairs to his waiting wife.

***

The cremation was held a week later. Utterly simple and without a service of any kind, Chandu, Meera and Vasu stood and watched as the coffin disappeared. Babita's body was wrapped in the quilt she had made, and when her ashes were collected the next day, they were scattered in the park that she loved so much.

Devastated by their loss, the three clung together in the bleak winter months that followed, all waiting for a spring that would bring new hope, and lift away the clouds that had hung over them for so long. As Babita thought, Mr Gupta, or Krishna, both one and the same, did all he could to remain strong and provide shelter for Chandu and Meera. He was indeed a fortress at the top of a mountain, and with this care, the ice slowly began to thaw.

CHAPTER
FIFTY-TWO

1976

'Vasu? I need to talk to you.' Meera walked into the bedroom where her husband was lying on the bed, watching television.

'As always, my dear, I am all ears. What is it?' he asked, turning down the volume and sitting up.

'Manju and Delilah will be here in four months,' she replied. 'Where will they sleep? With the paint and screwdrivers? Or shall we put them in the storeroom and they can unload the deliveries straight from their beds?'

Mr Gupta smiled. To hear his wife talking like this again was an enormous relief after so much misery, and he felt like bursting into song. 'I imagine you already have an answer prepared for me,' he replied, 'so, please just tell me what it is. I will agree and there is an end to it.'

'This is serious, Vasu. We must move. Even if Chandu was not here, there would still be no room. A girl of seventeen cannot sleep on a sofa for six weeks, and Manju has a bad back.'

'We could sleep in the storeroom, and Chandu on the shelves with the paint! There is your solution. Finish my dinner – I am starving.'

Meera took a few steps forward, and raised a hand as though she were about to slap him.

He laughed, reached out for her hand, and kissed it. 'Stop! Very well. Tomorrow you must get house details. I agree that it is time we moved. Somewhere nearby and Chandu can have the flat.'

Now happy, she heaved a sigh of relief, and went back into the kitchen. At dinner, she broached the subject with Chandu, not wanting him to feel insecure or worried in any way if he overheard them discussing it.

'You would rather I left? I can find a room – I have stayed too long.'

Meera knew he would respond like this. She had already given it a lot of thought, and began to execute her strategy with all the cunning she had... 'Chandu, you do not understand. For you to leave would not be possible. The shop could have no insurance with the flat empty, or if it did, the cost would be too great. To rent it to others is also impossible because there is no separate entrance. If you do not stay, then we cannot move, and my brother and Delilah will have to cancel their holiday.'

Mr Gupta watched and listened. His wife was a master of manipulation, and he could do nothing but sit back and admire her skill.

'Then I will stay, but I must pay rent. I know that I give money for food, but to stay here and pay nothing will make me very unhappy,' replied Chandu.

Mr Gupta sat up. Now here was something. Chandu was fully aware of what was going on and was coming in with a counter offer.

'Very well,' said Meera, 'but not so much, because to have you here will save us money in the end. There will also be more responsibility for you, with Mr Gupta elsewhere at night.'

'Please, can this negotiation be concluded and then I can eat in peace,' interrupted her husband.

'Patience, Mr Gupta, these things cannot be hurried,' replied his wife. Eventually a sum was agreed, and Meera let out a long breath, finally free to pursue her move with an easy conscience. Yes, she thought, it was a fresh start for them all, and this could only be a good thing.

Chandu had never gone back to the room where he lived with Babita. The things he wanted to keep were brought over in a van, and the tenancy was surrendered. Babita would never be left behind. They spoke about her every day, remembering things she had said and done, and still shed tears for what they had lost. Chandu had changed, and never smiled or played the clown like he had done before, but not so much time had passed, and maybe he would find some happiness in his life again? She hoped so...

As Meera's own hurt crept further to the back of her mind, her relationship with her husband came even more to the fore. He was now at the centre of her life, and she, his. She knew that this type of relationship wouldn't suit everyone, but for her it was the very essence of happiness, and her joy in this was without measure.

Her friendship with Babita would never be matched or replaced – she was quite sure about that. The two had shared a bond so strong that when severed, she was flung to the outer reaches of reason, and to the margins where all those who have loved and lost wandered; some for a short while to heal their wounds, and others for eternity, unable to repair the damage that had been done.

As he threatened to do if she stayed in India for too long, Mr Gupta watched and waited, and when she was ready, he had indeed brought her home.

CHAPTER
FIFTY-THREE

The Guptas bought their new house. Just a few minutes' walk from the store, it was an Edwardian end of terrace, with a large bay window to the front, and small walled garden at the rear. Meera loved it, and decorators were brought in to be bullied and harassed by the striking Indian lady dressed in glittering saris, who wore her hair in a twisted plait on the top of her head.

At first, they were somewhat intimidated by her direct approach, and took it in turns to ask questions, as well as taking extra care to meet her exacting standards. As time went on they began to relax, appreciating the Indian delicacies she made, her constant good humour, and genuine interest in their wives and children. Soon, they started to replicate her style, bringing news from home, and replying with banter and teasing of their own.

The move changed little in their working lives, and

several evenings each week Chandu would arrive for his dinner and stay for a while, watching television with Mr Gupta or playing cards. Meera kept a close eye on him to see if living alone would send him into a downward spiral, but this had not been the case. He shopped for food, kept everything clean, still enjoyed his work and remained very popular with the customers. He seemed to revel in having his own private space, and welcomed their visits to the flat; his own television now proudly displayed in the sitting room, and almost always on.

Manju and Delilah had arrived three weeks ago; the Guptas' new house providing ample space for them all. Manju looked tired and his spirits were low, but this improved as the days went by, and he seemed genuinely happy to be there. One afternoon when Delilah was helping out in the shop, he told Meera about his divorce from Suvi which was already underway.

'We both knew it had to happen. She was as miserable as I was and, as you know, spends most of her time with her family anyway. We have spoken to the children, not that any of them are that anymore. Delilah is the only one not at college, and she wants to study in London next year. The house will be there for them, of course, in the holidays or whenever they need it, and don't forget – it is your house too. I shall be buying an apartment in the city for during the week, and will go back there at weekends. That's it.'

'You are sure you want this?' Meera asked, studying his face carefully for any emotions he might have that hadn't been voiced.

'Of course. We simply couldn't keep up the pretence any longer.'

'Do you think you will marry again?' she asked, relieved to see him speak calmly, both resigned to and accepting the unavoidable.

'Highly unlikely. I shall throw myself into doing good works, which is where I see my future, as well as spending time with the children if they want it. I shall come here more too. I'm hoping to be working less, and am trying to sort something out about that.'

'This is your home, Brother. Come anytime.' The previous week they had all gone to Oxford to see Devi, Manju's eldest son, who proudly showed them around the ancient city as though he had lived there all his life. Soon there would be more of their family here than in India! Meera sighed. Everything kept changing, and she struggled to keep up with it.

'A big sigh, Sister.'

'Yes, it will be strange to have them both so near, and also a joy. You will be alright there on your own?' she asked, imagining him in his empty apartment each night, his family all far away.

He thought for a moment. 'Yes, I think so. There will be plenty to occupy me, and the two youngest will still be around every now and then. Don't worry. It will all work out, you'll see.'

***

Delilah had become a very attractive young lady, with her father's intelligence, and the sharp tongue of her grandfather. Deciding not to cut her hair, it hung down her back in a thick, shiny plait, and was much admired in

333

the trendy boutiques of Carnaby Street that she dragged her bemused aunt into. She now shunned traditional Indian dress, wearing only western clothes; her tall, slim frame suiting the styles well. Meera hoped that one day her niece would appreciate the fashion of her homeland again, and not disregard it altogether.

Manju and Vasu did their best to get on. Although the two would never be best friends, some acceptance of each other slowly took place, and the peace had so far been kept. Privately and correctly, Mr Gupta thought that Manju was jealous of his relationship with his sister, and noticed his possessive behaviour on several occasions; Meera usually shrugging it off with a joke. Even Delilah noticed it, and one evening after witnessing her father's rudeness, went into the kitchen to talk to her aunt.

'Auntie, I think you need to tell Daddy to get lost,' she said, looking at Meera sternly. 'He is very bossy and even makes demands of Uncle Vasu.'

'Delilah, this is no way to talk about your father,' replied her aunt, shocked. 'Where did you learn this language, "get lost?" It is not a nice thing to say.'

'Oh, we all say it at school. I heard it yesterday in the street too.'

'Hmmm, anyway, be kind to your daddyji. He has worries of his own, you know. Life is not always easy, Delilah.'

'You mean getting divorced? Why worry? They are not dying and will be happier. We will also be happier no longer listening to them argue all the time!'

Meera realised that this was the truth of the matter, and gave a shrug of acceptance.

'Anyway,' continued Delilah. 'I want to live here – in London. I have made up my mind. This is where I shall study, and I shall make my applications when I go back.'

'Well,' said Meera, 'if your mind is made up, perhaps you should go and talk to your daddy very kindly, and if you are lucky, he will let you come.'

***

One afternoon, not long after this discussion, Meera took her niece to the park that Babita had loved so much. As they walked, arm in arm, a group of young people strolled by, one carrying a radio which blasted out the latest hit, *Dancing Queen,* by the pop group, 'Abba.' Delilah pulled her aunt along so that they were walking in time with the beat, then began to sing, her Indian accent giving the song an altogether exotic edge. Meera thought how fitting the tune was to the young girl by her side, who was so young and hopeful, and oblivious to life's knocks that she would no doubt encounter at some time in the future. She wished that she could protect her from them, and keep her cocooned and safe, but knew that this was impossible. Delilah would have to take her chance along with the rest of them, sometimes winning, sometimes losing; each time things went off-course, dusting herself down and starting again.

It was a hot afternoon, and she led her to the shade of the cedar tree where they both lay on the dry grass, just as she and Babita had done the previous summer. Memories of her dear friend flooded through her mind, and deeply moved Meera began to cry. Hearing the stifled sobs, Delilah quickly turned onto her side to face her aunt.

'Auntie, what is it? Why are you crying?' she asked, her smooth forehead furrowed with concern. She reached out to hold her aunt's hand, upset to see the usually strong and outspoken woman by her side in so much distress.

Meera sat up, and pulling a tissue from her bag, mopped her wet face and began to recount some of the story about her wonderful friendship with Babita, the immense loss she felt, as well as the guilt at not being there for her when she was so sick. 'I loved her so much, Delilah, more than I can say. She was so special to me, and now I have a hole so large that it cannot be filled.'

'Not even by Uncle Vasu?' Delilah asked.

'Oh no, not by him, or anyone – not ever,' replied her aunt, appalled by the suggestion that Vasu could somehow take the place of Babita in any way. 'She was so beautiful, you see, and tiny... about the same size as when you were ten!' At this memory Meera smiled, then continued. 'Her hair was thick and went into ringlets if let loose, and her clothes were bought from a children's store. She had so little – oh, I feel so upset by this. She had so little, yet asked for nothing... this is the way to be, I know it, but she was like a saint. And so clever...'

'Tell me again, Auntie, how did she die?' Delilah's youth and lack of tact made this question a very direct one, but rather than taking any offence, Meera felt as though a gate had opened, and as she answered and cried, the tension held in her body for so long began to be released.

'She had cancer. The diagnosis was very late in coming, and although she had treatment, it was unsuccessful. I was with you in India because of grandfather, and Chandu had to manage alone. Uncle Vasu helped, and the doctor, of course, and a friend called April, but Babita refused hospital. She was always very headstrong.' Meera shook her head.

'And then what happened? She was dead when you arrived back here, Daddy told me.'

'Yes, she killed herself, Delilah. I was too late... too late to save her.'

'If she wanted to kill herself, then I am thinking that she would do this anyway. No saving would have been successful, Auntie.'

Meera looked at her niece in surprise. The child had grown enough to have an adult's insight, and although Meera had frequently told herself that Babita would have done as she wished, whether her friend was there or not, to hear it said in such a frank way somehow sounded so honest, that it must surely be true.

'How did she kill herself, Auntie? Can you tell me?'

'She took an overdose of her pain medication. Her suffering came to an end, and now she is gone. Poor Chandu, he loved her so much that he almost went mad with grief.'

'But he has survived, no? Come Auntie, let us walk and you can tell me more stories about your tiny friend with curly hair.'

She pulled her aunt up from the ground, and arm in arm they walked towards the lake, Meera continuing to recount the years that had passed, and time spent with Babita. As they were about to leave they heard an almighty noise above them, and with flapping of enormous wings a swan landed on the water, skidding along for quite a distance until it finally stopped, its mate already there waiting patiently on the bank. As they walked home, Meera told Delilah about Babita's love of the swans, how she would come here often to watch them, and of the last postcard she sent her from India with two swans swimming towards a beautiful sunset...

They had agreed to call in at the store, and picking up their pace began to head in that direction. Having regained her composure, Meera was just about to open the door when her niece spoke.

'You can talk to me anytime, Auntie. I know that I am a spoilt brat, Daddy says so, but I can listen. Soon I shall be here again. I am so happy about this, and so happy that I shall be with you.'

'So am I, Delilah,' replied Meera, looking at her niece's beautiful young face, her eyes shining with excitement at what the future might hold. 'So am I.'

CHAPTER
FIFTY-FOUR

A routine of playing cards on a Friday evening established itself, and it was the turn of Chandu to play host to the Gupta family. He enjoyed these evenings and the company very much, and found it distracted him from the ever-present and smiling face of Babita that so often lingered in front of him. Sometimes at night, when he was in bed, he chose specific moments of their shared lives and re-enacted them – thus compiling a living collection of happy times that he could view at will.

Not in his control at all, and disrespectful of where he was or what he was doing, were images that came like a lightning strike; his mind shying away from them like a wild horse trying to escape capture. He saw Babita screaming for help at the loss of her baby. He saw her lying in a bundle of rags, like a street urchin in India. He saw her naked body, the bloated stomach at odds with her protruding bones. He saw her sitting in the armchair, dead, yet with eyes open and mouth smiling. And the worst image of all – he saw her standing in front of him, the handstitched quilt pulled over her head to obscure her face from view.

Dr Greene told him that he was traumatised, and had suffered a breakdown of sorts, brought about by the strain of coping with Babita's illness. It was this that had sent him into denial when he first found her after the overdose. The noise of Dr Greene breaking into the room appeared to bring him round, and he fled, driven by fear and shock at what he had done, as well as the sudden and horrifying realisation of Babita's death. Each week, Chandu went to the surgery to talk about and share the darkest moments from that time, as well as the current ever-present flashbacks.

He enjoyed having the flat above the shop to himself. It gave him the space to do as he pleased without having to keep up any pretence. Meera became very distressed if she saw him crying, and without this restraint he allowed his emotions free rein and felt much better for it. The nails taken home from the store each day, and kept in the cupboard, remained in his memory but were no longer a part of his life. Without doubt they would have been found when the flat was cleared, but nothing was ever said, and neither did he ask.

To him, the Guptas were his parents as well as his friends. They were his family, and their lives were as intertwined as the strands of Babita's golden bracelet, now in the drawer beside his bed. His love for her would always remain; as fixed and unchanging as the cycle of life, forever spinning in a universe that was indeed without beginning or end.

***

Hearing voices in the shop below, Chandu opened the door at the top of the stairs to let his visitors in.

'Uncle Chandu!' shouted Delilah. 'We are here. I hope you are ready to be thrashed! I have been practising, and this time you will stand no chance.' Running up the stairs she hugged him, and then went into the kitchen to fetch herself a drink.

'Delilah, you must ask before you take something,' reprimanded her father.

'No, Manju. I buy these for her, and she takes when she wants to,' replied Chandu. 'This has already been agreed.'

Delilah came back into the room, a bottle in her hand. Drinking through a straw, she sat at the table and began to shuffle cards ready for the game.

Meera and Vasu had come more slowly up the stairs, and into their old home. As usual, Meera carried a large bag filled with cakes and snacks that were made earlier that day; her husband following closely behind, holding a plate filled with fried chicken left over from their dinner.

'For tomorrow, Chandu,' Meera said, before going to put it in the fridge.

'Sit down, sit down,' shouted Delilah. 'We have come to play cards, not arrange dinner for a starving man. Sit!'

Watching Delilah, Manju thought how like Meera she was. 'Stop being so bossy, Delilah,' he said. 'Soon you will be giving us lists of jobs to do and telling us when we must go to bed.'

Delilah thought for a moment. 'Not such a bad idea, Daddyji. I will definitely give it more consideration!'

Everyone laughed.

'She is like her aunt,' said Mr Gupta, and they all laughed again.

Two hours later, the final hand had been played, and a large pile of pennies sat on the table in front of Chandu.

'It's not fair,' complained Delilah. 'Uncle Chandu, you always win! Are you sure you are not cheating, and have special cards pushed into your sleeve?'

Chandu smiled, his head moving from side to side; so very Indian, so very him.

It said it all – no words needed.

Acknowledgements

Firstly, I would like to thank everyone at my publishers, Troubador, for their endless patience, support and professionalism at all times. I would also like to thank Jonathan Bayly, Gilly Johnson, Julie Devine, Lynne Pinder, Lesley Kuliukas and Stan Sanders. I also thank my son Tom, who is at the centre of everything. There are too many others to mention here, including each and every one of my readers. You know who you are, and I thank you all.